Sangre
DE LOBO

Sangre
DE LOBO

ETHEL M. HALSTEAD

"Your story is our priority"

LitPrime Solutions
21250 Hawthorne Blvd
Suite 500, Torrance, CA 90503
www.litprime.com
Phone: 1-800-981-9893

Published by LitPrime Solutions   04/19/2023

ISBN: 979-8-88703-173-6(sc)
ISBN: 979-8-88703-174-3(e)

Library of Congress Control Number: 2023902936

CONTENTS

CHAPTER 1

HARRI SAT CALMLY ON HER gray gelding studying the Holland estate from a small knoll above a private lake. Perspiration escaped from underneath Harri's hat brim and trickling down the back of her neck. It was ninety degrees in the shade, the air was still as death. From where Harri sat, the lake could have been a mirror; it reflected a perfect blue sky. In any given direction heat waves slithered like gigantic lizards across the horizon.

In spite of the heat, Harri remained motionless, her eyes scanning the landscape. It was one magnificent sight. *Why can't I love it? It truly is incredible!*

Yes, everything beautiful and convenient had been built into the three-story mansion and its surrounding landscape. Harri's father had planned, and executed to the peak of perfection, every last detail.

That's the problem; the whole place is just too damn perfect. There's nothing left to do, nothing to look forward to. Everything is already done to the nines! Everything except my life. My life can't be done! Or can it?

Harri thought about her silent question and came to a single conclusion: *If I don't move on, my life will be done.* After contemplating that thought for several minutes before moving on to another, this time using her conscience as her guide she added: *But what about dad? Every move he's made since I was born was made with me in mind. Could I abandon him now, even for a real life? I wonder what a real life would be like here in the states. Most likely not worth a damn. Half the people I 've met here are just phony imitations of real people. Guess I'll never stop missing my old life. Maybe there's something wrong with me, a missing gene or something. And maybe I'd better get my ass back to my room.... get ready to meet Mr. Prince Charming....*

"God, how I hate this Cinderella crap!" Harri whispered through clenched teeth as she lightly touched a spurless boot heel to her gelding's flank.

Harri entered her home through the service entrance, it being the nearest entrance from the riding stable. She went in search of her father and found him in his study. He had company. She didn't recognize either of the two men with him, and having barged in without knocking, she felt a little awkward.

As usual her father treated her intrusion as if it were the coolest thing that could happen to a private conversation. He introduced her to his visitors and then he explained to her why they were there.

The two men had just informed her father that the missing Cessna 310, which had left her former homeland and birthplace in South America three years earlier, had been located. The small cargo plane had departed the jungle outpost, with noted research scientist, Dr. Orville Singly, engineer Ted Tolver, and the pilot. Unfortunately, the three people on the aircraft had never acquired the attention, or the importance to the media at large, as the two crates of very precious cargo the small plane held in its cargo compartment.

That particular cargo had been recovered from a sunken riverboat just hours before it had been loaded on the Cessna bound for the US.

The two men had just informed her father that the remains of the pilot and the two passengers had been found in the plane's cabin, but the crates were missing.

Harri could well remember all the fuss about the airplane that had disappeared after leaving the landing strip near her former home in South America.

After being forced to leave her beloved home, her father had arranged for Harri to see parts of a world that had been denied her in her early youth.

Traveling with her world-renowned companion, had offered Harri

2

a front row seat to worlds she had only known about through books her teachers had brought into the jungle.

After returning to the United States from her six months abroad, Harri had read all the clippings from local and national newspapers her father had saved for her. She had heard her father discuss the few known details about the missing plane with friends and associates, male and female. And Harri had been aware that most of those friends had more than a passing interest in the fate of that aircraft and its cargo.

Harri could still remember the disbelief in her father's voice when he spoke of how the plane had mysteriously lost radio contact after leaving the dredge site at the jungle outpost, then seemingly vanish from the earth.

For several months the missing plane had been the topic of conversation at practically every get-gather and cook-out Harri could remember. She could well remember getting irritated with the subject because nothing new had been discovered and the repetition was getting to be a real bore. Harri was glad when it finally began to die down.

In the beginning, there had been much speculation that maybe the plane's crew had made other plans for the priceless cargo, and that eventually they would let the world know of those plans. That belief had been so strong among the investors who had supported the project for so many years, that they had waited for months to hear from the crew, never loosing faith that eventually they would.

The investors had been willing to forgive the plane's crew for their transgressions the moment they came forth with the crates. They had even been willing to fork over whatever price necessary to recover their precious cargo.

Over the past three years, even after the main heat had died down, the subject of the Cessna and its crew had resurfaced periodically, but all anybody could do was theorize the fate of the Cessna and its cargo.

Now, according to these two visitors, it appeared as though the most logical thing that could have happened, had happened; the plane had gone down in the jungle, apparently within minutes after takeoff.

Harri wanted to ask the two men about their real reason for being here and why they were discussing this subject with her father. He had nothing to do with the disappearance of that aircraft or its recent discovery in the jungle.

Could they possibly believe he had something to do with the plane or its cargo?

She decided to wait until the two men had left before asking her father about the true reason for their visit.

"No Harri, they were not accusing me of anything," said Ward Holland, amazed at his daughter's incessant and exasperating habit of jumping to conclusions. "Actually, they wanted me to help them."

"Help them?" Harri asked, sounding skeptical. "And just what sort of help were they expecting from you, dad?"

"They want me to find the missing crates," said her father. "They think I could find them if anyone could because I know that part of the jungle so well. That plane went down close enough to that terrorist camp known as 'Sangre De Lobo,' to make it accessible to the ruffians who run the place. The two men who just left here believe someone planned for the plane to go down at that particular location. And the logical conclusion would be that it had been one of my crew who planned it. The sponsors of the project have offered sizable rewards in the past, to anyone in that three thousand square mile area, for information about the plane or its crew. Not a single person has come forth, even with the huge reward as an incentive. Now that I know where the plane went down, I know why."

"Who found the plane?" Harri asked. "And how do they know it's the plane they've been searching for?"

"The plane was discovered by a small army of soldiers. The original sponsors of the project hired the soldiers. Finding the downed craft wasn't easy. Pieces were scattered over several hundred feet of jungle— mostly wings and tail section. The fuselage and cabin were still intact, but severely damaged. The remains of the crew were still inside the mangled cabin. The soldiers managed to gather enough numbers from the wreckage to identify it, and the crew had identification on them. They know they have located the right plane."

"Isn't it possible the plane's cargo was lost in the jungle when the plane crashed?" Harri asked.

"Not the cargo in that plane," said Ward. "If those men were leveling with me about the condition of the plane's cargo department, there's no way the cargo could have left it without being physically removed through human effort."

"Wouldn't the crates have been destroyed by the crash?" Harri asked. "After all, the crash did kill the crew!"

"True, but it didn't necessarily destroy the crates," said Ward. "The content of those crates was packed securely in several layers of heavy foam, and then placed in very solid wooden structures that were also wrapped in three layers of heavy foam, then bound with steel bands. They may have bounced around a bit, but I doubt they would have sustained a great deal of damage."

"So, are those men positive the crates were taken by someone in that terrorist villa?"

"No, they're not certain," said Ward, "but they have sufficient reason to believe the crates were removed by inhabitants of the villa, and that they were carted to the villa for storage. And that is their only lead at the moment to the possible whereabouts of the crates. Also, it's likely that someone did plan that crash site. I hate to think that one of my crew planned it, but who else could have?"

"Did your crew know the value of the crates?"

"Only four people were supposed to know about the contents of those crates," said Ward. "Two of the four were Dr. Singly and Ted Tolver, which were killed in the crash, and Cedrick Grinzak—Dr. Grinzak's son—and myself. Grinzak left the site before he had an opportunity to talk to anyone. Ted Tolver didn't trust anyone enough to give them the time of day without a four-hour deposit. And I damn sure didn't tell anyone. That leaves Dr. Singly. He could have talked to all of the crew for all I know. It did seem that his only purpose for living was to recover those crates and return to the states with them… and he always talked too much!"

"Dad, doesn't it seem a little strange that a group of hired soldiers just accidentally located that plane in such a vast, remote part of the jungle?" Harri asked. "Especially when it was most likely overgrown with jungle foliage by the time it was discovered. You know how the jungle swallows up anything that doesn't move for an hour."

"I don't believe it was entirely an accident," said Holland. "According to the two men who asked my help in recovering the crates, rumors had begun to trickle out of that terrorist camp. The rumors, according to hearsay, were that the villagers had something of value to sell if the right people were interested. I guess it took a while to reach the ears of the 'right people' but when it did, they went to work immediately, gathering a crew of soldiers to go in and check out the area. The sponsors must have demanded some sort of proof from the villagers before forking over a fortune for the crates. And they must have gotten the right answer. However, at some point, the soldiers decided to go in and check out the crash site before completing their negotiations with the terrorists. The soldiers found the plane—much to their regret. That must have been one bloody scene. The terrorists let the soldiers reach the plane, check it out thoroughly, make whatever notes possible, and then they set upon them with everything they had; wiping out most of the soldiers. The terrorists gave one of the soldiers a message and sent him on his way. The message read, *'Don't call on us with an army of soldiers—but do call!'* The terrorists wanted that message to get back to the supporters so there would be no more misunderstandings as to their intentions of collecting for the prize they heisted three years earlier."

"Maybe that would be a good plan," said Harri. "The sponsors could send only one person in to negotiate for the crates."

"Yes, it would be a good plan," said Ward, "except for one big problem, finding someone willing to go back in there. None of the surviving crew that went in on that first junket will go back in—not for any amount of money. Sangre De Lobo shelters the toughest, most violent terrorist guerrillas in the whole jungle. Nobody in their right mind would volunteer to go near the place. I know why even the wealth of the sponsors can't entice any of that crew to go back in. They know that surviving one trip was just plain luckier than any man has a right to be."

Harri looked at her father and almost put her foot in it by offering up a solution that even she would not have liked; she almost asked

SANGRE DE LOBO

Ward if he had considered speaking with Keil West or Brent Mathson about negotiating for the crates. Realizing her error, she clammed up quickly and waited for her dad to finish his statement.

"The sponsors are now, as we speak, trying to put together another group of soldiers." Ward said, looking grim. "They want the soldiers to set up a camp several miles from the Sangre De Lobo, and send one person in under the pretense of negotiating for the crates. However, what they really want is to learn if the crates are still in Sangre De Lobo. If so, they plan to send in enough soldiers to wipe out the terrorist guerrillas and just take the crates.

Suddenly something occurred to Harri that took her breath away, *Oh my God..!!!* "Dad, you wouldn't be considering...

"No Harri!" Interrupted Holland, "I wouldn't be considering such a thing!"

Harri studied her father's expression for a long moment. From the look on his face, she believed he was mentally revisiting another time, another place. *Was his mind trekking through a terrorist village from his past? If so, he wasn't at all happy with the re-run.*

What did her father know about that village that he wasn't talking about? Harri suspected that the two men who had asked for his help knew something about her father that she didn't know.

"You've been in that terrorist camp, haven't you dad?" Harri asked suddenly. "You know something about it...something those men want to know. They want you to lead that group of mercenaries into that terrorist camp. Right?"

"That's about the size of it." Her father said quietly as he gazed at some distant horizon through a window of his study.

"You just said you wouldn't do it! You won't go back! Will you, dad?"

"Harri, please pay attention, I said I won't do what those men are asking of me. What do I have to do, put it in writing?"

Harri knew that to push for further information would be a mistake. However, she was her father's daughter, and she was determined to get an answer. Angry and bewildered at her father's outburst, she stood stiffly, staring at him as he stared thoughtfully at something visible only to him.

7

"What is it, then?" Harri asked, more sharply than she had intended. "What's eating you, Dad? Something about this whole scenario is skewed! What do you know that you're not telling me?"

"Nothing! Nothing at all!" Holland snapped. "Let's drop the subject. We should be getting ready for dinner, Harri. Our guest will be arriving soon."

Harri stood with her thumbs hooked in the back pockets of her riding pants. Grimly, she watched her father's back as he walked from the room.

Suddenly her father looked older; his shoulders sagged wearily. Harri had never thought of her father as old, but now, watching him walk away, a chill winged through her spine. Everything around her felt out of sync. Something was terribly wrong; she could feel it. She didn't know what it was — but her father knew...

Harri stood in front of the full-length dressing mirror studying her reflection. The girl in the mirror was more than pretty, she was almost beautiful. Her shoulders and mouth were a little too wide, and her eyes were a little too knowing. They didn't have that soulful, mysterious look that was prevalent to truly beautiful women.

Harri approved of what she saw in her mirror because she knew her father would approve. However, she knew it wasn't a true reflection of Harri Holland. The girl she viewed in the mirror was created for special moments only. Like Cinderella she was wearing an evening gown. The gown had been designed especially for her. There was not another like it anywhere in the world. Everything about this girl was cosmetically perfect. From her beautiful shiny hair, to a perfectly made-up face and manicured nails.

Harri wondered how she, Harri Holland, could reflect such an image, one so different from the real Harri Holland. She sighed, no doubt she would impress this new Prince Charming that she would be meeting in a short while. Didn't she always impress her father's friends? As she turned away from the mirror she said vehemently, "Aren't most of them just too damned easily impressed?"

Suddenly, on impulse, Harri turned back, looked closely into the mirror and crossed her eyes. With her eyes still crossed, she stuck her finger down her throat, pretending to gag at her reflection. That action, as silly as it was, put her in a much better mood. She truly felt better now, almost human. Now she could greet her guest with a smile. There was only one problem, she still had almost ten minutes to wait before the guests would begin to arrive. By that time, she would be out of the mood again.

While she waited, she walked to the very back of her walk-in closet and pulled the zipper down on a clothes storage bag. She removed a set of fatigues from the bag and checked them over carefully for any signs of damage that might have occurred from being stored for three years in a plastic bag. Underneath the hanging bag was a pair of much pampered combat boots. Those boots were an object of her true devotion. She spent a lot of time keeping them conditioned with saddle soap and polished.

She replaced the fatigues in the bag then slowly zipped it up. She stepped from the closet, but looked back longingly before closing the door, "That's where the real Harri Holland lives," she said to herself. "She lives in a zip-up bag in the back of a walk-in closet."

The dinner party was a sweeping success. Her father looked proud and happy. Harri had to admit that the event had been pleasant, even for her. She had noticed during the evening how relaxed and happy the guests were as they hovered around her dad. He was a charming man, easy to converse with, easy to love.

In the past three years, Ward Holland had acquired many devoted friends here in his carefully chosen domain that lay within a forty-five-minute drive of Houston, Texas, the fourth largest city in the US, and still growing. He was loved and respected by most of the people in this grandiloquent, rural area.

Harri could well understand why, he was the type of man who attracted devotion and respect.

Grudgingly, Harri admitted she had even liked the new 'Prince Charming', Sid Grainer. How could she not like him? He was just like her father. Not really so much like her father now, as like her father before he so completely mellowed out.

Sid, like herself, had known about his intended role for the evening, and the two of them had laughed at their parents' obsession for matchmaking. Sid was no more interested in a steady romance than she was. He had too many plans for his own future, and he fully intended to follow through with them. His plans didn't include any permanent attachments to another human.

After meeting Sid, Harri was convinced the man had a great deal of respect for his mother and her wishes, otherwise he would never have agreed to attend this social. He was a vibrant, and obviously restless, man. Right off, he recognized Harri as a kindred soul. The two of them hit it off instantly. Aside from Sid's obviously charming virtues, she learned he was a very interesting conversationalist and an excellent dancer. She would keep Sid on her list of friends that she could call on if she ever needed an escort for a special occasion—but never for emotional support or a shoulder to cry on. She could truthfully say she was looking forward to seeing him again, and she knew Sid felt the same way about seeing her. She was no threat to his future, and he was none to hers, and each of them had recognized the advantage of developing their friendship. As allies they could put a stop to their parents' meddling.

The party ended with everyone promising to return to the Holland estate for an up-coming fourth-of-July extravaganza.

<hr />

CHAPTER 2

ONCE AGAIN, HARRI WAS GETTING an eerie feeling that something was wrong. The feeling had settled around her like a dismal fog. And the fact that her father had been acting strange ever since the dinner party—actually ever since the visit from the two strangers—wasn't helping to relieve the feeling.

Harry knew some of his incongruity could have been attributed to the stress of making sure everything was in ship-shape for the social. But the overall affair had been a whopping success, and he had seemed relaxed and happy with it, so what was bothering him now? *Maybe it wasn't the party,* she thought, *maybe it was something else.* She decided to ask him, point blank, what was eating him.

"Nothing is bothering me!" Ward snapped at his daughter. "It's just that there are a few chores that need to be finished before the fourth-of-July cookout, and I've been preoccupied. I'm sorry I've ignored you, Harri, I'll make it up to you when things have settled down around here."

But even as he spoke, Harri knew he wasn't leveling with her. He seemed to avoid looking directly at her when he spoke, and he quickly resumed work on his present project—mending things that weren't broken. And twice within the week, she had walked into his study while he was on the phone, and he had put his party on hold while waiting for her to leave the room, which was another strange thing for him to do, he had never let her presence interrupt his telephone conversations before.

Harri stood her ground, staring at her father while he put a coat of sealer wax on a picnic table. She wondered why Mario, her foster brother, wasn't doing the chore. Mario was very sensitive about his position in the family home. He would be hurt when he discovered her father had redone the tables, that didn't need to be redone, without even asking his help.

Harri's quiet scrutiny was making Ward uncomfortable to the point he could no longer ignore it. He looked up briefly and asked her if there was something she needed to be doing elsewhere.

"Well!" said Harri, miffed but still trying to smile. "I can take a hint! Guess I know when I'm not wanted!"

She walked away, straight backed and mumbling to herself, "I didn't learn a damned thing there! But I have to find out what's eating him before the suspense kills me. Secrets ought to be against the law!"

The following morning, Harri slept late. When she finally made it down for breakfast she discovered her father was ready to leave for Houston.

"Well, I was wondering if you would wake up in time to say good-bye before I leave," he said to a still groggy, Harri.

"Where are you off to so early in the morning?" Harri asked, yawning.

I have to pick up a few supplies in the city," he told her. "I may not be back before late tomorrow evening. There's a list in the utility room—a few things that still need to be done. If you'll see that Mario gets the list I would appreciate it."

Absently, Ward hugged Silana, his live-in housekeeper and the only mother Harri had ever known. Silana was trying to force another cup of coffee on him, and Ward was trying to escape. He quickly brushed a kiss across Harri's forehead and reached for the keys to his truck.

Silana watched Ward as he walked to his truck. She compressed her lips tightly, slowly turned her head from side to side, and then said softly, "It will be nice when he returns to us!"

"What is the matter with everybody around here?" Harri asked, looking distraught. "Even you're acting weird, mom. I mean…after all he'll only be gone for one day, two at the most!"

"But he has already been away for such a long while," said Silana, staring through a kitchen window at Ward's truck as it pulled from the driveway.

When it dawned on Harri what Silana had really said, Harri hugged her close, letting her know she understood.

Before sundown, a storm moved in, creating almost complete cloud coverage over the area. Harri realized how badly the area needed rain, so it didn't bother her as much as it would two weeks from now. She didn't want any rainstorm interfering with her dad's fourth-of-July cookout. He was putting so much work into the event; it must be very special to him.

Harri moved through the house one room at a time, checking for open windows and closing shutters. If this was a typical summer storm, the wind could cause a lot of damage to anything it could get at.

Harri, Mario and Silana, ate a quiet dinner in the eat-in area of the large kitchen at the Holland house. For the most part, they remained quiet as the relentless wind shook windows and howled mournfully around corners. Frequently, brilliant flashes of lightning burst through the huge bay window only a few feet from their table. The thunder that followed the flashes struck with magnum force, rolling over the earth with reverberating rumbles.

In the jungle Harri had heard loud, booming thunder that was nerve-racking, but she couldn't remember ever hearing the booming, rolling thunder that was so common here. She was thankful she was not easily frightened.

After dinner, Silana cleared the kitchen table as Harri rinsed the dishes and placed them in the dishwasher. Mario returned to the garage to finish some project he had been working on.

After Silana and Mario had retired for the evening, Harri sat in her father's study writing letters to friends she had parted with when they all left the jungle post over three years ago.

Harri was still feeling resentment toward one of those friends who she believed had abandoned her for more interesting pursuits. Keil West had been one of the most important people in her life, except for...

"Oh hell!" She said angrily. "Why bother even thinking about them. Everybody has a right to choose their own life's ports, and eliminate any person or thing that doesn't fit into those ports. Maybe I should be brave enough to find my own port!"

While concentrating on her writing, Harri had lost track of time. She was surprised when she noticed it was nearing midnight. The wind had finally died down, and the rain had ceased. The only noise now was a steady dripping from the eaves. *I might as well go to bed. There's nothing to do at this late hour except watch a spook movie on an all-night channel—and this is definitely no night for a spook movie.*

Harri was reaching for the light switch when a rock came crashing through the window of her father's study.

"What in hell...?" Harri gasped. Startled by the sudden crashing sound. She quickly stepped away from the window and waited to see if there would be further action. Deciding it was over, she picked up the stone. It had a note wrapped around it. The note was secured with a heavy rubber band. Harri removed the note and noticed the message was address to for her father. Written in a large scrawl, the message read: *Mr. Holland. Your friend, Keil West, needs your help. He's being held in a stockade near Sangre De Lobo. I'm told that you know of this terrorist camp. Your friend's life is in great danger. He will be executed, soon!!!*

Harri was struck senseless. She felt physically ill right down to her soul. This had to be the worst situation she had ever encountered. There was no way she would let her father go into that terrorist camp for any reason. *But someone must go. Someone had to go!* If there was even a small chance someone could get into that terrorist camp and find Keil, there was an equal chance they could get him out. Who could she ask to do such a thing?

Harri was certain there was nobody in her immediate circle of friends that could, or would go into that vile place...except her father. She was not going to let that happen. Not even if she had to go in herself. Harri froze in her tracks at that thought. Then she asked herself, *why not? Why shouldn't I go? After all, during our jungle survival training, wasn't I better at locating and capturing the enemy than most of the men? I was also better at evading capture. I should be the one to go! I'm more qualified than anyone I know!*

As Harri climbed the stairs to her room she kept the idea running in her mind, afraid to even look at another view of such an impractical picture. She had to convince herself she was right, no matter how her decision might appear to someone even pretending to be rational or sane.

There's no reason why dad should even know about this, she told herself. *I'll leave him a note, explaining that something came up—that I must be away for a few days. But what about the broken window the rock came through?* Snapping her fingers as if that action would yield up an immediate fix, she said aloud, "I'll tell him the storm blew something through the window." Besides, she reasoned, Mario would most likely have it repaired before her father returned from Houston, but she would leave the note anyway, just in case.

Harri laid out fatigues, combat boots, her 9mm Glock and several spare clips of ammo. She added a fairly new, AK-47 to the pile. She had never looked at the AK-47 closely, and still couldn't imagine why she had decided she wanted the thing in the first place. Her father didn't even know she had it. However, in spite of her original thoughts on the purchase of the evil looking weapon, at the moment she was glad she had it. She added another hundred rounds of ammo to the pile. She quickly sorted through other survival gear, things she had brought with her from the jungle, then quickly added the selected gear to her collection. Harri had never known why she had kept all that stuff. Maybe some sixth sense or premonition…

Harri pushed a sleeping bag into her large backpack then added a change of clothes and all the gear she had laid out: machete, dried foodstuff, weapons and ammo clips. She was cursing herself now for not buying that thirty-round drum for the AK-47. She had considered it and then decided against it. It would have been easily obtained at the time, but there had been nothing in her life to justify buying it.

Harri knew she could pick up some of her needed supplies in Villa Guano, which would be her departure point to Sangre De Lobo, but finding the clip she needed was not a likely prospect. To obtain specialty weapons and supplies in the jungle, you had to know somebody who was dealing the stuff. She didn't know anybody in Villa Guano who dealt in weapons, and she wouldn't have time to look. She had to find Keil West before he was executed.

In Villa Guano she would purchase, or lease, a vehicle of some sort. That is, if one should happen to be available. If not, she would hire someone to take her as near to her destination as she dared go in a vehicle. She knew enough about the terrorists' operation to know that all roads accessible to the terrorist camp would have soldiers guarding them. Vehicles entering the area that didn't belong there would be stopped instantly.

She would need a lot of cash to buy favors from the locals. She hoped she would be lucky enough to find locals that didn't play both sides against the middle. Getting the cash would be no problem. Her father had set up a checking account for her that she seldom touched, and the account was getting fatter by the day. She would have to stop by her bank in the morning before she boarded her chartered plane.

Harri paced the floor in her room as she mentally put together her plan for her trip back into the jungle. She happened to catch a glimpse of herself in a mirror as she paced, and she was half surprised when it dawned on her that she looked like any number of candy-assed girls one might meet on the streets of Houston. She needed a hair cut. The jungle was no place to have to worry about hairdos. If she could conceal the fact that she was a female, short of growing a beard and mustache, so much the better.

The following day, sporting a new haircut and wearing her combat boots and fatigues, Harri threw her stuffed bag into the cargo department of the small chartered plane, then stood staring at it, trying to convince herself she really wanted to go through with this madness.

For the first time since she had learned of Keil's situation, she was having some genuine second thoughts about her plan. *I must be using shit for brains*, she told herself as she boarded the small plane and fastened her safety belt. *But I can't wait around hoping for a change in conditions because the only change likely will be Keil's execution.* Just thinking that Keil's life might end made her violently ill. But getting herself killed before she could locate him wouldn't help his case any.

Harri was feeling even less sure of her decision when the plane landed in an isolated outpost to refuel before it began its last two hundred miles into Columbia's massive jungle. Harri decided not to leave the safety of the plane while it was being refueled, even though she would have used the facilities at the station if the people there had looked a little friendlier. She noticed that even the pilot refused to use the facilities. Also, he was careful not to venture more than a few feet from his plane.

When the plane was filled with fuel the pilot pulled some bills from his pocket and waved them at the attendant who grudgingly walked over and snatched them from his hand.

The pilot stepped back into the plane and began taxiing away from the pumps without looking back. Harri saw him breathe a sigh of relief. The pilot was likely surprised that they had been permitted to leave the place without being attacked, or at the least having to pay someone off before continuing with their trip. It seemed that every person in this part of the world, who was in a position to meet people with cash in hand, was a self-appointed agent of some sort, and, for the most part an agent that had to be "paid off" before one could pass through his territory. Harri was seriously considering asking the pilot to return to the states now, with her on board.

Harri had been watching the scenery below, trying not to think about her future. She knew it was highly possible that she had no future.

She looked at her watch. They would be landing in Villa Guano within the hour, and the closer they got to the villa, the more certain she was that she was a raving, freaking fruitcake. When she departed from Villa Guano, she wouldn't have a guide to turn to if she should get lost. In a jungle, getting lost was easier than staying on tract. Everything looked the same for miles, and one could pass within a few feet of a destination without seeing it.

The pilot would drop her off at the landing strip at villa Guano and from that point, sink or swim; she would be on her own. Once the pilot flew out of her reach, having second thoughts would only be taxing brain cells.

Few people outside the jungle had ever heard of Villa Guano, even though it was the largest and most civilized of all known villages in this jungle. The people of Villa Guano had even set up an advisory board, and had a law, of sorts, governing its people. Villa Guano was about forty miles southeast of the jungle outpost where Harri was born;

where she had spent her life up to the age of sixteen. She had been to Villa Guano with her father many times during her sixteen years at the outpost.

When the plane landed at the Villa Guano airstrip and taxied up to a hangar, Harri noticed the few people milling around the hangar had stopped whatever they were doing to study the plane that had landed with only the pilot and a single passenger.

Harri sat for a moment letting her gaze roam over the motley crew that was staring at her. She was glad she had managed to look almost as scruffy as the men who were watching her. Her combat fatigues and boots, along with the dirty fatigue cap she was wearing backwards on her head, had served their purpose well. If any of the men could tell she was a female, then their observation from a distance was better than the pilot's who had spent several hours with her in close quarters.

Her thick, close-cropped hair was sweaty and sticking to her head. She removed her cap and ran her fingers through the short, tangled mess, which looked an awfully lot like a drowned weasel. However, she wasn't trying to win a beauty contest, she wanted to look as scruffy as the local men she would be dealing with, but she knew she couldn't look as tough as those hombres who were watching her now even if she could grow a beard and add a hundred pounds to her slender, five-foot ten-inch, frame.

Another thing she was certain of, she had to find a private facility and soon. She needed the privacy now for more than to relieve herself, which, in itself, was becoming an emergency. She also needed to remove some of the cash from the bundles that she had taped to her torso. She would keep a portion of the cash handy to buy or lease an automobile. Or to pay a driver, whichever was available. She also needed cash to purchase additional supplies for her trip to Sangre De Lobo.

Speaking in Spanish, she asked a guard for directions to the nearest 'John'. He gave her a sour look and told her to use the wall behind the hangar like the other men did. Looking as mean as possible, which was getting easier by the second due to her emergency, she told the guard that he wouldn't want to clean up after her if she used the wall just now. Grudgingly, he pointed to a small outhouse near the hangar.

She made a dash for the wood-framed building, which was covered over with strips of ratty looking, corrugated metal. Harri opened the door and stopped short. The inside of the outhouse easily convinced her she should have used the wall, but the guard was watching her, so she stepped cautiously inside, seriously doubting her boots would ever be the same again. To take her mind off the stifling odor while she relieved herself, she tried to read some of the many bits of wisdom and philosophy that was haphazardly etched upon the walls of the privy. Many of the signatures and bits of poetry, along with confessions of undying love, were overlapping each other. She decided that only a cryptographer could decipher it all. Most of the words were written in Spanish, and misspelled. One rather common phrase, also written in Spanish, she found to be amusing on this particular wall: "A bird in the hand is better than two in a bush."

When Harri left the foul smelling, little building she was relieved to discover the guard had found other interest for the moment. She wondered if there was a water hose nearby that she could use to wash the crud from her boots. She decided not to ask, someone might wonder why she would bother. She doubted she would offend anyone other than herself with the smell. The boots could wait.

Harri had left the outhouse in time to watch the chartered plane disappear into a distant blue yonder. A sudden panic held her in its grip. That plane had been her only link to civilization as she had known it for almost four years now.

Doubt and fear were slithering through her head like slimy eels. Suddenly, Harri realized that all the years she had trekked through this jungle alone, and the countless hours she had spent participating in jungle survival training, had not prepared her for this moment. She was totally alone in an alien world.

Harri's pessimistic thoughts were yanked back to the present by three young boys who had gathered around her, each had tried to lift her heavy duffel bag. None had totally succeeded, although the tallest of the three had managed to get it off the ground. They looked disappointed. They wanted to earn pesos, and their foremost opportunity was to offer a service to the few people who flew into the airport. Harri's plane had been the only one to land in two days, and the boys were convinced their services were not needed here. They didn't want to resort to begging unless it became necessary. Harri saw the disappointment written on their faces and decided maybe the boys were the answer to her problem.

After a short chat with them, Harri gave each of them a few pesos and told them there was more if they could help her with information. She needed to learn as much as possible about the local environment and what it had to offer her cause. She watched the face of each boy as she talked. The oldest boy, Mando, looked as if he knew everything there was to know about Villa Guano.

Harri decided that if there was something this kid didn't already know he would learn it quickly if the price was right. She could see endurance and pride written all over the kid. She liked him immediately. Harri asked him if he knew where she could purchase an automobile, or hire one and a driver for a day or two. He told her his uncle had a truck and would take her anywhere she wanted to go if she could pay. Then he informed her that he expected to be paid for taking her to his uncle.

"Where does your uncle live?" Harri asked.

"He lives that way," said Mando, pointing east. "Our casa is within walking distance of the airport!"

Harri learned that the boy lived with his uncle, and that his parents had disappeared when he was a baby. She handed the two younger boys another fifty pesos each—about five US dollars—and sent them on their way. She told herself that just having them there had made her feel safer. It was worth the few bucks she had shelled out to them.

She and the older boy walked toward the uncle's home, less than a mile from the airport. The boy was impressed with the tall soldier who carried the duffel bag as if it were a sack of feathers.

As the two of them walked, Harri kept looking over her shoulder to see if they were being followed. Two men at the airport had shown more than a casual interest in her presence there. One of the men looked as if he could slit a person's throat just for breathing his air. He was not an exceptionally large man—no Sumo wrestler for sure—but there was something about him that could put a chill on the hottest day in hell. The man had a square face that was heavily lined and a 'Fu-Man-Chu' mustache. His hair grew low on his forehead and his neck was short and looked as if it had been created from heavy, knotted rope. Harri had glanced at him several times from the corner of her eye and each time he was staring directly at her, not even attempting to conceal his questioning look.

When she and the boy walked away from the airport, the man looked at his watch, gave it a light tap and then walked behind the hangar and out of sight. Harri had become so involved in watching the man with the mustache, she had forgotten to keep an eye on the other man, the skinny one, and he had disappeared from sight also. She hadn't felt any particular fear of the skinny one, he just gave her the creeps. She had seen things crawling around in dead animals that looked more pleasant. She decided she would rather sleep with that mustached dude who had scared the hell out of her, than live on the same planet with the beady-eyed creep who looked a lot like a six-foot-tall, wharf rat.

Harri acquired a bad case of jitters while being welcomed into the uncle's home. She felt that everything in her immediate realm was operating in slow motion. That time was running out for Keil. She was anxious to settle her business with the uncle and be on her way to Sangre De Lobo before sundown. Her agitation was playing wholesale destruction with her nervous system.

The uncle, whose name was Kiko Manillo, was a warm and friendly person. He had a quiet, matter-of-fact manner that appealed to Harri. He listened as she stated her needs and then told her he could take her to her desired location.

"Yes, I am familiar with the area," said Señor Manillo. "I know a way into the terrorists' camp that is not watched by the guards. Nobody uses the old road now. It will take us within ten miles of your destination."

That was a suitable arrangement for Harri, she wouldn't dare to go any closer than ten miles to Sangre De Lobo in an automobile.

From where Señor Manillo would drop her off, Harri would travel the rest of the way on foot, which was the only way a body could hope to get near the terrorist village and live to talk about it.

"We will leave here about two hours before daybreak," Señor Manillo informed her.

Harri was aggravated when she learned that they couldn't leave immediately, and asked, "Why must we wait until morning?"

"We will gather the supplies you will need to take with you into the jungle, my young friend," said Señor Manillo, "and while we do this, I will answer your question."

Harri wanted to travel as light as possible. She already had nearly all she needed in way of supplies. She only needed a few first-aid supplies and two containers of bug repellent. There were no foods available in either of the village's two stores that she could take on a trip through the jungle. She would have to survive on the dozen Granola bars, a box of crackers, and six tins of beef jerky she had packed before she left the states. Harri hoped she would be able to find fresh water. Her water supply wasn't going to last long on a hot day, and her few canned sodas would most likely taste like dishwater after a few hours in the jungle's heat.

"You were going to tell me why we can't leave for Sangre De Lobo today," said Harri.

"Si!" said Señor Manillo, "I do not wish to travel at night in the jungle. It is dangerous to use the lights; they can be seen for miles. Even on the old road, we must go in while everyone is still sleeping. Within an hour after we begin our travel, we will leave the good road and turn into the bad one that leads to Sangre De Lobo. From that point we cannot use the lights. We will be driving for almost an hour where the road will be hard to see, and that road is not good to travel even when it is visible." Suddenly, Señor Manillo chuckled at his own remark about the road, then said, "Actually my friend, the road is even more bad when it is visible. It will take us about two hours to reach the location where I must leave you. From there I can only pray that you will return safely from that horrible place. This mission must be very important to you. I do not know another young man who would go into Sangre De Lobo alone. You do not appear to be loco, so I must believe something else is compelling you to make the dangerous travel to that terrible place."

"How do you know so much about Sangre de Lobo, Señor Manillo?" Harri asked.

"When Mando, my nephew was only a baby, his parents were taken away to that village by one who wanted information about the factory where Mando's father worked. Mando's father was my brother. He worked for a chemical plant near Bogotá—Bogotá is over four hundred kilometers from Villa Guano. My brother visited with me as often as possible. Once, when he was here, he told me about someone who wanted information about his work. He said the man was threatening his family. My brother confessed to me that he did not have access to the requested information, and he was afraid. Within a week from that visit my brother's wife disappeared. In another week my brother was missing also. I believe my sister-in-law was taken from her home to frighten my brother into stealing information from his company. I know my brother was not taken by force because he took little Mando to his best friend's home and asked the friend to bring him to me if he did not return for him in five days. As you must have already guessed, he did not return to pick up his son. Sangre De Lobo is the largest terrorist operation in all of Colombia. If one has enough money and the right contacts, anything can be purchased from the murdering ones who run that camp. I knew my brother and his wife had been taken there, and like you, I felt compelled to go to that place which my people have chosen to call *Villa Diablo.* 'Devil Village'. Even if there was only a small chance my brother and his wife were still living, I felt I had to go in and search for them. The sad truth is, I almost lost my own life before I could get away from that horrible place. If that should have happened, little Mando would be in a more terrible situation than he is now. At the least, as long as I live he will have food and shelter, and with the few pesos he can earn at the airport, well…we manage. He is a good boy. He is like my brother. Maybe one day, he too will go to the big city and find a good job there."

After eating a late dinner of bean burritos and fresh vegetable soup, made from home-grown vegetables, Señor Manillo gave Harri a stack of quilts and a small pillow. She made herself a bed on a porch that once had been covered with screen mesh. The screen had long since lost its usefulness as protection against tiny, night flying critters. Over the years it had become shredded in many places and had been re-woven with strands of the screen's fine wire, but now the edges of the screen were beginning to pull loose from the rotting framework. A tattered blanket served as a covering for the only exit leading from the porch. A small outhouse set sadly alone near a wooded thicket some seventy-five feet behind the humble dwelling.

Harri rolled onto the pallet fully dressed, mindless of the bulk of the handgun that remained in its holster under her loose shirt, or the bundles of cash that were still taped to her body. Somehow, even though she couldn't bring herself to remove her supplies from her body, she felt at peace with her surroundings. Earlier she had even managed to clean the crap from her boots. They looked almost as good as before she entered the airport's disgusting john.

For several moments Harri lay on the hard pallet smiling, and wondering why she was feeling a thrill at this opportunity to spend a night on Señor Manillo's porch. *If I were sane, I would be feeling fear or repulsion at this whole crazy production.*

For a while, Harri lay sleepless on her pallet, thinking back over the years of events that had brought her to this uncertain moment in her life. She wondered if it would all end here in the jungle, only a few short miles from where her life had begun just over nineteen years ago...

Harri Holland knew her father had been a soldier of fortune. A hired gun. She knew there had been a time in his life that wherever he spent a night was home. It mattered not if nighttime found him in a sleeping bag on a jungle's floor, or enjoying a snooze at Club Med. Ward Holland had been an adaptable soul. Occasionally, he might be found nestled in the arms of some nameless female he had encountered along life's highway of diversified sins and thrills. For Ward Holland, life had been an adventure. He had lived it to the fullest without regret or a backward glance. He had traveled the globe with danger as a partner, and he had enjoyed every minute of his precarious life that he could remember. Ward had lived his life on the edge; and he had earned the right to believe he was invincible.

Harri knew that her father had held a low tolerance for weaker humans, and had somehow managed to prevent such from becoming a part of his element. In his regime, every man had to carry his own weight or get off the playing field. He didn't have the time or the incentive to coddle the weak. Then fate had intervened and Ward Holland had unwittingly placed himself in a situation where he would become one of the lesser beings he had always loathed.

In order to survive and keep his infant daughter alive Ward Holland had been forced to become a mere human, an every-day-run-of-the-mill, being. And he had multiple reasons to doubt that he could handle such a roll. The only thing that kept him directed was the simple fact that he had to 'handle it'. There were no alternatives.

Harri had heard the story from Silana many times. She had even heard bits and pieces of it from her father, and she had wondered if she would have liked her father if she had known him before she was born. Perhaps not! But she would have admired him!

Harri smiled now as she recalled the story, beginning with her birth:

<hr>

CHAPTER 3

"I WILL NOT—I CANNOT—GIVE THIS BABY the care it needs!"

Ward Holland had all but yelled out those words in desperation and panic. "Don't you understand, Silana? I couldn't even keep his mother alive here in this stinking piece of hell, and I don't know a damned thing about babies. This is the first one I've ever seen up close. If my life depended on it, I couldn't even change his diaper!"

"Her diaper, Señor Holland! The little one is a girl," Silana had told him softly.

"A girl? In this friggin' jungle...?"

Ward, had settled back heavily on an antiquated steamer trunk, a look of total disbelief and horror spreading over his tired, unshaven face.

"How could this be happening to me...of all people?" he had asked in despair. "I'm Ward Holland! I've spent a lifetime avoiding this crap. Things like this happen to normal people with normal lives and normal jobs. They don't happen to Ward Holland!"

Ward had cast an incredulous glance at Silana as she held his infant daughter close to her breast. Without a single thought as to a plan for himself or the small, always-hungry bit of screaming flesh, Ward dashed from his quarters. Within minutes he found himself pushing deeper and deeper into a tangled humid jungle; a miserable, mucky, portion of earth that he had come to hate.

Farther and farther, he pushed, full speed ahead, away from all sounds, smells and thoughts of the vile outpost. He tore a path through tangled vines with his bare hands. He wanted to keep moving until he reached some place where the air smelled fresh. A place where he could breathe, any place that didn't smell like rotting bract and open sewers.

Without warning, Ward's pain-racked brain changed courses. To his consternation, something inside him began pulling at his senses and dragging his booted heels to a standstill. Whatever it was had compelled him to slow down; forced him to stop and think. The nameless something was insisting he turn around and go back. He hated it. Whatever was controlling him now, he hated it with a passion that was making him ill.

"Whhyyyyy... ?" He shrieked into a dense surround that absorbed his agonized yell without so much as an echo in return for his desolate outcry.

CHAPTER 4

THE OUTPOST WAS A GREEN, gaseous piece of earth that Ward and his new bride, Lydia Malone Holland, had unwittingly become residents of. It was a crummy piece of overgrown turf that lay forty miles northwest of a large settlement that had been appropriately named, "Villa Guano".

The growing company outpost that Ward had found himself totally in charge of, had been established on the highest, and the only, tract of solid earth for ten miles in any direction. All around the new company camp were seeps, bogs and sinkholes that smelled like open sewers when the wind blew from any given direction. After a while, Ward had gotten used to the smell, but the problem with the company's supporters was an ongoing thing that no sane person could get used to. And if he was seeing the picture clearly it wasn't going to get any better.

The men working this project had no representatives on the outside that could speak for them. As of yet, *nobody* had found a channel of communication to the outside world. In short, there was nobody to complain to about their intolerable situation. At any rate, nobody who could improve it. Ward himself was the Big Cheese at the post, and he didn't even know who was paying his salary. In truth, he wasn't even sure he was being paid a salary.

The only access to Villa Guano, a fairly large settlement where the crew acquired some of their supplies, was by way of a poorly constructed dirt road that had to be reworked after each heavy rain. The more Ward explored the area, the more he was convinced the whole jungle was a large piece of repugnant earth that God had never heard of and only the very strong survived long enough to complain.

"I have to survive it," Ward said vehemently. "I have to survive, and I have to ensure that my daughter and my men survive, too.

It didn't take a bundle of wisdom to deduce that Ward Holland had made a major mistake in bringing his wife along on this assignment; even a fool could have figured that one out. Now, after the fact, Ward was feeling the full impact of his foolishness. After reading the fine print on his contract he discovered that a promise of needed supplies and additional personnel, such as a company medic, was just printed words on a piece of paper and didn't mean diddly squat to the workmen at the post. They had already discovered their contracts were meaningless. Meanwhile there was a doctor, of sorts, at Villa Guano. "The "Medicine Man".

Villa Guano was the center of all civilized activity, if one could call it that, for over two hundred miles in any direction. Also, in every direction lay treacherous jungle that no sane person would dare tackle, and especially not with a family. With a few rare exceptions, Villa Guano was made up of primitive and ignorant people, and infested with money-grubbing yahoos that were getting filthy rich screwing the primitive and ignorant.

Ward and his bride had been flown into the jungle five weeks after the original crew had been flown in. Their small plane had landed at the airstrip in Villa Guano and they had been trucked to the company's post where their living quarters had been prearranged for them. When Ward and his bride arrived at the company post, Ward saw two men supervising the construction of a small landing strip near the post. The two men helped Ward get settled and explained present procedures. A few weeks later when the landing strip had been completed, the two men left the post on a twin-engine Cessna and nobody saw them again after their departure.

Now that the company had its own runway, all the company's supplies were flown directly into the compound, thus eliminating the haul from Villa Guano.

Due to the eternal rainfall and the rapid growth of jungle greenery that overran anything that stood still for a moment, the small runway was a total bitch to keep up.

"I'll contact my agent," Ward had told his troubled wife. "If I explain the problems we're having here, surely, he can contact the dirty sons that are in charge here and maybe *he* can get some action going. We have a contract Liddy, there must be a way to force those suckers to be responsible." Ward's words sounded hollow, even to his own ears.

Lydia smiled, but her smile wasn't convincing. She had sensed the problem from the start, and she was wise enough to realize that the situation wasn't getting better—that it wasn't going to get better. Lydia brushed her lips lightly across her husband's cheek, and just for a moment she held onto him tightly. She knew that pretending a brave front wouldn't work with him. She had never been good at acting, and Ward could read her like a book. Everything about this jungle was a nightmare and she couldn't pretend otherwise.

Ward held his wife close for a moment, angry that he couldn't summon up even a few encouraging words for her.

"I'll be back soon, Liddy," he told her, pushing her away before he said something stupid that would only add to her doubts and uncertainty. "There's a few things I need to check on at the construction site."

Ward placed his hard hat on his head and headed toward the crewmen who were preparing a foundation for a metal storage building.

As he neared the area, he heard one of the company's planes coming in. Without stopping at the construction site, he walked on to the landing strip and waited for the pilot that, hopefully had brought the supplies Ward had ordered days before. He waited until the plane taxied to the newly erected hangar, then he walked over to the twin engine Cessna that glistened in the noonday sunlight and waited for the pilot to step down.

A sullen looking man, thirtieth in years, stepped from the plane. This was not the pilot he had given his supply list to.

Ward introduced himself, and the pilot acknowledged his introduction with a grunt, not bothering to return the introduction.

After unlocking the cargo compartment of the plane so the crew could unload the supplies, the pilot turned to Ward and said, "Your foreman, Wolf Haden, will be arriving tomorrow around three in the afternoon."

So! The man can talk! Thought Ward... *But obviously he limits that ability to a self-determined necessity.*

Ward watched as the crew unloaded the supplies, then noticing that some of the requested materials hadn't been unloaded. He walked back to the pilot and asked, "Will there be another shipment of supplies soon?"

"As long as this project lasts there will be other supply deliveries," the pilot answered without further comment.

Ward decided he was right about this man, he was definitely not the chatty type, which further aggravated Ward's sense of cooperative harmony. At least the pilots, up to now, had all been friendly. Even though none of them dared to deviate an inch from the instructions they had landed with.

"You're new," said Ward. "Will you be flying all the supplies into the post now or will the old pilots be working the project also?" Ward knew his questions were unwelcome, but now he was just enjoying pushing this jerk's buttons.

"Other pilots will deliver supplies, but what makes you think it's any of your damned business? The boss decides who he'll send in," the man answered, brusquely.

So, a civil conversation is out of the question. Ward's jaw set angrily. *I'll bet this bastard kicks his dog!*

Ward turned to walk away, but on second thought decided to toss the guy something to chew on: "I'll be needing to fly back to the states in a few days..."

The pilot's back was turned to Ward, but Ward saw the man stiffen as if he'd been punched in the breadbasket.

Ward had no idea why this jerk was reacting with such hostility, but he hoped to find out. "I suppose some of you guys could make room for me on one of the company's planes." Ward felt a small satisfaction when he realized he had finally managed to get the pilot's attention. The man turned quickly around, looking at Ward with raw malice, and just for an instant, Ward thought he detected a trace of fear in the man's eyes. Ward watched as a muscle worked in the pilot's jaw, and he knew the man was trying to recover his composure. About the time Ward decided the dolt wasn't going to respond, he saw a twisted smile pulling at the corner of his mouth, a smile that gave Ward the distinct impression that the lout was hoarding a private joke. Disgusted, Ward turned to walk away.

"Nobody leaves this post until they get permission from the boss," the pilot said bluntly to Ward's retreating back.

Ward turned back to the man with a puzzled frown: "Exactly what does that mean?" he asked, not sure he had heard correctly.

The pilot calculated the distance to the door of his plane and then said, "You're a smart man Mr. Holland, you figure it out," then he climbed back into his plane. Ward saw the man remove an automatic weapon from a boot inside the plane. He placed it on the passenger seat, gave Ward a long menacing look, then closed the door with a determined yank. Ward guessed the creep was almost as scared, as he was belligerent. Ward scowled at the asinine pilot then threw him a bird before he could taxi onto the runway.

The next afternoon Ward sat in the shade of a newly erected metal hangar, waiting for the plane that would bring his foreman to the post. He fully expected that Haden would have information about the delay in the arrival of needed supplies and personnel, especially the company medic and extra guards.

While waiting, Ward made notes of problems he would discuss with Haden, problems that Haden would most likely be handling.

Also, his foreman had to be informed of the growing disquiet among the men who had signed on with the company and were now working hazardous positions they were not trained for.

Ward could easily understand why the men were pissed. After looking the project over they realized this assignment was not even close to what they had signed up for. None of them were working jobs they had been trained for, and most were working jobs they wouldn't have touched had they known the score up front.

Ward was angry about the whole set-up and, even he, wasn't sure just what was expected here. He had read the package of information several times, and it didn't agree with his contract. Something was way out of kilter.

Past assignments that Ward had signed on for were cut and dried, nothing left to the imagination. His agent would pull together a highly trained crew of men who would be dropped by parachute, or trucked into areas where riots and uprisings were running rampant. Or where opposing groups of rebels were out of control and causing embarrassment for some ruler that was willing to pay a fortune to regain control without loosing face with powerful allies or political supporters.

Ward wasn't the least worried about not being able to handle this new assignment—anyhow, he wasn't worried at the moment. He had never met an assignment he couldn't handle. Still, he wanted to know what he would be handling. This project was not what he had expected and the wording in his contract didn't exactly clear it up. All he could glean from reading the half-dozen pieces of paper in the package was that he was suppose to supervise the construction of a landing strip that would support the weight of large and fully loaded cargo planes. The contract specified the need for trained sharpshooters, combat soldiers, construction workers, and heavy equipment operators. The dimensions of the runway were clearly established but there was no mention of where he would obtain supplies or equipment for such a project.

It was obvious the small craft that delivered the prefab units would not be delivering the heavy equipment. He could only hope that somebody on the outside would recognize the problem and respond with some answers. Also, there was no mention of why said cargo planes would be landing at this remote jungle outpost, or why the workers here would need the heavy equipment? What was the purpose of the equipment? Drugs could be ruled out. Nobody in their right mind would go the expense of such operation when the smaller and faster planes would work better. So, the *why* of such endeavor was still up for grabs?

So far, the crew had managed to erect all of the requested buildings: three storage buildings, one large repair shop, and the aircraft hangar that housed not only small aircraft for pilots that found the need to remain overnight, but it also held the only communication system the crew had access to. Unfortunately, the post's communication system extended only to approaching aircraft that was landing on the unstable runway.

Sometimes, after a heavy rain, all company aircraft would be directed to the airport at Villa Guano because whole sections of the company's landing strip would wash out, leaving behind bogs and opening up sinkholes.

All of the buildings, including the hangar, had been flown in as packaged materials. The packages had been such that fit into aircraft that could land safely on the inadequate, temporary runway. Ward was certain that if the proposed landing strip were ever to become a reality, much heavier, more sophisticated equipment would be needed. Ward had no idea where that equipment would come from. The present runway would barely support the weight of the smaller planes that landed almost daily now.

After considering all the things he wasn't sure of, one thing remained that he was sure of: he wanted to get all the problems squared away, get organized into a working unit and get this assignment completed on schedule, or sooner. This on-the-job-training was clearly not his type of operation.

After picking up his new foreman, at the hangar, Ward took him around the post and introduced him to the crew, learning as he began introductions that Haden already knew many of the men.

After he had clued Haden in on current events at the post, he asked him about the medic, the guards, additional supplies and crew members that should have arrived two weeks ago.

"I'm sorry, Holland," said Haden, "but I'm a new man on the job, too. I have no knowledge of this company's policies. Frankly though, I've never heard of guards being offered for personal protection of employee's families, not in this line of work, but I suppose it's possible. I'm sure there will be guards, but their duty will be to protect the company's equipment from invasions by native looters and terrorists. I've been told the jungle is full of both."

"And the medic?" asked Ward.

"Nobody has informed me if a medic will be available at this post," said Haden. "I'm not used to having a doctor around, so it never occurred to me to ask. As you most likely know, most of us are trained to do emergency medical procedures. If anybody gets sick or injured, one of our own can usually handle it. If not . . ." Haden left the sentence hanging, knowing Holland would grasp the unspoken implication.

"And as for company contracts," Haden said, shaking his head, "the only one I've read is my own. There's no mention in my contract about protection for family members. My contract explains my personal responsibilities. It also informs me that I will be supplied with shelter and a bed. That could mean almost anything, right down to a tent and a sleeping bag, and, if I'm really lucky, an oil burning hot plate; although, in my contract there's no mention of that particular luxury. My own contract does not include protecting other company employees or their families."

"Those sons-of-bitches!" said Ward angrily. "It looks like we've been had."

"You may not be aware of this, Holland," said Haden, looking Ward up and down, "but you've acquired quite a reputation among some of the men I've worked with. You and I have never crossed paths before, but I've tripped over your reputation a time or two. If you're telling me this is the first time you've been lied to about an assignment, well... you still have a lot to learn, and you don't deserve the reputation that follows you like an armored shadow. Personally, I learned a long time ago that every man is responsible for his own survival when he signs on with the Rat Patrol. That's why we're paid the big bucks—to take big chances."

"I've been lied to by the best and the worst," said Ward, "but I'm not used to being lied to by the people who pay my wages. I've signed on with some strange and, occasionally, brutal assignments, but the people who supported the assignments have been pretty straight with me, barring some unforeseen events that nobody could have predicted."

"You've been a lucky man, Holland," said Haden. "The assignments that I've worked have offered two conditions, very rich for the lucky and very dead for the less fortunate; which leads me to believe that you have had more than your share of good luck, or a very short memory. Or maybe you've just had some really posh assignments."

Posh assignments? Ward shook his head. In his line of work there were no such a thing as posh assignments. Ward had known from the onset of his chancy career that only the alert and the lucky survived the test of time. It didn't take a genius to figure the odds when one signed on with an outfit that promised only two options: riches beyond the average man's dream, or sudden death. When people got careless on the job, they got removed, one way or another. Ward feared he had fallen into the latter cast this time around and again he wondered how it could have happened to him.

In truth, Ward knew how it had happened. His agent had called him about the assignment and before the man had finished speaking, Ward had already said yes. The offer was too good to even consider passing up. When the dollar signs had reached six zeros, and his agent was telling him it could all be his for hardly more than a year's work in a remote portion of earth that few people outside of its local populace had ever heard of, it didn't sound half bad. But his agent had forgotten to mention, or maybe he never knew about, the appalling conditions that came with the job. One of the details he forgot to mention was the fact that the company had set up camp in the heart of nine thousand square mile of uncharted, savage jungle. Most of which was made up of silty mud, sink holes and anaconda that easily measured up to thirty feet in length. Every body of water, large or small, was infested with giant size piranha, and nobody dared run short of mosquito repellent. Ward was used to working in such environment and for the most part he found it intriguing. He could cope because he was trained to cope. Coping was what Ward Holland did. He couldn't remember an assignment, no matter how wretched, that he hadn't realized a great deal of satisfaction from. As a man alone he had laughed at danger—even loved it. But Ward was not alone now, he had a wife, a wife that would be a part of his life forever, and he had been married less than two months.

Ward still couldn't believe he had actually taken that final step to the altar. After deciding upon his field of employment some ten years ago, he had never once courted the notion of having a family. In his line of work a family was a luxury he couldn't afford. That is, until met and fell in love with Lydia Malone. Lydia was everything that Ward was not. She was the perfect specimen of humanity, a woman that could make Ward Holland a whole person. She was the opposite side of all that was dark and ugly about his life. She was brightness and sunshine; she was softness, beauty and gentleness; she was unadulterated class.

How easily he had forgotten everything connected to his career. After meeting Lydia, the single most important thing in his life was to make her his forever.

Ward contacted his agent and explained his circumstances.

"A wife!" His agent blurted into the phone. "Surely you jest! You don't have a wife—you're not the marrying kind. What are you trying to pull here, Holland? Are you holding out for more money?"

"No, that wasn't what I had in mind when I called," said Ward, "but I'm open to any new offers, or additional fringe benefits you might arrange for me. And I am married! Any assignments I consider now will have to be considered with my wife in mind."

In a matter of hours Ward got a call from his agent notifying him that arrangements had been made to provide acceptable quarters for Lydia at the company post. She was to be supplied with domestic aides from a nearby villa and guards would be made available for her protection. Lydia found the arrangement acceptable and followed her husband down a one-way passage into a nightmare from which, for her, there would be no return.

<hr />

CHAPTER 5

WHEN, AFTER ALL HER PRECAUTIONS, Lydia discovered she was pregnant, she had to accept it as an irrefutable fact, there was nothing she could do to undo her pregnancy.

"A baby!" yelled Ward. "You must be out of your mind, Lydia. You can't have a baby! Not in this friggin' jungle. It's out of the question—you can just forget it!"

"Obviously, you misunderstood what I said, Ward." Lydia was trying to be patient in spite of her husband's outburst. "I'm not asking permission to have a baby; I'm telling you we're going to have a baby."

Ward looked at his wife as if she had gone mad. He was speechless as he tried simultaneously to deny and accept what she had just told him. If she was pregnant there was nothing, they could do to prevent the birth of their child.

Still, a part of his mind was silently yelling, *how could this have happened?* He shook his head. *Dumb question.*

"I'm getting you out of here Lydia. Like I said, there's no way you can have a baby in this stinking jungle. There's no hospital here—there's not even a doctor here."

Much to Ward's dismay, he discovered that getting his wife out of the jungle would take more than a few bucks to buy a plane ticket. Too late, he discovered the gaseous, overgrown parcel of earth was like hell in more ways than one; when you got there you couldn't leave.

Now, he fully understood what that pilot had been trying to tell him. Nobody could leave this place, dead or alive. He and Lydia, along with his whole crew, were being held captive in this jungle.

Silana Ociano, a resident of a nearby villa, had practically adopted Lydia from the beginning of her pregnancy. Silana was the local midwife, and the only person in the area to have any medical knowledge, and her knowledge was limited to setting broken bones and treating her patients with herbal remedies.

When Silana worried about leaving Lydia even for a few minutes, Lydia would assure her, "I have Mario Akio and he is more responsible than many adults" Mario could speak a bit of English and Lydia adored him. She would be okay with her two friends, even without a doctor. Mario was always with her, and Silana would be there when needed.

At first, Lydia had overlooked young Mario as a personal aid because he had been with her from the day, she moved into her quarters at the company post. Also, he was hardly more than a child.

Mario had followed her around from the day she arrived at the outpost. Without asking permission, he had carried all the suitcases and heavy items into their quarters. He had helped them move the furniture around until Lydia was satisfied with the arrangement. From the beginning, Lydia and Ward had believed Mario was a part of their domestic help, and both were happy with the choice.

The Hollands were surprised when they discovered there were no domestic aids. Mario had been helping them in exchange for the food they gave him each day.

"If he wasn't sent to us by the company's supporters, then where did he come from?"

"I have no idea," said Ward, "but if I were you, Liddy, I wouldn't put a lot of faith in him staying around for long. If he's just a jungle waif, the only thing he's looking for is a handout for a while then he'll move on to other parts, and sometimes these youngsters have no qualms about stealing the shirt off your back before they move on. It might be wise to keep an eye on him."

Time proved her intuition to be right, and Lydia was happy she had trusted Mario. The boy was sharp and eager, and learning English much faster than Lydia was learning Spanish; and Lydia was convinced that Silana was a true saint. Possibly the only saint that ever existed in a jungle.

Ward discovered Mario had constructed a small hut for himself only a few hundred feet from his and Lydia quarters. When he checked inside the hut it was neat and clean. The bed, which was nothing more than a few tattered blankets, was made up neatly and his foodstuff was placed on a thick, hand fashioned piece of timber that he was using for a table. His few dishes were clean and placed neatly beside the foodstuff. A small bag was hanging from a peg on the back wall. Ward guessed the bag contained the boy's clothing and other personal effects.

Ward and Lydia learned from Silana that Mario had been abandoned by his parents at the age of eight. According to Silana, Mario's father had fallen ill and could no longer provide enough food for his family, fearing for the welfare of their younger children, Mario's parents decided the boy was capable of providing for his own needs, and had sent him away to fend for himself. Silana had helped him as much as possible, but her own livelihood was far from secure. Often, she had worked through a day and sometimes half a night, with only a cup of herbal tea to sustain her.

Silana taught Mario how to survive on plants, roots, wild fruit, and small, edible critters. She had even taught him to recognize the difference between the poisonous and non-poisonous species of both plant and animal life forms.

Ward and Lydia moved Mario into their spare bedroom. The room had an outside entry, and Ward closed off the inside connecting door, creating private quarters for the boy and themselves. Lydia was glad Mario had found her before moving on to other parts of the jungle.

Silana and Mario looked forward to the baby's arrival. They watched over Lydia with a singular, attentive vigilance and kept Ward posted on all activity in the area. If either of them detected anything unusual in the proximity of the outpost, they informed Ward immediately.

Two weeks prior to her baby's arrival, Lydia knew something was wrong. Reluctantly, she confided her fears to Silana: "It is possible I have a problem Silana," she told her friend warily. "I might not have an opportunity to watch my baby grow up. If my baby survives and I do not, I fear for what will happen to him. Without a mother he doesn't have a chance of surviving more than a few days in this jungle."

"No! Señora. No!" said Silana, alarmed. "You must not speak of such things. I am fearful of why you tell me this. I wish to be with you and the Señor and the little one as long as you need me, but you must remain with us also, you no can go away, Señora!"

"If what I fear should become a reality, I will not have a choice Silana. You are a wise woman and you are aware of the possibility. I know you have delivered many babies and you have watched helplessly as mothers and babies die. You know I'm telling you the truth; I can only pray that I'm wrong."

"If the Holy Mother should find a reason to take you away and leave the infant to earthly mortals, you must not worry Señora, I will care for the little one as if he were my own. I will care as long as I have life within me."

"You have said the words I was hoping to hear, Silana," said Lydia. "I do not wish to place such a burden on you, but my fear for my baby weighs more heavily on my heart than my pride. I willingly ask this favor of you. My wish is that you will take my family as your own, Silana, my husband and my baby. My wish is that you will keep them close to you always and care for them as if they were your own. If I should have to leave them behind, you must remember, I have given them to you. They are yours from the moment of my demise. If you would make me this promise I could leave this world in peace—that is, if I should have to leave it at all."

"I promise Señora, and I do not break my promises," Silana vowed solemnly as she closed her eyes and made the sign of the cross.

"Silana, if my husband does not agree to this, you must make him understand that it was my wish for you to remain with him and our baby. In time, both he and our child will love you as I do, of that I have no doubt. You, Silana, are the dearest lady that I have ever known."

✦ ✦ ✦ ✦ ✦ ✦

CHAPTER 6

SILANA WAITED UNTIL THE INITIAL pain of Lydia's funeral had dulled, then she approached Ward in her usual courtly manner. When she was sure she had his attention, she said softly, but firmly, "Señor Holland, I must speak with you. There is much I must tell you. What I have to tell you is very important, and I have decided it is time for you to know."

"Yes, Silana," said Ward, sensing she was uncomfortable with whatever she was trying to tell him.

Suddenly, Ward felt a chilling dread of what Silana might be trying to tell him. He had tried to hide his growing anxiety that soon, Silana would tell him she could no longer care for his child and his household. The thought of her leaving him was appalling, but in spite of his fears, he urged her own, he might as well face the inevitable and be done with it.

"Please feel free to speak, Silana," said Ward, wishing he could cut this moment from his life. "There's no reason for you to feel uncomfortable—does this concern the baby?"

"Yes, and it also concerns you, Señor Holland" said Silana, softly. "It is time that I must tell you that you and the little one belongs to me, now." Silana stopped and placed her hand over her heart as if in prayer, then she continued in an almost whisper, fear causing her voice to tremble, but her resolve pushed her on.

"I shall care for the two of you as long as I am living, or until you no longer need me."

"Ward stared in confusion at Silana as she spoke. When he thought he understood what she was offering he walked to her, placed his arm gently around her shoulder and said, "Silana, you couldn't possibly understand how much I appreciate what you're offering, but you must understand that we are not your responsibility. Maybe your people have different customs about these matters, but I could never place such a permanent responsibility on your shoulders, or such restrictions on your future."

"I do not think of you and the little one as just a responsibility, Señor Holland," said Silana. "I spoke the truth to you. You and the little one is now my own, the same as you would have been Señora Holland's own if she were with us. My heart weeps because she is not with us now, but it was her wish for you and the little one to belong to me when she went away. You must abide by her wish Señor Holland, as I must also."

After Silana had convinced Ward that Lydia had indeed given him and their child to her, he was baffled at Silana's simple acceptance of such a fate. This beautiful woman had readily accepted a lifetime commitment and was totally willing to donate her life to a family she had known for less than a year.

Ward's attempt to dissuade Silana fell on deaf ears. He realized she was not accepting any argument from him, and the only thing that mattered to her was the love she felt for her new family and the pledge she had made to Lydia. He was overwhelmed and humbled at the gravity of it all. Silana had accepted him and his child with a deeply emotional commitment that Ward couldn't even begin to understand. And he remembered a time when he thought of Silana's people as something very close to savage.

Ward knew, without giving it further thought that he would be proud to be *owned* by this wonderful, caring person. He also realized it gave him a solution to an otherwise impossible situation.

While Ward was trying to adjust to an entirely different way of thinking, Silana began talking again: "We must give the little one a Christian name, Señor Holland," she said softly. "She must have a name suitable for a girl child. Do you have such a name, Señor Holland? Maybe one that has held a great importance to your family?"

"Her mother's name was the only name that ever held a great importance to me," said Ward.

"Then it is settled. She shall be named Harriet Lydia, for her mother," said Silana. "I am so glad you approve, Señor, because that is what I intended to name my little girl."

"That's a good name, Silana," said Ward, "but I hope you don't mind if I call her Harri as long as she's living in this Jungle; and I would appreciate it if you would always dress her as a boy. As a girl, her life would be in constant peril. I would feel better if nobody knows that our baby is a girl."

"Silana gave Ward the first genuine smile he had ever gotten from her. He could almost see the tenseness melt away from her angelic face as she picked little Harri up and held her close to her heart. Silana turned and headed toward the kitchen with the baby and Ward heard her whisper softly, "Our baby, our little girl. Little Harri!"

CHAPTER 7

WARD KEPT AN EAR OPEN for any mention of a possible slack in operational procedures of the few aircraft that were permitted to land in his vicinity.

"I'll never stop trying to find a way to get you and little Harri out of this jungle," he told Silana. "There has to be a way. There has to be someone, somewhere in this jungle, that's brave enough to buck this freakin' system. If I can find one that's even willing to discuss it with me, I'm sure I can offer him enough money to take you and the baby out of here."

The more Ward learned about the rigorous rules attached to the few airplanes that were permitted to land on any of the accessible landing strips, the more he realized the hopelessness of his situation. Occasionally he noticed a new face in the vicinity of the post, and often new workers from the states and other countries were flown in to work the post, but none of the faces ever left the jungle—not alive anyway. Getting his daughter and Silana out, was not going to be easy, even if possible.

It had become obvious to Ward that all the airplanes landing in the area were small passenger planes except for the few, also small, cargo planes. The reason for all the small aircraft was no secret; none of the unstable landing strips would support anything larger.

Flying supplies into the remote area was a lucrative business for the few pilots that dared to chance it. The guerrilla and terrorist armies, drug cartels, outlaws hiding from the laws of their homelands, to say nothing of the native-born families just trying to survive, made the place a very lucrative spot for peddling their wares. All of the jungle residents needed food, clothing, alcohol, tobacco, medication and weapons. Over the years, they had all learned to depend on the pilots who could supply their needs. The pilots who landed with medical supplies, weapons, ammunition, or good whiskey, could, within reason, name their price. Most of the ammunition and medical supplies were sold to the highest bidders. Some of the foodstuff, such as fresh fruits and vegetables, had price tags that shocked the natives, but someone was always willing to pay the outrageous prices.

From the beginning, Ward decided to send some of his crewmen into Villa Guano on a weekly shopping trip. That is, as long as weather conditions would permit it. The two food markets in Villa Guano had a variety of foodstuff to choose from; at much more reasonable prices than the greedy sky jockey's fare.

CHAPTER 8

H OW EASILY ONE COULD LOSE track of time: Ward scanned through the tattered calendar that was barely hanging on a nail above a water cooler in his prefab office. The original hole in the calendar that fitted over the nail in the wall had been torn through long ago. Additional holes had been punched into the soft cardboard. Now the calendar hung at an angle on the wall. Its curled pages were covered with greasy fingerprints and penciled notations. Somehow, the sight of the calendar really pissed Ward off this morning. Or maybe what pissed him off was the fact that the jungle project was well into its second year and the runway wasn't anywhere near completion. The problems Ward and his crew had encountered were numerous and expensive. Most of their construction supplies were coming in by aircraft, but the planes that could land safely on the small landing strip didn't have sufficient cargo space to carry the heavy equipment they needed to finish the project.

"We've got to find some machines capable of moving large amounts of earth," Ward informed Haden. "We'll never finish this damned landing strip without better equipment. This junk we're working with is not only too small to do the job, we can't even keep it running. Trying to move large amounts of earth with this under-powered, beat-up crap is impossible, we could just as easily remove the Nile with a soup ladle."

"I have two more places that I'm checking for equipment," said Haden. "But as you know, there are no reputable companies to deal with in this jungle. Most of the conniving dealers want their money up front, using the excuse that they need money to deal with. The last time I trusted one with the company's money I never saw him again; somehow, I wasn't greatly surprised; and I wouldn't bet my lunch on ever finding the equipment we need. This junk we're using now, as you know, is the result of my last dealings with a local. It sure doesn't inspire a lot of hope."

The irony of his situation left Ward in a rage at times. He couldn't get the equipment he needed until he'd built a landing strip that would support the weight of a large, heavily loaded cargo plane, and he couldn't build the runway without the damned equipment.

However, once the runway was completed, the cargo planes would bring in heavy equipment and tons of steel and cement, and Ward had no idea what he would be using the heavy equipment and other supplies for at that late date. That part of this operation was still a big secret.

Ward had to have better equipment, now. He had to have cement and steel and a lot of other construction supplies that the company wasn't providing, if he were going to finish building a mile and a half of runway that would support a C-130.

The strip was to be constructed over some very unstable earth, and it couldn't be done with hand tools. But a bigger problem still, was in trying to make the people who were supporting this project, understand the problem.

Ward walked by the hanger and picked up his mail from the small company post office his crew had established inside the hangar. His mail, when he got mail, was never more than two or three pieces. His financial statements from the states, an occasional up-date from his agent, and twice he had gotten his tax records. The pilots, who brought in the smaller equipment and the building supplies, also brought the mail. Unfortunately, neither Ward or his crew was permitted to send anything out.

If the statements he had received from his U.S. accounts were correct, Ward's wealth was growing to mind boggling proportions, and his taxes were being paid by an appointed CPA. He had received his tax returns, complete with his signature, and everything was in order and up to date. In fact, it all looked great. Somebody associated with this damned company was taking care of business. Ward's agent had faithfully kept him informed of what was happening in other parts of the world, and somehow the information came to him uncensored.

I supposed there's no harm in my knowing what's happening in the world as long as I can't respond to it or disapprove of it. If this freakin' runway is ever completed, maybe things will lighten up a bit.

But after seriously pondering the situation, Ward realized that getting the materials to complete a landing strip that would support the repeated landings of huge cargo planes was going to take more than wishful thinking. The undertaking of such a project in this location, using irregular and under-powered equipment and faulty materials, was absurd if not insane. Most of the terrain was not just unstable, sink holes were a common problem he dealt with on a daily basis. As if those factors were not enough to discourage their efforts, for many consecutive days during the rainy season the whole area would be flooded with several feet of water.

✦ ✦ ✦ ✦ ✦ ✦ ✦

CHAPTER 9

AFTER MONTHS OF WONDERING WHY he was building a landing strip in this damned jungle, and wondering about the motive behind such an expensive project, Ward had finally been informed of the purpose for the landing strip. However, it still didn't make sense to him. The strip was going to be used in the future to fly in bulldozers, backhoes, dredges, cranes and other earth moving machinery. Ward was already aware of that part of the endeavor. What he wasn't aware of until this morning, was that the equipment would be used to change the course of a three-mile stretch of a wide, piranha infested river. The main objective behind the mind-boggling project was to build a channel around the portion that was to be drained. The river's water would be directed into the channel and then reverted back into the mainstream below the section that would be drained.

"Why in hell would any sane person pour hundreds of millions of U.S. dollars into such a senseless project?" Ward asked Haden. "What, in that three-mile section of river could possibly be valuable enough to justify such skewed quest? And that's to say nothing of the unquestioned financial support? This whole friggin' jungle isn't worth what's already been poured into this rotting sink hole."

In the beginning, Ward wasn't looking for answers to the whys and what fors of this project. All he wanted was to finish the project and get the hell out. Supposedly, he was being paid a fortune to see that the mission was completed, and that was his original goal. Complete the mission, get the hell out. But now, after every conceivable thing that could go wrong, had gone wrong, it was getting more important to know why he was fighting so hard to accomplish this ludicrous mission.

Somebody, somewhere, was renewing contracts without the knowledge or consent of the crew. Wolf Haden and a few of the crewmen that had followed Haden from one assignment to the next, didn't seem to have a problem with the automatic renewal policy. As long as they received their monthly financial statements and could watch their wealth grow, they were content to go along with the program without questioning it.

"Don't you ever wonder what's really happening back in the states?" Ward asked Haden. "Do you think the people who are supporting this project are leveling with you about your bank deposits? Do you trust them even when you know you've been lied to and jerked around by those ruthless pricks?"

"Being lied to in this business is standard procedure for me, Holland," said Haden, "but as long as I get my paycheck, they can lie to me until their tongues fall out—or as long as it makes them happy. I have a few more years to work these slimy assignments then I'm getting out. I never want to see another stinking sinkhole, or hear another bloody mosquito as long as I live. When I walk away from this bloodsucking hell, I'll never look back, but that's a few years down the line. If, at that point in time, I'm still here, then you'll hear some yelling—the likes of which you ain't never heard before. As for my paycheck, you can bet that the crew and I are being paid. I knew the procedure well enough to take care of that matter before I signed on the dotted line. And since you and I were using the same agent to procure our assignments, I'd bet half of my pay that you're being paid also."

"It's encouraging to know that you're so confident," said Ward. "I've never had to deal with a situation like this before, and frankly I'm not at all convinced. I hope you never have a reason to regret your trust."

"I can understand that you're feeling enraged with this company's underhanded tactics, Holland," said Haden. "Your anger is certainly justified. What I find hard to understand is that you didn't give this outfit a closer check before bringing your wife into it."

Ward was shocked at Haden's statement. It was the first time anybody had ever dared to mention his wife in connection with the company or its problems. Haden had spoke in a half disgusted, half tired, and more than a little disappointed tone of voice. While Ward was trying to digest Haden's verbal assault, he heard the man speaking again: "The personal mistakes you've made here are not consistent with your reputation, Holland. If making mistakes had been standard procedure for you, you wouldn't have lasted a week in this business, so what's the deal? You obviously know your stuff. I could never have brought this project as far as you have—not with the equipment you've had to work with, and yet, you seem to be totally out of sync with the human aspect of this project. You must have known what to expect. In this business every man is responsible for his own safety and that of his crew, but the bottom line is, every man's first responsibility is to himself. We were all taught that in survival training. Did you really believed this company would supply your family with bloody bodyguards? If you did, that type of thinking would be contrary to everything you should have learned in survival training. People who make the sort of personal mistakes you've made here get killed—or get someone else killed. You're the boss here, and I can't tell you how to run this project, or your personal life, but I can tell you that your life and the life of your child wouldn't be worth a plug nickel if you separate yourself from the company. There's a certain amount of protection for company employees simply because there's safety in numbers. But anyone who wants to chance their luck outside the company would need more than a few bodyguards. In this damned jungle, they would need an army to keep them alive twenty-four hours."

Ward was too angry to speak. He had never understood Haden's total acceptance of the situation here. The man was intelligent, level headed and a damn good leader himself. Haden's men, the ones who had followed him from one site to another, were loyal to him and accepted his word as gospel. And as much as he wanted to deny it, Ward knew Haden was right. Disconnected from the company he and Harri would be on their own as long as they remained in the jungle. They would be sitting ducks for jungle scum and assassins. The assassins could come from almost any corner of the jungle, even from his company's supporters—or maybe, especially from his company's supporters. His only hope was to stick until the mission was completed or abandoned. If either of those conditions became a reality, he and Harri, along with the whole crew, would at least have a fighting chance of getting out.

✦✦✦✦✦✦

CHAPTER 10

T HE PROJECT WAS WELL INTO its third year. The runway was not yet completed, and there was still no end in sight for its completion. More and more, Ward wondered about an organization that was obviously wealthy beyond reason, but somehow failed to understand that they were pouring good money after bad by keeping this project going under its current conditions. A company with as much money, or backing, as this one obviously had, should be able to get some decent equipment to the project, equipment the men could work with. That is, if they did indeed want this project to be completed. It seemed as though the people who were supporting this operation had an endless supply of green and absolutely no concept of time.

From the beginning, the crew had been working under a severe handicap. Civilized people should not have to tolerate the debasing conditions his crew had to deal with. However, the men working the project had few choices. Only the people who planned and executed this project had multiple choices, and they had chosen to allow the working force only two—work or die.

Ward and his crew were not only trying to build a landing strip, which in itself was an apparent impossibility, but they were doing it in a war zone. Each day his crew walked onto the work site, they had less than no assurance they would walk away from it alive. It took weeks, sometimes months, to replace equipment that was broken or destroyed in skirmishes with the terrorist from other sectors of the jungle. Sometimes the equipment couldn't be replaced, and the men would have to do the backbreaking work by hand that they had been doing with the faulty equipment.

Half way through the fourth year, Haden managed to obtain a few pieces of antiquated heavy machinery that actually worked. He had purchased it from a man known only as 'El Hombre'.

El Hombre worked for an organization that could only be contacted through him. The equipment, for which Haden had paid a premium price, was not really what Ward would have purchased if he'd had a choice, but it wasn't bad, and El Hombre could be contacted in Villa Guano. The man was obviously a rogue, and Ward's opinion of El Hombre didn't improve when he learned that one of his employees, a mechanic he had hired locally, was terrified of El Hombre.

Ward had taken the mechanic with him to Villa Guano to look at a piece of equipment he planned on purchasing if it checked out okay. The mechanic was checking the machine over when he spotted El Hombre. Ward saw the sudden look of fear that leaped into the mechanic's eyes. Ward was surprised when his mechanic turned his back to El Hombre and hurried from the scene. As he scurried away, he was mumbling something in Spanish. All Ward heard was, "El Hombre...Sangre De Lobo..."

The mechanic stepped around a corner and out of sight, and remained out of sight until El Hombre had departed. Ward decided not to mention the incident. Sooner or later the mechanic would volunteer the information if he wanted to. The mechanic knew that Ward had watched the action with curiosity. As it happened, it was sooner.

"Is very bad Hombre," said the mechanic. "El Hombre, he from Villa Sangre de Lobo. He see me, he send someone for me, and you, Señor Holland, would need new mechanic."

"Why would he send someone for you?" asked Ward.

"Because once I live in Sangre De Lobo. Most people there not permitted to leave. I was not given permit to leave."

"Why would anyone at Sangre De Lobo want to prevent you from leaving there?" Ward asked, frowning.

"The bad ones that run the villa do not trust all the people who live there and they will not let them leave the villa—unless one of the leader's say is okay. They are afraid if the people leave, they will pass information to others outside the villa."

"What sort of information?" Ward asked.

"Much bad things happen in Sangre De Lobo," said the mechanic. "If ever enough information of bad things should reach the ears of people in our government, the government might send many soldiers into the villa. Maybe the soldiers could prevent the bad ones, such as El Hombre, from doing bad things."

The mechanic glanced around nervously as he talked, as if he feared unseen ears were listening. Ward could sympathize with the man's fear. He was familiar with some of the activities in Sangre De Lobo. It was indeed a very bad place. But Ward needed the equipment El Hombre could supply, so he would overlook the man's choice of residence and his underhanded operations, and he would continue to deal with the rogue until this jungle project was completed. It irked him to know he needed a man like El Hombre; that he had been forced into a position to have to deal with his type. But each skirmish with outsiders could destroy pieces of their equipment, and without El Hombre he wouldn't be able to replace it, and even if he could, it might take months. He would keep El Hombre as his supplier, and try to forget the ugly bastard was also a terrorist. However, forgetting that might not be easy. El Hombre might see to it that he didn't forget.

Ward was beginning to see why his company couldn't get needed equipment into the jungle. It couldn't be flown in at the present time, and the terrorist would seize anything as valuable as heavy equipment if someone dared to bring it into the jungle from a city such as Bogotá. Ward knew that El Hombre, or some other terrorist, could steal the equipment that Haden had purchased and Ward would have no choice but to buy it back again.

"Beginning today we're going to keep our own soldiers posted at the construction site—around the clock," Ward informed Haden. "If we expect to maintain anything close to a steady progress, that's the only way we can manage it. While we've never entirely lost a battle to any of the jungle's warring populace, too many of our men have been taken out by jungle snipers, and it's getting harder to recruit good men to work the project. As you know, some of the men we brought in to replace the ones we've lost can't be trained to eat with a fork."

Ward's inability to control the situation with the snipers and the growing discord among his crew was weakening his authority on the job. His men were not showing up for work and, more often than not, some failed to offer an excuse for their absence. He knew he had to tighten the reins on the crew if he expected to complete the landing strip. Even if his sentiments lay heavily with the men. He recognized the danger they all faced each day, and he was tired of losing good workers.

While Ward mulled over the problem, Haden approached him with a possible solution. His proposal would be expensive and time consuming, but workable.

"You could stop the work on the landing strip for a while," said Haden, "and have the crew clear away all the growth near the new strip. The heavy growth around the strip offers concealment for snipers. I know it'll be a grueling task. Every piece of bush large enough to cast a shadow will have to be removed for at least two hundred yards in every direction. We could also string more floodlights along the perimeters of the cleared area and leave them burn during the night, that would discourage some of the scavengers and maybe even the snipers that use our guards as targets."

"You're talking about weeks, or months, to complete such a project," said Ward, "but it will give the crew a fighting chance to survive the snipers' bullets. It's a good plan, Haden. Tell the crew to begin the clearing today. I'd like to hold onto the competent men we have left; the last two men I hired have to be retrained every day…to find their way to work."

CHAPTER 11

"DAMN THIS SLOW-MOVING PROJECT!" GRUMBLED Wolf Haden, as he watched the endless land clearing operation. "Do you realize we've been putting in sixteen-hour days for over a month now, Holland?"

"Yes, I'm fully aware of the time we're spending on this project, Haden. But the thing bothering me most is we've just begun to make a dent in the growth—we'll be on this project at least another month, even if it doesn't rain. If it rains, the cleared area will re-grow before we finish clearing the rest."

"You know something, Holland," said Haden, "I'm really getting sick of this damned place. I don't know what the hell we're doing here, and if my guess is right neither does anybody else. I've never felt so completely worthless in my life. If anybody has even a foggy notion of what we're supposed to be accomplishing here, I'd like to hear it. If there was any purpose behind this operation maybe I could go along with it. I'm not a difficult person Holland, but I do like for things to make sense—even when I'm being paid."

"No, you're not difficult Haden, but for a man who has never complained before, you've done your share of it lately," said Ward. "But I agree with you. There should be a way to speed up this project; and it would be nice if we had some idea what we're doing here. But while we're here the crew's safety has to be a priority and trying to rush things could be dangerous; someone could get careless. Actually, even this slow pace could be dangerous. I haven't mentioned this because I didn't want to cause any undue alarm, but there's a good chance that we'll never finish this clearing project without someone outside the company getting wind of it, and when they do, it will become even more risky to keep the crew working in the heavy growth areas. Even the machines that we have equipped with bullet proof shields will only protect the equipment operators, we can't keep the whole crew working behind shields."

The land clearing was completed, and the crew was celebrating, everyone was feeling more confident now that they had a shot at surviving the assignment. Some of the crew was even grumbling about petty, discomforting things that were not life threatening. Ward took that to be a good sign of their growing confidence in their safety.

The pilots who flew food and other supplies into the jungle often bore the brunt of the crew's gripes. The pilots were free to listen if they chose to do so, but orders from the big bosses were more important than the gripes of the project's crew. Even from their best complaints, all the crew could expect from a pilot was sympathy.

Ward was certain a pilot's sympathy was never as genuine as his desire to keep flying his plane and raking in the big bucks. Ward made a point of not complaining to them. The pilots who were bringing their supplies in now were a pretty good group. Ward found himself wondering what had happened to that jackass that had only flown a few missions then vanished. But whatever, or whoever had kept that jerk away from the project had his vote.

The men who flew in with supplies always looked the project over while they were at the post. If there were suggestions from any of the crew that could speed up the action a bit, it was noted. Whenever a valid suggestion was relayed to the people who were supporting the project, often there would be a positive response, and the suggested items or tools would be added to a future shipment of supplies. However, the only information that was permitted to leave the jungle was that which was directly related to the completion of the project. Personal complaints and grievances were still kept safely inside the jungle's protective province. Even men who were dying were not permitted to leave—a growing graveyard attested to that fact.

The project was heading into its seventh year. The runway had just been completed, and heavy equipment was being unloaded daily. A few more men from the states had been added to the staff—men who had expertise on the operation of modern, heavy equipment. Some were family men, who, like Ward, had been promised safe living quarters in order to entice them into the jungle's operation.

One man, J.C. Mathson, who brought his family into the jungle post a few months prior to the completion of the runway, had actually brought guards with him to protect his wife and eight-year-old son, Brent. Ward wondered if the man had some inside knowledge of the company's underhanded policies and had insisted on bringing guards in with him.

Another family man, Robert West, who had recently joined the ranks of the uninformed, had been promised protection for his wife and seven-year-old son, Keil, only to discover later, as had Ward and other family men, that no guards were available. Any person in the jungle who was capable of handling the position of guard was already taken.

Ward was forever thankful that he had Mario and Silana. He wished there were others like them. Ward knew it was a wasted wish, others of their type didn't exist.

Ward knew for certain that, without Silana little Harri would not have survived the first weeks of her life, and Mario had been more than a bodyguard for Harri, he had been her teacher, her companion and her friend. The long ridiculous hours Ward had spent on the project had prevented him from even being a father to his child, and there was no end in sight to that unpleasant situation.

But in spite of Ward's hellish work schedule that demanded most of his time, Harri had survived. She was now six years old, and she was one tough little package.

Silana had been her mother and, like Mario, her teacher. Mario began training her to run when she was three. He played hiding games with her at least two hours daily. If Harri could evade him for five minutes she was rewarded with a cookie or a bit of Silana's candied fruit. Now, at the age of six, if she could get a thirty-second head start on him, she could disappear like the wind. On more than one occasion Mario had searched, panic stricken, for several minutes while wondering if he would ever find her. If she ventured too far from their quarters, she could step into one of many sinkholes that swallowed up unsuspecting victim without leaving a trace.

Harri had super hearing and eyes like an eagle. She always knew where Mario was as he searched for her. She would let him wander through the jungle until he was ready to call Silana in on the search, then she would jump out from her hiding place and surprise him.

Harri loved her life in the jungle and couldn't understand why her daddy wanted them to leave their home and go to some strange land that she knew nothing of, except from books.

After Harri met Brent Mathson, who was almost eight-years-old, and Keil West who was barely seven, she knew she would never want to leave her jungle home—not in a million years—or, at least, not as long as Brent and Keil were there.

From their first meeting, both Brent and Keil believed Harri was a boy. With little effort she became the leader of the group. She taught them the tricks of jungle survival, and the three of them were inseparable.

Brent's mother, Ellen Mathson, was appointed post teacher for the three jungle urchins and two older boys. There were other children at the post now, but none old enough to attend school. Ellen Mathson also believed Harri was a boy. Harri was taller and stronger than either of the two boys she had made fast friends with, and it was obvious to anybody who bothered to notice that she was head honcho.

By the time she was nine years old, Harri was sure that Keil West was the best friend she would ever have. He was her buddy, her confidant, her soul mate. There was but one secret she had not yet revealed to Keil, she had never told him she was a girl.

Brent Mathson was another story. Harri knew Brent could never be the pal to her that Keil was, simply because she loved Brent with a passion that was reserved for only one male in a female's lifetime. She simply could not treat Brent like a brother, or even a close pal.

As Harri grew older just being near Brent stirred up emotions in her that ran from sweet ecstasy to violent anger, and her inability to control those emotions created more than a little conflict between the two of them, and caused her to hold back on being completely open and honest with Brent.

Being a female was not easy for Harri. When she began to feel the frustrations and emotions of a normal female, she couldn't understand that those emotions *were* normal. She couldn't deal with them. When she felt her pride, or even her position with her friends being threatened, even in the slightest way, she became angry, often when there was no real cause for it.

It seemed to Harri that Brent was constantly looking for new ways to rile her. He was forever competing with her in games that required tremendous strength, or some stupid mind games that required mental skill or extreme willpower. Harri couldn't accept it when Brent won at any of those games, which he did, more and more often. Then, suddenly, Harry was failing to win any games that required sheer strength.

Those last six months were the most difficult for Harri. Everything around her began to change, even Brent did a one-eighty. Almost overnight Brent grew taller and heavier, and even though Harri could hold her own with any other challenger, she failed when the challenger was Brent.

Harri stayed angry at Brent most of the time now. She couldn't understand why he was suddenly treating her as if she were some fragile piece of crap that would break if he treated her normal; normal being all those years that Brent had no qualms at all about winning at any competition, no matter who had to lose in order for him to win. And he had expected nothing less from Harri, and she had seldom disappointed him.

Now, Brent was making her crazy. He was causing her to doubt her own identity, and that was wrecking her self-confidence. She was having strange dreams about him. In her dreams he would hold her in his arms. *How could I ever dream such a dumb thing?* Brent still believed she was a boy, and she didn't want him to touch her. All she wanted was to find a way to get her relationship with him back to where it was before all this craziness began. Back to where she was comfortable with him as a friend and worthy opponent.

Then suddenly Harri's world came tumbling down around her in a single day. Brent and his parents had disappeared from the jungle post.

Harri cried. Since she was a baby, she had never cried. The salty tears were foreign and disgusting, but she couldn't stop their flow.

Silana found Harri weeping into her pillow. The sight was so uncommon it startled her. "My baby, what is wrong? I'll find Mario and ask him to go for the post medic and bring him here".

The thought of the doctor coming to her home and probing into her most secret feelings was, in Harri's opinion, the only thing that came near to being as bad as losing Brent.

Harri felt a great deal of sympathy for the old doctor, but she didn't feel enough sympathy for him to want him in her personal life.

Each time she saw the doctor walking from his metal office building to one of the workman's quarters she always felt as if she should assist him in some way. He always looked as if he were in pain.

The doctor had appeared at the jungle post about four years ago, and even then, he looked as if *he* needed a doctor. The people at the post had been happy the company had found a doctor willing to offer his services to the remote outpost. That is, until they saw the poor man in person. Actually, he was a good doctor, and had at one time been among the very best. It was just that he was getting along in years and had been considering retirement until he was offered the post position.

Accepting the position in a remote jungle had been a last-ditch effort at doing something worthwhile for his fellow humans before he died. At the same time, it added a little adventure to his own boring existence.

The man was a noble old soul, but Harri had no intentions of adding any adventure to his life, not now, not ever. He had her sympathy and that was all he would be getting from her. Just thinking about the doctor probing into any part of her life helped bring her tears under control. Wiping angrily at her red eyes, she managed to convince Silana she was not ill—just angry with herself for losing an important contest to Keil.

Harri was angry at everything in the jungle that might have taken

Brent from her. Brent had been yanked away without warning. He never knew she was a girl. He never knew she loved him.

After Brent's disappearance, Harri and Keil became even closer. Keil's mother took on the responsibility of teaching the post's children. She was not a certified teacher but with all the textbooks Mrs. Mathson had left behind, she had few problems.

Both Harri and Keil were extra bright teenagers, and had no problem with the change in teaching methods.

By the time Harri turned fourteen, the jungle project had leveled out to a stable forward motion. Ward was finding more spare time on his hands and was spending it all with his daughter. He was amazed at how much she had learned without his being available to teach her. She was a whiz at English, math and world history, and at the same time she could hold her own with the best of the older boys who indulged in jungle survival tactics.

Ward knew some of the older boys were taking their survival training seriously while others were participating just for the sport of it. He believed Harri was serious about her training, but he suspected she also relished the competitive action.

When Ward joined in the training sessions and began teaching Harri the finer arts of hand-to-hand combat, he was surprised, but impressed, at her ability. Not only could she learn swiftly, but she already knew more than he ever suspected. She could teach him a few things now. He wondered if maybe he was getting a bit rusty.

Ward wasn't nearly as worried about his own ability slipping, as he was worried about what might be happening to Harri. He was certain she needed all the defensive skills she could acquire as long as they remained in this jungle. She needed to be prepared for any dangerous thing she might encounter. But along with his desire for her safety was another deep-rooted concern; he saw something happening to his daughter that wasn't at all what he wanted for her.

Ward looked at his daughter and saw himself at that age, and the recognition ignited a cold fear inside him. Ward had seen the same traits in young Brent Mathson, and had wondered how long the kid would survive if he didn't develop some common sense to go along with his survival skills. But Ward remembered all too well that good old common sense was not common to people like himself and Brent. They would never listen to people who had already been there; they were destined to learn by surviving whatever they encountered along life's hellish highway.

All too often the young and the brave didn't survive long enough to set the world on fire. Brent was smart, but he also fit that old cliché, "Fools Rush In." Words of wisdom would be wasted on him. Now, as Ward watched his daughter, he saw something in her he hoped to deter, or at the least, he hoped to instill in her the importance of thinking each new idea completely through before putting it into action.

It had taken Ward years to learn that simple lesson. Some of his acquaintances had never learned it, and most of them were dead. Ward wondered if he was already too late. Granted, there were times a person wasn't permitted the luxury of thinking every thing through before acting on it. Even young Keil West who always tried to think things through, had also learned to act on instinct. It was just one of the things people do when they're living in a jungle.

Just before her sixteenth birthday, Harri decided to tell Keil she was a girl. Harri had fostered an unrelenting fear that her whole world would change when, and if, she could summon the courage to tell him her secret. As it turned out, Keil's only response was, "I know! I've known for years you were a girl. Even Brent knew. We didn't care. You were always gutsier than anyone we knew, so why let a little thing like you being a girl spoil our friendship?"

"That really pisses me off, Keil!" Harri said angrily. "You could have told me you knew. It would have made my life a lot easier. I've spent so much time trying to conceal it from you that it was making me ill. Now you stand here telling me you have known for years...that even Brent knew!"

"Brent did know! I'm not joshing you, Harri. Actually, Brent was a pretty smart guy, but not nearly as smart as I am," he told her with a dimpled grin. "I knew a lot of things, even back then, that Brent didn't know."

"Such as?" Harri drawled, trying to sound as though she couldn't care less what Brent didn't know.

"Well . . . such as . . . you loved him. He never knew that," said Keil. "I think he was in love with you, too. But he never knew you loved him."

"Love...? What in the...? Love?" Harri, sputtered angrily. "You guys were my friends, Keil! There was no place for what you're talking about in our lives!"

"Not between me and you," responded Keil, "but Brent was different. You must have recognized that difference and loved whatever it was."

"I always thought you liked Brent," said Harri defensively, neither admitting nor denying his accusation.

"I did like Brent!" Keil declared emphatically. "Brent was a great guy, and I still miss him a lot. But there was always something about him that was...almost scary. Much too deep for me to understand. Even when he was eight years old, he had some rather subterranean ideas on what made the world rock. He couldn't wait for the day he could hit the world with all he had, and gather from it all he thought should be his. But I won't fault him for wanting to be a part of the action. Lately, I've been giving this big world some serious thought, myself. I can understand Brent a lot better now."

"I hope you're not thinking about vanishing too, Keil West, because if you are I'll feed you to the friggin' crocodiles."

"Chill out, Harri! I'm not going anywhere for a while."

"Well, okay." Snapped Harri. "Sorry I yelled. But I don't want you dropping off the earth like Brent and his family did."

"There has been talk recently about what happened to them, but my guess is you won't want to hear it," said Keil. "None of it's very flattering for Mr. Mathson."

"Okay, so it's not flattering. I can take it. I'm not a baby, you know!"

"Just remember you asked for it," said Keil. "The rumor is, that Mathson joined up with a group of hard-core, mercenaries when he left here, and that their training camp is somewhere here in this jungle. Some of the men who work the dredge site believe Mathson is a brother to the leader of the group, and that Mathson's brother, Brent's uncle, had plans to bring Brent into the league as soon as he was old enough to enlist. Personally, I didn't find any of the gossip so terribly offensive until one of the men took it upon himself to accuse Mr. Mathson of spying on the operation here."

"What is there here to spy on?" Harri asked.

"Darned if I know," Keil said. And actually, it was only that one man who mouthed the bit about Mathson being a spy. He said Mathson was yanked from here and placed in a more worthy position after it was determined there was nothing here worth spying on. But you know how talk gets around, Harri. I'm sure it was all just speculation and gossip. Nobody knows what Mathson's reason was for leaving here. Most of the men who work the dredge site liked and respected Mr. Mathson. They were happy he found a way to escape this operation, that he had the guts to get out. If that's what happened."

"Do you believe that's what happened?

The plain truth is, Harry, that nobody here knows what happened to that family. I for one, would like to know. Sometimes at night when I can't sleep, I find myself thinking about them. Mrs. Mathson was a great teacher, and Mr. Mathson was one cool dude; and I suppose I'll never stop missing Brent."

CHAPTER 12

HARRI'S SIXTEENTH BIRTHDAY WAS A mixture of pleasure and frustration. Silana had planned a grand celebration for her, and had insisted that Ward, along with Keil and his family, be present to celebrate the occasion. Silana knew Ward would have to take time off from his work to attend Harri's party, but he had promised her he would be there.

"He should be here now," Silana said, sadly. "That ugly mud place and those noisy mud machines could not possibly be as important to the Señor as his daughter's very special birthday. Every girl should have a grand party for her sixteenth birthday, and her father should be present for the occasion."

Silana wiped angrily at a defiant tear that had manage to escape in spite of her best efforts to keep smiling. But no matter what, she would see to it that Harri was happy this day.

Mario had worked for days putting the finishing touched on the presents he had hand crafted for Harri's special day. Now he placed her present, along with a large container of freshly cut flowers on the table. Silana had everything under control, and a frolicsome air was becoming infectious. That is, until someone came by from the dredge site to inform Silana that Ward would be delayed for a while.

"Some VIPs are flying in from the states." The man told her. "Mr. Holland has to meet them at the landing strip and take them to the dredge site. He said to tell you he would be home as soon as possible."

Silana turned her oven off and covered the platters of food she had spent hours preparing. Learning about the delay was bewildering, but once more Silana managed to suppress her hurt and anger. The delay was no big surprise to her. It had happened too often in the past.

But just this one time, she had been hoping, even praying, that Ward would be home to participate in his daughter's birthday celebration. Just this one special day. Was that too much to ask?

Ward sat on the tailgate of an ancient pick-up truck and waited for the plane to land. When it taxied up to the hanger and two men stepped from the plane, Ward greeted the two men with an air of impatience. After introducing himself and exchanging a few quick pleasantries, he asked them to walk with him to the dredge site. He understood that he was to explain in detail to one of these men about his proposed method of retrieval of a recently unearthed riverboat. Actually, as Ward had learned, the contents of the riverboat was the real treasure.

These men believed the boat held something in its aged hull that a large number of people were willing to kill for; and it had become apparent to Ward that the supporters of this project were willing to kill a large number of people for it.

Ward had known three days ago that this engineer, Ted Tolver, would be flying into the jungle post to examine the pending procedures of recovery. Ward didn't know, or care, what Dr. Singly's role was in this operation, but he did care that they had shown up on his daughter's birthday.

Tolver and Dr. Singly were convinced that the hull of the recently discovered boat held two crates, and inside those crates should be the priceless objects of their concern.

The boat and its treasure had gone down in what was now a drained section of the river well over thirty years ago. Tolver and Singly were well aware of the condition of those crates. At this point in time, even a fool would have to assume the crates were, at their best, partially decayed. Even if they had been constructed of the hardest, most decay resistant wood, wrapped in heavy oilcloth, waxed over before and after being placed into the crates, there was still a good possibility the contents had been destroyed over the years.

At the worst, the crates would have been lost long ago; they would no longer be lodged in the boat's hull. Or, the whole nine-yards could just fall apart upon contact with human hands. If one of the earths moving machines should accidentally touch the crates, the result could be total disaster.

Tolver and Dr. Singly knew the fragile contents of those crates could disappear like dust in the wind if the crates were mishandled. While they were not at all sure of the present status of the crates, they wanted to give them every chance of survival this recovery effort could offer. They had come this far with this project, which had cost the project's supporters well over a billion dollars, and now, if there was even a remote chance the crates had survived the past thirty years, Tolver's job was to ensure their survival until they were safely on U.S. soil. Those crates were what this past seventeen years had been about.

Now that they were this close to succeeding in this phenomenal venture, he couldn't let anything jeopardize this chance of a perfect recovery. There would be people jumping out windows if this operation failed. Those people had taken every conceivable chance known to humankind in hopes of recovering the crates, to say nothing of dumping millions of their precious dollars into the project just on the off chance the crates might still be intact and retrievable. Now they were close to success. Now they actually had their dream at their fingertips.

Tolver didn't even want to think about anything going wrong. The recovery of those crates had to be planned right down to the last grain of sand. If he let anything happen to them, he could never go back and face the mob of people he'd left behind only this morning. The very thought was unnerving.

Ward was hesitant to inform Tolver that there was nothing more than options available to them. There was no definite proposed method for the recovery of their treasure. Ward had been protecting the find with his own life since the discovery of the boat five days ago. He had followed orders to the letter, stopping all operations at the dredge site. But he hadn't made any definite decisions about the recovery of the crates.

The boat would have to be exposed and the crates would have to be located inside the hull before he could make a decision about how to remove them. At the moment, he wasn't even sure the old boat was still intact. Or that the crates were still inside its hull. Ward hadn't been fooling himself into believing he could rush in, bring up the crates and hand them over to the anxious group who would undoubtedly be waiting for them with open arms. The removal of those crates was going to be a very delicate operation, and referring to it as a delicate operation was an award-winning understatement.

As they walked, Ward explained briefly what procedures had been used in discovering the location of the elusive riverboat.

But Tolver wasn't interested in the boat's history, he only wanted to know about its immediate future.

Ward knew that Tolver and Singly's main concern was for the safety of those packaged objects that, supposedly, lay within the deteriorating hull of the old boat. In spite of his anger at their bad timing, Ward sympathized with their concerns. He had to admit to himself that he too was concerned about the objects. He and his crew had spent ten years of their lives dredging that empty riverbed in search of those objects; it was natural to feel some concern for the future of their spectacular accomplishment.

Ward had no idea what treasure was concealed in those old crates, or how he should feel about them, but he did feel something, even if he wasn't sure what. He was convinced that there were innocent people back in the states who had helped to finance this project. He didn't believe for a minute that all of the people associated with this operation were aware of what had happened here in the jungle. He would even bet that some of them would have violently disapproved of it. Some of those people were just normal people who had money to invest in something they believed very strongly in. And whatever that something was, had created an exorbitant, feverish desire for success.

Their hope had been kept alive by some infinite, burning desire that wouldn't permit them to admit defeat. It had kept them hanging on for seventeen years, just as his desire for freedom had. Ward wasn't sure if he should feel any personal responsibility for the crates, or any real sympathy for those people, but he did, and he would make damned sure that he did everything possible to ensure their safety.

Putting responsibility and sentiment aside, he needed those crates now as much as anybody needed them; those crates were going to be his and Harri's, and his crew's, ticket out of this jungle.

But, at this very moment what Ward wanted most was to leave these men to do their fact gathering without him. He wanted to go back to his quarters, and just this once, he wanted to keep a promise to his daughter and Silana. He had given seventeen years to this damned company, and during those years he had lost his wife and been forced to ignore his daughter. He had been forced to remain in this jungle for a single reason, to find that sunken boat and extract those crates from its bowels. Now the boat had been located and made as secure as possible, and without the aid or the ingenuity of Tolver and Singly.

They could wait a while longer if they wanted his opinion, or his advice. The crates were not going anywhere and neither was he—at least not today.

Ward knew that if Tolver wasn't satisfied with the proposed method for the recovery of those crates that he would take over the supervision of the recovery. Ward was not happy with the idea of anyone taking over a project that he had poured his sweat into for seventeen years.

Ward, along with Haden and the overworked crew, had long since changed the river's course. The river had been diverted away from the dredge site for almost a decade now. For years his crew had fought everything that created a problem for the project, from terrorist guerrillas, to violent acts of nature. On many occasions the crew had worked from twelve to fourteen hours a day while building the runway, and after the runway had been completed, the battles had continued. The men had turned up ton after ton of mud and silt with bulldozers and other earth moving machines. From daybreak until well after dark the steady roar of the huge machines could be heard as the crew inched their way through the unstable earth. Each night, Ward returned to his quarters totally exhausted, his body a mass of tangled nerves. The roar of the monstrous engines would linger in his head long after he had eaten a warmed-over dinner and retired for the night.

Most of the earth was being turned up from depths of ten, to up to thirty feet below the surface, depending on the stableness of the soil in the immediate excavation area. Weariness was permanently etched into the faces of the crew as they continued their relentless search for the elusive boat.

Ward had lost count of the skirmishes the crew had been involved in with the natives and the terrorist guerrillas that operated in the Guano region. He had worked short handed for days while his men recovered from bullet and knife wounds, and even when he was working with a full crew the going was slow and difficult. All of the men had learned to keep at least one part of their mind on the nearby terrain as they inched their way through every square foot of the ever-changing riverbed. They had learned to keep an eye out for more than a sunken boat. Staying alive depended on staying alert. Even with their own guards keeping watch, it was still impossible to know from which direction the sniper's bullet would come. The snipers operated like ghosts, they would strike for no apparent reason and then disappear into the jungle. Ward had decided long ago, that for the most part, the snipers used his men as targets; what they did was just a game—a sick sport.

Ward had often thought about clearing all the jungle growth from the dredge site, as they had from the landing strip. But somehow the crew had managed to keep up their work on the dredge site in spite of the endless skirmishes with the jungle inhabitants. None of the crew had ever again refused to work, not without a good reason, and many of them had gone to work even when they had good reasons not to. All of the crew had come to a unanimous, unspoken conclusion that the sooner this project was finished, the sooner they could all leave this hell.

The dredge site was almost three miles long and several hundred feet across in its widest breadth. One of their worst, and for sure, their most frequent enemies, had been the rains that filled the empty river bed to the max, as if it had never been drained. Each time the area suffered from heavy rains, the crew had been forced to start over from square one. There were times when the silty mud had, overnight, swallowed up vital pieces of their equipment. The sinkholes had an uncanny habit of devouring anything that crossed their path. The crew would dig the equipment from the mire and build a path with timbers for the machinery to travel on until it reached more solid ground. It only took a few incidents of that type for Ward to learn that the best time saving device was to wait until the rains ceased and the river bed dried up enough to resume their work, even if it took months. Ward and his men had worn out many a deck of cards during those years, waiting for the rains to stop and the land to dry up.

Now after seventeen long years—years that to Ward would have been the best remaining years of his life, the day he had dreamed of had finally arrived. This day had kept him going even during those times when he had been convinced that the whole crew was wasting their time, working their lives away, on a project that would never reach a successful conclusion.

Not once though had Ward been tempted, for any length of time to abandon the project. Not once did he lose sight of why he had to keep going; or what kept him in this rotten jungle; he had stayed for Harri.

Now Ward had to get Tolver and Singly off his back as quickly as possible. He had promised Harri he would be present for her birthday party and he damned well planned to be there. This day was a very special occasion for him as well as for Harri. He had hoped that he would have Harri out of this jungle before this day arrived. Since that couldn't be arranged, he had planned to spend every minute of his time with her on her birthday. He had been forced to neglect his daughter during her baby years and her pre-teens.

Harri had managed to survive without his care or his supervision and had grown into a young woman—a very beautiful young woman, and she didn't even know she was beautiful.

He should have, at the very least, told her she was beautiful. And he could have told her, if he had taken the time to notice it himself.

Ward had been so determined to keep Harri and himself alive, that their survival had become the most important thing in his life. In Ward's mind, their survival had hinged on getting the project completed so they could at least have a shot at getting to a place called civilization while Harri was still young enough to enjoy some of the freedom she was entitled to by birthright. But right now, at this very moment, Ward just wanted to be with his daughter while she was celebrating her birthday. There would be another day to plan their future, but Harri would never have another sixteenth birthday.

Tolver and Singly had other plans for Ward's time. They wanted to go over his every plan of operation. They wanted to know today, in detail, what his plans were for the resurrection of the boat and the handling of the crates. Tolver wanted to fill his notebook with information that would satisfy all the investors back home. He wanted to finish his assignment today and, if possible, and be gone by nightfall. But he had to be wholly satisfied that Ward Holland's plan for the crates was foolproof, that Holland's plan left no room for doubt or error. It had to be a plan that the investors would understand and approve of; and Tolver wanted this mission completed ASAP; he wanted to get the hell out this stinking steam bath that was crawling with loathsome critters.

Tolver never believed himself to be a tenderfoot or a coward, but he took pride in the fact that he had enough sense to know that this environment was never meant for civilized people.

Ward agreed completely with Tolver about one thing. He wanted Tolver and Singly to be gone, even before nightfall, if possible. What Ward didn't want was to go into lengthy details of his future plans for the crates, at least not now. He didn't want to tell Tolver that their treasured crates were buried ten feet deep in river silt; if indeed, they were even still inside the old boat. He didn't want to tell them he had no immediate answers for their questions and he hadn't given a thought to a plan of recovery. Ward had been informed that stopping everything until Tolver arrived had been an injunction from headquarters and no further plans or actions were expected until Tolver's arrival. But it would be much too time consuming to argue points with Tolver if he tried to explain that.

Even trying to explain that he had a prior engagement he needed to attend to was becoming a formidable problem. The two men were persistent and barely civil in their demand for his undivided attention. Ward had felt put out from the moment of their arrival and the feeling grew as the minutes were threatening to turn into hours.

Ward turned to the two men and said, "Gentlemen, I have a birthday party to attend. If you need more information than I have offered,

Then we can discuss the project until you're bored stiff with it, but
for now I'm leaving the site. You're welcome to come along—or stay
here—it's your choice!"

Ward placed his hard hat on the seat of a bulldozer and walked
rapidly toward a company vehicle that he planned to drive to his
quarters. He opened the door to enter the vehicle and discovered the
two men were still with him. He had just learned something more about
the brass who were associated with this project, don't issue invitations
to them unless you seriously desired their company.

Ward was amazed at what Silana had accomplished with so little to
work with. The dining table was covered with a lace tablecloth and a
huge cake adorned the center of the table. There were bright packages
and a container of beautiful flowers setting at one end of the table, and
a colorful bowl of punch at the other. But the most amazing display of
her magic was the sixteen colorful candles that were artistically arranged
on top of the cake. Ward knew that Silana had hand crafted each of
those decorative candles that glowed on Harri's cake.

Harri was radiant: she looked as happy as if this was the absolute,
coolest birthday party a sixteen-year-old female had ever known. But
somehow, in spite of Harri's happiness, Ward was depressed. This
birthday should have been spent among dozens of debutantes and male
suitors, in a ballroom with colorful streamers and balloons flying from
the ceiling. A band should be playing dance music and Harri should
be wearing delicate lace and dainty slippers.

Ward made himself a promise that he would make it all up to her
as soon as he could get her out of this jungle. And if things would just
hold together a few more hours, Harri would be out of here. Within a
day or two at the longest.

Harri noticed that her father looked unhappy. She walked to him
and hugged him close, then asked, "What's wrong dad? You look
as if my party isn't exactly your idea of a ball—or is something else
bothering you?"

"No honey, I'm just tired and a little disgusted at how the day managed to get out of control. I had planned on being here over an hour ago. This birthday party was, and is, very important to me, Harri. We're going to do this all over again when we get to the states. You'll see what your old man can do when given a free rein and some operating space."

"Please don't be disappointed dad," said Harri. "You have nothing to regret, and if your sympathies are for me, you're wasting them. I've been very happy with my life here. My only concern is with the way you feel at being stuck here. I have nothing to compare it too, except pictures in books, and compared to them this is paradise. I'm happy, dad—very happy! I only wish that somewhere along the way you could have found some time to be happy, too."

"The fact that you've had nothing to compare this place to is one of the problems, honey. I hope you'll have many choices in your future, and as for my happiness, it will begin the day we leave this jungle. When you see what it's like to live in a civilized world with every possible convenience at your fingertips, and shopping malls on every corner, then you'll understand what I'm trying to tell you. I can hardly wait for you to begin your life in that world Harri. You'll love it! I know you will!"

Harri hugged her father close, then pushed him back at arms length, looking directly into his eyes she said, "Dad, for your sake I sincerely hope that neither of us are disappointed. It's your world that you want to return too. God knows I want to love it as much as you do, but please try to understand, this is my world, the only one I've ever known. My mother is buried here!"

Ward felt a chill rush down his spine. It had never occurred to him that Harri might not want to leave this jungle. He couldn't even grasp the notion that she may even love it. That to her this jungle was home; and it always had been.

Ward fought back a growing foreboding. He even tried to understand his daughter's feelings for this stinking spot of turf, but something about the overall big picture just wasn't working for him. The place had been nothing but a total hell for him since the day it took his wife.

"There you are!" exclaimed Ted Tolver. "We—Dr. Singly and I, want to apologize for disturbing your daughter's birthday party, but we are operating on a limited time schedule and we would like to finish our discussion about the recovery procedure of those crates. As we all are well aware, the safety of those crates is the most important part of this whole project. If they are damaged or destroyed in the recovery efforts, all the years that you and the others have put into this project, to say nothing of the hundreds of millions of dollars that have gone into it, would all have been for naught. I can assure you that the people who have invested their wealth into this endeavor would not take kindly to such news."

While Tolver was still speaking, Ward placed his arm around the man's shoulder and walked him into his office. Dr. Singly followed behind without an invitation. The office was small and the three men filled most of its space. Ward had built the tiny office onto his quarters several years past.

It was obvious that neither Singly nor Tolver were wholly comfortable with their positions at the moment, but they were prepared to bluff their way through it if necessary. Ward asked them to be seated and offered them coffee. Before either could refuse, he filled two cups and handed one to each man, then before either man could speak, Ward spoke in a voice that sounded much more patient and composed than he felt.

"Gentlemen," he began, "when you speak of time schedules and your desire to rush from this jungle, you could be speaking from the very soul of every man, woman and child at this post. Leaving this jungle is a subject that is very close to the heart of the people who are being held prisoner here. And I want the word "Prisoner" to register with both of you because that's exactly what we are—prisoners! Personally, I've been stuck in this friggin' jungle for seventeen years. I've been lied to by upper management and many other management types who have a stake in this operation. When you speak of anger, you speak in a general sense. None of you could really know the meaning of anger until you've lived with the endless degradation, corruption, terror and sheer hopelessness that exist here. All of us who are stuck here are fully aware that someone else pulls the strings that control our existence, and that our recourse has been nonexistent. My daughter and I are here, not by choice, but by the underhanded rule of the people who are in charge of this operation. I can assure you that I would have been gone years ago if not for her. Whoever is responsible for this operation can be thankful she was born. Aside from my fear for her safety, nothing could have held me here under the present conditions. She is the reason—the only reason—that I'm still here. She is the reason your damned landing strip got built, and the river's course was changed. She is the reason your boat has been located, and the reason that you might recover whatever in hell you're looking for. I'm sure, if you really try, you can understand why I have so little sympathy for your present time schedule or with any anger your colleagues back home may feel due to unclear answers on how this project is being handled. And now that we understand each other, I'm going to rejoin the festivities in the dining room and celebrate the birthday of the one responsible for your reason for being here. After the party is over, I have a proposition for you. So why don't you two stick around—have some birthday cake?"

"Why not?" said Tolver, "After all, it's not as if there are a hell of a lot of choices around here; we have to depend on you for our sleeping arrangements tonight. And while I can't speak for Dr. Singly, if I could fly out of here before sundown, I would never consider staying the night. So, in case you think I have no sympathy for your situation here, you're wrong."

"You'll have an opportunity to put that sympathy into effect shortly—so be prepared," said Ward.

Ward, along with Ted Tolver and Dr. Singly, rejoined the festivities.

Harri walked to her father's side and took his arm. She walked him to the table and cut him a slice of cake. While he was swallowing a mouthful of the delectable treat, Harri said, "Dad, I don't know what's going on here, but I don't like the vibes. Who are these men? Why are they attending my birthday party? And why do I have this feeling that whatever is happening—or is going to happen—is something I'm not going to like whole bunches?" She handed her father a glass of fruit punch and a napkin, and waited until he had swallowed the last crumbs of his cake.

"These men are our ticket out of here, honey," said Ward. "Although, they don't know it yet. After your party has ended, I'm going to enlighten them of a few important facts. You will be leaving here tomorrow if all goes as planned. I'll join you in the states, as soon as this project is finished—and we shall live happily ever after."

"Dad!" said Harri with a gasp. "What in hell are you talking about? I can't just leave here without making plans. Where would I go? What about Silana and Mario? Am I to just leave them here in the jungle? They're my family, dad. I won't leave them—or you! You must be mad to think I would. How could you expect me to live in a strange country where I'm an outsider, and try to survive among total strangers until you join me? As you well know, if one might judge the future by the past, that it could be years before you could join me."

"It won't be like that, Harri," said Ward "I'm flying with you to the states, so will Silana. I will return here as soon as I get you and Silana settled into temporary quarters in the states. I'll finish my assignment here—which will go rapidly from this point. Mario will remain with me until the project is finished and then he will be with me when I leave this jungle for the last time."

"What about Keil, Dad? Am I supposed to just leave him and never look back? You know I won't be able to communicate with him once I leave here."

"Harri, please listen to what I'm saying. When this project is finished there's no reason for Keil to stay on here. He couldn't stay here even if he wanted to. He and his family have remained here for the same reason we have, because they couldn't leave. The West family will be just as anxious to get the hell out of here as I am, and unless I'm mistaken, Keil is ready to move on. They have a home to go back to in the states. Keil has been working the dredge site for months now, and he's doing a great job, but the project is all finished—except for some clean-up work. He can't stay on here. None of the men can stay. Keil will be going to college in the states, or looking for another assignment. What I'm trying to say is, it's over, Harri, and I have but a single ace to play, and I'm going to play that ace to the hilt. I talked to the crew before Tolver and Singly arrived. The crew has agreed to go along with whatever I decide, and I have decided to go through with the plan we contrived. The only way that I can be certain that you and Silana are safely out of here is to get you out before the last part of the project is finished. If you and I, along with Silana are not on that plane tomorrow the project will not be finished to the investor's satisfaction. All of the crew are aware that once I get out with my family that I will, in turn, guarantee their safety out of here."

"Dad, are you sure that the people who are supporting this project are such monsters?" asked Harri. "Do you really believe that they wouldn't live up to any part of their contract with the people who have put so many years of their lives into this project?"

"No Harri, I'm not sure," said Ward. "It's possible that we would be treated fairly even if we do nothing, now that the project is all but finished, and the supporters have in sight all they ever wanted from it. It's possible that since we have no proof of what they've done, up to this point, that they wouldn't jeopardize their future position by creating a problem for us now. I have believed from the start that a large portion of the people who are supporting this project had no idea of what's been happening here, and after the project is finished, I believe those people may ask questions about the crew that finished it, and somebody had better have some answers. But there's still a lot that I don't understand about what has happened here, and I have decided not to take chances with your life. I want you out of here. None of the men trust the powerful supporters who have controlled this project from up front, and none of us have been able to determine their motive for keeping us prisoners here for all these years. We can't be sure of their actions once they have those crates in their possession. We don't even know who 'they' are, and we would have a difficult time proving that we have been held here against our will. Their knowledge of that fact gives us a certain amount of security, but not enough. As you well know, our distrust is justified. We'd be foolish to trust them now, no matter what we might want to believe. So, if you will gather what things you need for the trip and inform Silana of our plans so she can do the same, we can leave here early tomorrow—that is, if all goes as I have planned it."

At that moment Keil walked through the door, and seeing the look on Harri's face he knew that somebody had rattled her cage big time.

Harri spotted Keil and excused herself to her father as she walked to Keil's side. She took Keil by the arm and led him out of earshot of the others. In a hushed voice she said, "Keil, I have to talk to you, it's important. So please don't leave before we talk…okay?"

"Sure," said Keil, walking toward the cake table, "but what's the matter with you? You look like maybe someone just died!"

"I think someone just did! I think it was me—or at the least, a part of me did," she said, morosely.

"Okay! So, I'll stick around for a while. Meanwhile, here's your birthday present." He handed her a plate of assorted candies that his mother had made. It was obvious that his mother had also arranged them on the plate and wrapped them in clear plastic—they looked great.

"Sorry I'm late for your party. I really tried to get here earlier. It's all your dad's fault," he said with an impish grin.

Why is it dad's fault?" Harri asked, knowing that it most likely *was* her dad's fault.

"He kept me busy all morning moving all the idle equipment into the compound, then he threatened my life if I didn't have it cleaned and ready for repairs by nightfall. I had to clean the mud off those monsters; and before you ask, the answer is no. I don't know why he did it. I guess he's just mean clean through."

Harri's punch unbalanced Keil. She had to seize his arm to prevent him from toppling into the cake. When he regained his balance, she said, "Dad's not nearly as mean as I am, and don't you ever forget it pal!"

"How could I? You keep reminding me with these bruising punches," said Keil, rubbing his shoulder

At that moment, Mario handed her the gift he had made for her. Harri opened it with care. He had wrapped it so beautifully she hated to destroy the effect. When she finished unwrapping the box, which he had constructed of some sort of yellow and brown wood, she gasped at the contents. In the box was a hand polished jade stone set in a smooth silver base. The backside of the base was engraved with the words, 'happy birthday' Harri. Underneath the greeting was the year, month and day of the event. It was the only piece of jewelry that anybody had ever given to her for any reason; it was beautiful. Placed neatly beside the pendent necklace was a hand stitched leather sheath that held a beautiful, shiny knife with a six-inch blade. The knife had also been hand crafted. The handle was carved from bone, and the blade was polished to a mirror finish. A message was etched into the blade in microscopic, flowering letters. Harri marveled at the beautiful script. She could not read the message precisely, but she knew the design of the knife and the inscribed message held a religious significance to Mario. In essence, what the message said to her was: "Wherever on earth you should wander, hold fast to the hand of God."

Harri was fighting to keep tears from spilling from her eyes and embarrassing everyone present, but mostly herself. She hugged Mario and kissed his cheek and then she moved to Silana's side and hugged her so close that it startled Silana.

"What was that for, my daughter?" Silana asked, still looking surprised.

Harri smiled at Silana and shook her head. There were no words that could explain what she was feeling now, and even trying to explain would make her sound like a total dork. This sudden sentiment was causing her discomfort, and she hoped it was a temporary thing. If she had to live with it, even for a while, it would surely kill her. Expressing emotions should be reserved for the angelic and the genteel. People like Silana and Mario. But in spite of her objections, a portion of Harri's brain was spinning a web of memories, and forcing her to examine each one. As her thoughts traveled back through the years, she saw Silana placing those beautiful little candles in her room, and in Mario's hut. Silana had created those candles with love, just as she had the curtains at their windows, and the countless dinners she had placed on their table through the years. Harri could still feel the feather soft kisses on her cheek as Silana tucked her into bed each night when she was a child. Silana and Mario had always been the center of Harri's world, and for a while tonight Harri thought she had lost them. Maybe she had needed that jolt, it had awakened her to how very important they were to her life.

The party was over. As Harri and Keil stepped outside she heard loud voices coming from her father's office. She could tell by the sound of those voices that her father had not yet convinced the two men, who were acting on orders from a higher command, that he would stop the jungle operation entirely if he were not permitted to take his family out of the jungle tomorrow. Harri knew that her father would convince them that his intentions were genuine, and as an end result, she and Silana would be leaving tomorrow, or within a few hours at the most. She had to talk with Keil. She had to know if he and his family had any definite plans for a future beyond this project.

Harri and Keil sauntered slowly along a well-beaten path. Harri breathed in deeply, savoring the warm, damp evening air; and she was already missing this place that she hadn't even left yet. The rains would be coming soon. In the past she had always dreaded the arrival of the rain; but she wouldn't be here when it arrived this time, not if her father had his way. Suddenly she felt that horrid ache squeezing at her chest again—she was even going to miss the freakin' rain.

Harri was finding it difficult to accept that her life in the jungle, her home, was ending. That even if her father didn't succeed in his effort to take her out tomorrow, it was only a matter of days and everyone would be gone. Her world, as she had known it, would have vanished forever. This must be what dying is like, thought Harri. You wake up one morning and everything that you always took for granted has disappeared; everything is new and different; you're in another world and nobody cares if you don't want to be there.

Everything inside Harri was fighting to hold on to a portion of this world where she had been born, a world she had loved so completely. Soon there would be nothing left to hold onto. Everybody and everything that she had known and loved would be gone. Within a few months, even if she should return, she would not recognize the place where her seed had taken root and grown. It would all be swallowed up by the ever expanding, living jungle. Anything that stood still within its confines was devoured by the jungle within days.

Harri was suddenly aware that Keil had been talking to her and she hadn't heart a word he'd said, and now that she was listening, all she could hear was the raised voices that were coming from her father's office.

"Sounds like your dad has failed to create a good working relationship with those two," said Keil. "You have any idea what their problem is?"

"Yes. I know exactly what their problem is," said Harri. "But I don't want to talk about it just now. I want to ask you a question instead."

"Okay! So, ask away!" Keil told her.

"Do you know the project here is ending Keil?"

Harri knew he did know, but she was still hoping Keil would tell her he had it all under control. That he would always be where she could talk to him. That he would never be far away.

"Sure!" said Keil. "We'll be leaving as soon as the crew unearths that sunken boat that we located a few days ago. Sure, wish I could find out what's so important about that old boat. All the men on the dredge site are curious, and with good reason. Some of the men have put a lot of years into locating that thing. I believe it's only fair that they be told what they have located. We…me and the other guys who work the dredge site, have eliminated almost everything known to the modern world that could have enough value to create the interest this project has created. We know that it can't be guns, ammo, gold, diamonds, or drugs. It wouldn't be worth what has gone into the project, no matter how much of it went down with that boat. Mr. Evens is talking about maybe writing a book about the seventeen years he's been working on this project. It would be very important to him to know what they have unearthed and why there's been so much money and effort poured into this project."

"That's all very interesting," Harri told him, trying not to sound impatient, "but the reason I wanted to talk to you is to learn, if possible, if your folks have any plans for their immediate future—like maybe a new assignment in some other county—or even here in south America. I understand that there are assignments of this sort available to interested parties in all third world countries."

Keil laughed. Harri's statement was amusing.

"Did I say something funny?" Harri asked.

"Yes," said Keil, "you said, assignments of this sort. The reason I think that's funny is because, to my knowledge, there has never been another assignment like this one in the history of civilized humans. I doubt if any of the men working this project would be willing to sign up for another like it, unless they could change all the rules and have some sure-fire method of enforcing them. Maybe you haven't heard, but the men here were literally shanghaied into working this project. Well…maybe not literally shanghaied, because they did all signed up for the project in the beginning. But all of them were led to believe their assignment would last for a year or two at the longest. All of their contracts have been renewed repeatedly without their consent. I'm sure that the 'powers that be', the individuals who are in charge of this operation, have their asses covered from every angle, but that does not change the facts. Some of the men here would put a heap of hurt on those suckers if they could learn the identity of the ones who have kept them enslaved on this project. If not for you, I believe your father would lead the pack. I believe he would find them and hand them over to the men who would jump at an opportunity to even the score."

"You don't really believe my father is angry enough to do something like that—do you?" asked Harri. "After all, he's been paid a fortune for his work on this assignment, and he never appeared to be totally disgruntled with his lot here. But I suppose it's possible that everything he's endured since I was born has been for my safety and happiness. If so, it's a damn shame, because we could have found a way out. It would have involved some risk, but we could have made it."

"Your father would never have endangered your life as long as there was a safer way to handle the situation," said Keil. "My father thinks the same way as yours. He's always believed the safest thing to do was complete the assignment and get out in one piece, without risking the families. Recently, as you know, your father and some of the men have been making plans for removing all the families from the jungle before the project is completed. None of them fully trust the supporters. Not enough to place the lives of their families in their hands after the project is finished. None of the men are sure what will happen when there's no longer a reason for the company to keep us here. And it's not as if they don't have a reason to distrust those suckers. I think it's only natural that the men are not leaving anything to chance. That they're going to insure an escape route. Ironic as it seems, two of the women

86

are willing to wait it out with their men. My mother is one of them. She knows that Dad and I will be two of the last men to leave the site. She's refusing to leave without us."

"I wonder why I can't join the one's who stay?" Harri mused.

"That wouldn't be wise, Harri," Keil told her. "It's possible this jungle will turn into WW-3. If the company decides to send in an army of soldiers to pack things down here, it could get rough for a while. Personally, I don't believe there will be any problem at all from the company's decision makers, but I could be wrong; and there could be problems from other sources, we don't know what will happen when we start pulling out. It would be better if as many as possible of the innocents were out of the way."

"I can't believe that you just referred to me as an innocent," Harri said, smiling. "I could lick half of your crew with one hand tied behind me. Face it pal, I could be a valuable asset. And if it comes to a battle, you're going to need all the good men you can get!"

"Hey pal! Don't jump all over my case, you've had me convinced for years! But I'm not the one you're dealing with here, and if you start kicking up a fuss you're going to create a problem for everyone. So, why don't you go along with your father's program for a while—make him happy? He deserves that much from you. Remember, if you don't like your new life, you can drop it and move on to something else. It's not like you'll be locked into something you can't change. As long as you're free you can change your mind, or your location, as often as you like. That's what your father wants for you Harri, to be free to make decisions without any chains attached."

"Oh, okay! I suppose you're right," said Harri. "I'll try to go along with it for a while. That bring us to the question you asked earlier about what my father and those men were loudly disagreeing. My father started the ball rolling tonight. He has by now, told Dr. Singly and that engineer, Ted Tolver, that he plans on taking me and Silana out of here tomorrow. I'm sure he has informed them that if there's a problem the operation will stop until it's resolved—but you already know all of that. My guess would be that the two men are trying to convince my dad that his plans are not wise. But dad and the men who agree with him still have that lever that you mentioned, and that lever says his plans don't have to be wise—just approved. If we don't leave here on schedule, that project will be blown to hell. There's no other alternative available to the men except to carry out their threat. Dad can fly that plane, and if it should become necessary it will be seized by the crew and used to take the families from the jungle. I believe Dr. Singly and that engineer will see the logic of complying with dad's wishes. After all, he has managed to make me understand it, to some degree, and I don't want to get on that plane any more than those jerks want me on it. And now, I'm not going to beat around the bush any longer Keil, putting our folks and this project aside for a few minutes—what in hell are your plans after this project has ended? Surely you have some plans!"

"Why didn't you just ask," said Keil. "You always fly into warp mode and for the dumbest reasons."

"I did ask! You didn't understand the question!" Harri said irritably.

"Okay! I didn't mean to avoid your question Harri. It's just that I don't have any definite plans yet. If I continue with this line of work, my mother is going to be hospitalized with a coronary—unless I can convince her I'm working at something safer than the role of a mercenary would permit. When I decide, which will be after this project is finished, I will let you know. I won't be out of touch with you as long as I have control over my actions, and you must know that."

"Oh sure! How could I not know that?" Harri said angrily. "Now that everyone's free to make decisions, keeping in touch won't be a problem...like there's a communication system growing from every monkey's rump in this friggin' jungle."

"From this point on, there will be communication," Keil told her. "As long as we have our freedom there will be a way to communicate. Even the men who stay to finish this project will be able to communicate with friends and relatives on the outside, now. They will be staying on the project because they want to, not because they have no choice. Everyone has learned something from this project. Any future assignments that any of us sign up for will come with better contracts and some guarantee that we'll be able to make personal decisions about our lives."

"I don't know how you feel about contracts Keil," Harri, Harri said grimly, "but my personal opinion is that contracts aren't worth their paper if they're not issued by reputable people. Contracts have been broken before and I'll bet my best pair of boots that a few will be broken in the future."

"Maybe so," said Keil, "but I know these men are a lot smarter now. They won't be likely to repeat this mistake—not in this lifetime."

Why couldn't the men have done this before Keil? How come they waited so long to take a stand—to enforce some control over their lives?"

"Mainly because they had nothing to bargain with before," said Keil. "Sure, they could have taken one of the planes when it came in, possibly could have managed to get a few families out. But there could have been a bloody battle for the ones who were left behind, and for what? The men would have lost everything they had worked for up to that point and possibly would have lost members of their families. The wealthy people who are sponsoring the project would have regrouped and continued with the project like noting had happened. They would be doing the same thing to other men and their families while some of our bodies rotted away in this jungle. They would have convinced the outside world that we were the bad guys. It's possible that they would have killed everyone left behind and blamed it on the ones that fled."

"How could they have convinced the world of that?" Harri asked.

"Well, look at it from the world's point of view. All the contracts are in order, and every man here has been paid a fortune for his time. A bloody battle, that we initiated, would have made us look bad, not them. Now, we have something to bargain with—something the supporters want very badly. We control the situation now. We won't have to convince the outside world of anything. We only have to convince the people who want to retrieve those crates from that sunken craft that we mean business. Like you said earlier, they will see the logic to our demands or they lose everything. In the beginning they had the lever. They held something that we wanted very badly, our freedom, and the only way we could get it was to finish this bloody assignment. Now the table has turned and we hold the prize that finishing this assignment has produced. Now we have something they want very badly, and the only way for them to get it is to abide by our wishes. What we're doing will never atone for what they did, but it's as close as we'll ever get to justice, simply because we have no proof of what they did to us."

Harri walked in silence for a few minutes, kicking at small clumps of mossy looking loam as she mulled over the present inevitable and the uncomfortable unknowns of her future.

"What's it like, Keil?" she asked suddenly.

"What's what like?" Keil asked. Wondering if he had missed a part of the conversation somewhere along the way.

"That other world? Surely you remember something about it. You were seven years old when you came to the jungle."

"Oh, that other world! Meaning the good old U.S. of A.," Keil said. "Yes, I was seven years old when I left the states, but I had lived a very sheltered life until I came to the jungle. And what can a seven-year-old do to rack up memories? The few I do have are vague, and when I try to remember them it's like trying to read small print through chicken soup. It's been over ten years now, that's a long time for me to remember something that I never paid much attention to in the first place. I do remember that I was happy there—but then, I've been happy here, too. The only thing that I missed in the beginning of my jungle tour was 'McDonald's' and 'Dairy Queen'. Now, I can't even remember the taste of McDonald burgers, or ice cream sundaes."

"Do you think I'll like it there?" Harri asked quietly.

"Yes, if you'll give yourself a chance you could like it a lot," Keil told her. "But I know you pretty well, Harri. You'll never stop fighting it unless you have a good reason to. For your sake... as well as your dad's, I hope you'll find that reason. I hope you'll give it your best shot before turning your back on it. I know that I'll eventually live in the states. For me, there's never been an alternate plan. I'll find my spot of turf in the U.S. after I get rich fighting other men's battles and digging up their buried treasures."

"You're really sure that you're going to be offered other assignments that will make you rich, other assignments that you can handle and even survive, aren't you, Keil?"

"Yes, I'm sure. There will always be jobs for men who will go where the lily livers and weak of heart, fear to trod. And, it appears as if there will always be wealthy sponsors to support such speculative ventures."

"If the states are so great, why can't you work there?" Harri asked. "Why follow the mercenaries and freedom fighters? It seems to me it would be safer to work in the states."

"I would be dumb to waste the knowledge I have acquired from this project. You wouldn't believe how much I've learned just from listening to the men talk, to say nothing of actual experience. These men have an inside track into the operations of many strife torn countries. Both sides of the conflict have need for men willing to risk their lives for a cause, or a fortune, or both. Some of the newer men who signed on to work the project here have given me information about other jobs in other countries...even who's hiring and what sort of money I could expect to make if I decide to accept one of the assignments. Right now, me being foot loose and fancy free, knowing what I know, I could almost write my own ticket, call my own shots. Any position I could find in the states, at my age, without some college behind me, would pay me minimum wage. It would take me forever to buy an automobile—which isn't exactly a luxury item in the states. I understand that it's difficult to live without wheels there. Everyone drives to work. On the other hand, if I continue to follow this line of work, I could be rich by the time I would normally graduate from college. I could still go to college if I choose to do so, and I wouldn't have to worry about who pays my tuition."

"You're weird, Keil," Harri said. "You said a few minutes ago that there were no more assignments like this one, now you're talking about following this line of work. I suppose you could explain that!"

"Sure, I can explain it," said Keil. "When I said this line of work, I meant it in the most general sense. I didn't mean an assignment exactly like the one we're finishing now. What it all boils down to, is being in a position to earn big bucks doing something that I find personally enjoyable. Even though few men would consider it for any amount of money. Fighting other people's battles in strife torn countries doesn't fall into the category of coveted careers for most younger men. In this business a man may work alone, or with an army of soldiers. Depends on the assignment. The assignments all have one thing in common, though; none of them come with a guarantee that you'll survive it. But on the flip side, every assignment that I've ever heard of left a man with a choice of whether or not to stay with it—except this one!"

"You really are considering becoming a soldier of fortune, a mercenary, aren't you, Keil? And you were bad-mouthing Brent Mathson's father and uncle for their questionable activities in just such an occupation as you're considering for a career?"

"Let's get one thing straight, Harri," Keil said emphatically. "I have never bad mouthed Brent or his father for any reason, and I don't even know his uncle. I repeated gossip just to jazz you a little. I should have kept my mouth shut. You know there's a difference between repeating gossip and morally condemning a person. There's a lot of good men out there risking their lives for someone else's cause. It's been done since the year one. And aside from that, I have a personal belief that the only thing morally wrong with anything a body does lies within the personal opinion of the interpreter."

"You sound like you've been taking lessons from Brent," said Harri. "Do you ever act as your own interpreter, Keil?"

"Every day of my life!" Keil answered.

The two fell silent. Simultaneously they turned and headed back toward Harri's quarters, each absorbed in thought. For Harri, this was a turning point in her life. She would have to battle her father for the right to remain in the jungle until the project was finished, or leave here tomorrow. And regardless of the outcome of that battle, if she should choose to fight, she would still be leaving here very soon. She would leave behind everything she had ever known as friends and home. Except Silana and Mario. She would have to cope with a lifestyle that might prove to be impossible, and live among people who were total strangers. People that she might never understand or learn to communicate with. Thank God she would have her family.

Possibly the wisest thing she could do would be to get on that plane with her father and Silana tomorrow and never look back. She was certain she couldn't win a battle with her father, simply because her conscience wouldn't permit it.

As Harri and Keil neared the door of her quarters, Keil placed a hand on her shoulder and turned her to face him. "Harri, no matter what you hear about me in the future and most likely the gossip will flow freely, just remember, you know who and what I am. Don't judge me by gossip, okay?"

"Keil, for heaven's sake! Why would you even think something like that of me? I would never judge you by anything except what I personally know about you, and I know you pretty well. I haven't judged Brent by the gossip I heard about him," said Harri. "I know you much better than I ever knew Brent!"

"But you were never in love with me," said Keil.

Harri looked at Keil for a long moment and then said quietly, "I love you more than you'll ever know, Keil. I love you and I don't want to lose you, but you're right, I've never been *in love* with you."

Keil pulled her into his arms and held her close for a long moment, and then he pushed her back, slowly looking her up and down, as if to remember every last detail of her features. Then, more seriously and more softly than she had ever heard Keil speak, he said, "I love you too Harri. You've been the best buddy a guy could ask for. I'm going to miss you like hell, and I can't even imagine not ever seeing you again!"

Harri watched as Keil walked into the humid night. She cursed the circumstances that would separate them, possibly forever. Then she cursed the hungry mosquitoes that were attacking her—her repellent had begun to wear off.

✦✦✦✦✦✦

CHAPTER 13

FROM THE WINDOW OF THE DC-9, Harri had a perfect view of Houston. She gazed steadily at the panoramic scene until the plane dropped below a level that would permit further observation from the sky. The view of the city from the sky had not been a total surprise to Harri because she had as much knowledge of U.S. history and geography as most of its countrymen. Still, actually seeing it for the first time was rather startling. Houston was the first large city she had ever seen in daylight hours. The only thing she had seen of Bogotá when she and her family had landed there were the millions of lights that illuminated the sky when their Cessna 310 landing late the evening before. Harri had roused from her sound sleep in time to glimpse the city and see the huge airport just before landing. Then they were unloading luggage from the smaller craft. By the time they had checked their luggage for the trip to Houston, it was very dark. By the time they had eaten a snack at the airport, everyone was exhausted from the trip. Rather than look for lodging for the night, they all slept at the airport on whatever chairs and couches were available. In only six hours they would be boarding their plane for Houston; looking for lodging didn't make a lot of sense.

Harri turned away from the window and began searching for her handbag and other small carry-on stuff that that her dad had told her not to check through. After she had located her personal effects, she waited for whatever would happen next. Ward leaned across Silana and whispered to Harri, "You can relax for now. It'll be a few minutes before we leave the plane even after we land.

Harri heard the jet's engines reverse and had no idea what was happening. The plane slowed abruptly and the noise caused her to feel uneasy; she wondered if everyone felt uneasy on their first jet ride. Tolver had flown them into Bogotá in the Cessna 310, and other than being a little cramped, it had been a pleasant ride. Her dad had pointed out landmarks and bodies of water that were interesting from ten thousand feet.

Harri looked out the window again just before they touched down on the runway. She had been amazed at the view of the city from the sky, but up close the huge structures looked almost threatening. Houston was not the largest city in the U.S. but she was thoroughly impressed; there was certainly enough of it to suit her.

Yes, this was slightly different from the small photos of metropolitan cities in her textbooks. But then a picture of the whole city of Houston would hardly fit on one tiny page.

Harri smiled now; remembering those long, silent nights in the jungle when studying geography, history and math was her only source of entertainment. She was thankful that Mrs. Mathson and, later, Mrs. West, had managed to bring into the jungle the many textbooks they had used for teaching. Harri had often been permitted to take them home to study and she had absorbed the knowledge from their pages as if they were a life-giving food supplement. In later years she managed to obtain other books and magazines that found their way into the jungle. Those books offered only entertainment and had been worn to shreds by every person at the installation who could read. Then there was the time, when she was in her early teens, she had been introduced to the adult literature that had been flown into the jungle by the sky jockeys. She had spent hours pouring over those magazines, adding knowledge of an entirely different genre. Harri smiled again as she remembered her first reaction to the magazines that Keil had sneaked to her after ripping them off from the crew at the dredge site. The crew had passed the magazines around until they were tattered, but they were still visibly explicit enough to cause her to blush—even now.

The plane taxied into its slot at Intercontinental Airport and Harri was anxious to leave the craft. Again, Ward held her back until all the people up front had gathered their luggage and left the plane. She would have to get used to this procedure if she decided to make flying a career, then she laughed at the thought—fat chance of that. If she ever flew again, it would surprise her.

For once, Harri didn't even try to lead, she just followed her dad and was glad that he knew where they were going. Soon they were being directed through customs, and Harri couldn't believe the number of people who were pushing and shoving their way through the crowds. Many of them were rude and thoughtless, while others seemed to be moving around in a daze; daze she understood.

Then she discovered that a major football game between the Oilers and the Bills was being played at the Houston Astrodome later that day. It would be the last game the Oilers would play on Astrodome turf.

Many of the people at the airport were late arrivals who were trying to make it to the game on time. Never having seen a football game, Harri decided to give the game the benefit of doubt. Maybe it was worth all this hassle and maybe pushing and shoving was the only way to get to the game on time. Also, she decided it wasn't fair to judge the whole country's populace by this present few.

Ward gathered their luggage and placed it in the cargo department of the vehicle that would take them from the airport to their destination—a condo suite near the Trinity Bay area. The condo would be their home for the next few days.

As they were leaving the airport, Harri took one last look at the crowd. She smiled at the dress code and hairstyles of the many young sports fans—some of them were actually cute.

Ward directed the driver of their vehicle to their destination, which was several miles from Houston. As Harri gazed out the window of the rental car, she was still feeling a little awe struck by all the man-made splendor, and the condo was no exception. Their suite was superb to the last detail. Her bedroom, which was almost the size of their total quarters in the jungle outpost, had its own bathroom and an adjacent dressing room. The bath section was equipped with a huge garden tub. On a balcony outside the bathroom was a Jacuzzi hot tub. The dressing area had surely been designed for a queen, and three walls had floor to ceiling mirrors that were installed on pivots. Harri could see every detail of her posture when the mirrors were adjusted right. The wall-to-wall windows of her bedroom opened out over a magnificent landscape that wound its way to a beach section of a blue lake. The windows were adorned with dazzling window dressings. The king size bed was covered with a matching bedspread. The bedspread and the drapes were crafted from a rich, burgundy colored, satin brocade. Each separate piece, bedspread and curtain panels, displayed underskirts of delicate, dark cherry pink, chiffon.

Harri walked slowly through the three-bedroom suite, carefully inspecting the flawless structure and exquisite decor. Every room was finished to perfection. She wondered why she couldn't feel some excitement, or at least a small thrill at being in a position to observe such splendor. To actually be a part of it, now.

She could well appreciate the beauty, and even marvel at the talent that went into every element of the total structure, from the architectural design to the interior decor, to say nothing of the breathtaking landscape. As she studied the suite, she compared it with pictures she had seen in books during her social studies of both ancient and modern Europe. Her overall opinion was, that all of the structures she had observed in books and magazines, as well as this present one, were magnificent. However, none of it could mean more to her than what it was: inanimate objects of splendor and beauty that were to be admired as one would admire the paintings by the old masters that graced the walls and ceilings of museums and cathedrals in the ancient cities of Europe. Harri was quite sure that she would never be content basking in the glory of the achievements of others, no matter how much she admired their talent, or their magnificent creations.

The following two days were a blur in Harri's memory. Like a whirlwind the days passed, and in their passing they set the course for the next three years of her life.

CHAPTER 14

Ward discovered he hadn't lost his ability to get things accomplished when he was given a free rein without fear of having his family and friends murdered. After he had set up a checking account for Harri, he called for a driver to escort her to all the finest boutiques and dress shops in Houston.

While Harri was shopping, Ward sat at the telephone. For the next four hours he talked to every exclusive Realtor and building contractor in the state. By the time Harri returned to the condo from her shopping trip, he had managed to locate a contractor who had the experience and reputation that Ward was looking for. The contractor also had access to all desirable building sites that were still available in any area Ward might consider building his home.

Ward wasn't happy with the idea of living in a crowded city, and he didn't want Harri stuck miles from civilization. However, the contractor had among his property listings three separate sites that Ward wanted to check out before making a final decision. One of the sites, if the contractor had described it accurately, was exactly what Ward had in mind; and that site was only two miles from an exclusive residential area. There was a private lake on the property and grazing land if Harri should later decide she wanted a horse. He was sure she would want a large dog or two, and possibly a cat.

The following day, Ward met with the contractor and they drove to the building site. It was perfect in every detail except price—the price was outrageous. Not having the time to dicker, and not wanting to take chances on loosing the property, Ward agreed on the spot to purchase the acreage.

After looking through every floor plan available and not finding one that he was totally satisfied with, he and the contractor finally chose to rework one that was almost, but not exactly, what he wanted. Ward made notations of what he wanted changed, what was to be added and where. The contractor told him he would have to call in another architectural engineer to assist him in redesigning the plan, and that it would be several days before it would be ready for inspection. Satisfied that he was leaving everything in competent hands, he left the contractor's office, asking him to call as soon as the plans were ready for final approval.

After a scrumptious seafood dinner, Ward, Harri and Silana returned to their condo and settled in for the evening. While the two women were preparing themselves for bed, Ward eased himself into a soft, leather recliner and began calling a number of old friends that he hadn't talked to for almost two decades. One man on his list was not only an old friend, he was a retired building contractor whom Ward wanted to leave in charge of the construction of his home during the time that he, himself, could not be present to supervise the operation. But most of the calls were to female friends from his past—women that Ward had developed pleasant relationships with before he met and married Lydia.

Ward wasn't looking for romance, he was searching for a traveling companion for Harri, one that could teach her every trick known to female kind, about how to dress, what was in style and what to avoid—in wearing apparel and humanity.

While he was finishing his assignment in the jungle, and while their home was under construction, he wanted Harri to travel. His wish was for her to learn everything there was to know about the lifestyle and culture of every country which held any appeal for the socially elite, or the rich and famous. He wanted her to meet the best people, to learn first-hand, how the other side of this world lived—the side that had been denied her up to now.

He knew Harri was brilliant as well as beautiful. After all, hadn't her mother been brilliant—to say nothing of beautiful and charming, and the most fascinating lady of the twentieth century?

Harri had her mother's looks and charm, even if she were an inch or two taller. Ward was sure that with a little coaching she would fall right into the roll of society queen. After Harri had learned all there was to know about distant and exotic countries and lifestyles, and where to shop for the finest fashions in clothing, and after she had developed a taste for exotic food, they would settle into their new home. Once they were settled, they would invite everyone in the county to the most incomparable housewarming party the area had ever known. They would meet all their neighbors, good, bad and mediocre, and accept or discard them accordingly, then the two of them would settle down and discuss colleges.

Ward was sure that after a few months of tutoring from the best possible teachers, that Harri would be ready for the finest college in the country—and he would see to it that she was accepted, even if he had to buy the college.

After ten calls or more, Ward discovered that none of his friends from the past were available to act as traveling companion to Harri. However, he did manage to contact one his best friend from the past, Anisha Clayton. Anisha, as usual was full of information.

Anisha Clayton had been his best friend for many years before he married Lydia and disappeared into the jungle. At one time Ward and Anisha had even talked about marriage, but after looking more closely at their respective life-styles, and their individual desires for their future, each came to the conclusion that at best a marriage between them would only screw up their perfect friendship.

When Ward mentioned to Anisha that he was looking for a traveling companion for Harri she informed him that she had just returned to the states from an extended trip abroad and that she had acquired her traveling companion from an agency. She had been very happy with the results. Her chosen companion had been a charming young woman who was knowledgeable of every exotic place of interest and intrigue on any continent inhabited by the human race.

Anisha had been particularly pleased with the fact that the young woman could change their plans instantly to suit any mood that Anisha found herself struggling with. She admitted to Ward that as she advanced in years, she was becoming a moody person, and that she tried very hard to conceal her moodiness from the public at large. The young companion she had chosen was ideal because she could always sense Anisha's moods and possessed the ability to make the best of a bad situation. Anisha informed Ward that she would highly recommend this lady for any age traveler.

Three days later, after meeting with the lady, who's name was Raquel SaMone, Ward discovered that Raquel was not exactly a young lady, but it was easy to see why Anisha referred to her as such. Raquel was very bright and possessed the boundless energy of a teenager. Ward would guess she was well into her thirties and wise beyond her years; he liked her immediately.

Raquel spoke five languages fluently, and could cope in as many more. She did extremely well in English and within minutes she had Ward convinced that he need not look further for a traveling companion for Harri.

After meeting and chatting with Harri, Raquel approached Ward and informed him that she absolutely refused to address his daughter as 'Harri' if there was another name available to her. After Raquel learned that Harri's given name was Harriet Lydia, she repeated the name to herself several times. Deciding that Lydia was a beautiful name; she tried the name on Harri and smiled at Harri's response. Harri looked at Raquel blankly for a few seconds and then shrugged her shoulders. With an amused aplomb, Harri promptly accepted the title.

CHAPTER 15

Two weeks from the day of their arrival in Houston, Ward and Silana, along with Anisha Clayton, escorted Harri and Raquel to Intercontinental Airport in Houston. Silana held Harri's hand until she was forced to let go when Harri boarded the giant aircraft.

The three waited at the airport until the plane was airborne and continued to watch until it became a silver speck in a vast blue yonder. Silana wept softly as she watched the plane disappear. Anisha held her closely, assuring her that her beloved daughter would return to her safely.

After Silana had managed to get herself under control, she apologized to Anisha for her emotional breakdown. "So many things are happening to my family and I am afraid for them. I do not understand about these big airplanes, or these cities where so many people move around quickly in automobiles and buses. Since I was a child, I have lived in a small villa in the jungle. Once, when I went to Villa Guano with Señor Holland, it was a happy day for me because I had always wanted to go to a large villa, but this is different…It is so difficult for me to…" Silana placed her folded fingers across her heart and tried to find words to explain her feelings about the strangeness of this mysterious world she was trying to understand.

Silana had always been strong and proud. Seldom, if ever, had she let anything get to her emotionally for any length of time. But this was too strange, too much, too soon, for her to grasp it in its entirety. And watching the big airplane take her daughter away from her was the last straw. It had completely overwhelmed her.

For two days, Anisha had begged Ward to permit Silana to stay at her home in Houston until he completed his assignment in the jungle.

"What will it take to convince you, or make you understand that Silana doesn't need to be in that stinking jungle, Ward?" Anisha all but yelled at him. "Please for God's sake, give the lady a break! Let her stay with me! I need her more than you do now, and I'm certain that she needs me more than she needs you—at least until you are in a position to give her a real home!"

Ward stubbornly refused to give his consent to such an arrangement until he could get Silana alone long enough to consult with her about her feelings on the matter. He wanted to be sure in his own mind that Silana really would be content living with a beyond middle-aged lady who was almost a total stranger to her, and who admittedly, had an attitude problem.

"When Ward did find an opportunity to speak with Silana about her feelings, she responded with a question, "If I cannot remain here in the states with Anisha when you return to the jungle—and while my little girl is trekking all over the world—where will I live?"

"You can travel with me back to the jungle and come with me when I fly back here to check on the progress of our home," said Ward. "You know I will be happy to have you with me. I've grown so used to having you take care of me that it'll be difficult going it alone, Silana."

But Silana was not fooled by his phony plea for her support. She knew from the lack of sincerity in his voice that he didn't want her to return to the jungle—that in fact, he would be much happier and would feel more personal freedom if he knew she was living safely here in Houston with Anisha.

From their first meeting Silana had liked Anisha, and knew without question that Anisha was sincere in her offer. Anisha really did want Silana to remain with her in Houston.

Silana had no desire to impose upon Anisha's generosity with her extended presence, but she knew she could find a way to become an asset to the woman for the period of time she would be with her. She would not be imposing.

Silana had thought the matter over carefully and had, for the most part, already decided what she would do. Now, pretending a scolding attitude that she did not feel, she said to Ward, "Well! You will just have to take care of yourself for a short while, Señor Holland, because I will remain with Anisha while my little girl is away and while you are finishing your work in the jungle." Then giving him a look that she knew he would understand, she said softly, "I will pray to the sacred mother to bring my family together again, soon."

Ward looked long and hard at Silana, trying to see beyond her brave front. He wanted to know for certain that what she was saying was what she really felt. He wanted to be sure that he had everything straight before he made any commitment that he might regret later.

What Ward saw in Silana's face was what he already knew, that he had everything straight from the beginning. Silana would never permit him do something that he would regret. She would always insist on what was right for the people she loved, even when she had no tangible facts to work with, or proof of what was right or wrong. Her instincts were her guide, and they had never let her down. As Ward looked upon that beloved face, he wondered why he had never before noticed what a truly beautiful lady he had been living with for so many years.

Silana kissed Ward's cheek, and with a twinkle in her eyes, she said softly, "I have faith in you Señor, you will manage just fine and Anisha needs me now."

Ward smiled. As usual, Silana was seeing all sides of the situation and was making life as easy as possibly for him. Silana didn't want him to be worrying about her when he needed to give his full attention to finishing the jungle project.

Ward had not been wholly convinced that Anisha was really sincere in her plea for Silana's company. He knew it was possible that Anisha, like Silana, could see a problem for him if Silana returned to the jungle outpost. She was willing to make a temporary concession in her life style to prevent that problem.

Ward permitted himself to gloat a little. He was right about Anisha; she was one great lady—even with her attitude problem.

Three days following Harri's flight to new adventures, Ward said good-bye to Silana and Anisha. When he returned to his condo, he found a message waiting for him. Tolver's pilot would be picking him up at the Houston Intercontinental Airport at six the following morning.

Ward quickly packed his few articles of clothing and toiletries, then locked the condo's door and headed for Houston, where he spent the remainder of the night in a hotel. At six in the morning, he turned in his rental car and boarded the Cessna 310 for the long trip back into the jungle.

Many hours later, when they landed on the familiar strip near the dredge site, Ward stepped from the plane and stood still for several seconds waiting for that dreaded feeling of being trapped to reappear.

The feeling was no longer there. Everything around him looked the same as if he had never left; but now he was free. That was different.

Ward felt upbeat and lightheaded as he walked toward the dredge site. He ran his gaze quickly over the working men. They too seemed to have taken on a new awareness of their personal worth. They knew the control of this project was now in their hands, and they had waited the return of their leader to make their final move toward their final freedom.

Ward felt more than a little pride in these men that had held this project together and made it work, even when most of them were sure they were battling unyielding odds. These were the sort of men that held the world together. They were not heroes; they were not great men that authors write books about. They were simple hard working, men from every walk of life, who had for years been hammered almost beyond their endurance by a force that was not visible to them; a force they were powerless to fight. Each of them had, at sometime during their confinement here, become bitter and angry men. On numerous occasions these men had harbored murderous thoughts, directed at the parties who were responsible for their dilemma, but they had conquered their hate and learned to live with their fear and had completed an impossible mission. Ward understood the powerful creed that made up the majority of those men. He knew that in time, their hate, their anger and even their desire for revenge, would cease. They would move on to other assignments, or simply retire. The almost two decades they had spent here would be looked upon as just chapter of their lives, now written into the sands of time.

CHAPTER 16

D R. SINGLY'S NERVOUSNESS WAS APPARENT to Ward as he watched the crew setting up the equipment that would bring the treasured crates from their unstable grave. Somehow, Ward could find little sympathy for Singly's misgivings about the uncertainty of the recovery efforts.

Ward knew the doctor was making himself ill while fretting over the project when he didn't even understand the problems. Due to the doctor's lack of knowledge, the man certainly was in no position to offer any helpful suggestions. Also, Singly had an uncanny knack for always being where he shouldn't be, and hindering or pissing off the workmen who did know what they were doing.

Ward wished the doctor would leave the dredge site. There was no reason for him to be here, he was an obstacle that the workmen had to work around. Ward was convinced that even Ted Tolver wasn't happy with the doctor's presence at the site.

But even with his lack of engineering knowledge it was obvious to Dr. Singly that the equipment which the crew was using to recover the crates could not be stabilized in the shifting, silty soil. And, and while that knowledge was causing him a great deal of pain, he couldn't bring himself to walk away from it; to leave it in the hands of those who would, if possible, recover the crates intact.

Tolver's engineering knowledge left him in an even greater quandary. Tolver knew that the only way to stabilize the area enough to ensure the safe removal of the crates was to bring in tons of steel and cement, literally build a bridge and a platform for the heavy equipment to rest on. He also knew that such procedure would require weeks, possibly months to accomplish, even if the weather held. The heavy rains were due any day now and Tolver knew that when the rains came the whole project could be lost forever. Even the light rains that they had suffered recently had slowed the project to a crawl. They had accomplished little toward the recovery of those crates since Ward Holland had left the site over two weeks ago. But then they hadn't used any heavy equipment since Holland left, the men had been working with shovels and wheelbarrows. The crew had to unearth enough of the boat with hand tools to get at with the equipment without destroying the crates. Once they were sure what they were dealing with, they could then use their heavy equipment to finish unearthing the boat.

Tolver looked toward a sky that told him little about the weather as a whole, but he could feel the dampness in the air and a shudder ran through his body. Tolver wished he had never heard the stories of how long the rains lasted here in the jungle, or how long it took for the area to dry up after the heavy rains had ceased. But most of all he wished he had never of how much damage the rain could do to the dredge site. He also wished that his company could have found someone else to handle this part of their project.

After he had examined the project and its problems from every angle, he was convinced that he wasn't the man for the job. The company could have found someone else—someone who was more qualified than himself to take charge here. He even wondered why anyone needed to take charge. Tolver was more convinced than ever that, left alone, Ward Holland was capable of completing this mission without any help from the outside world.

Today, Tolver had watched from the dredge site as the Cessna 310 landed. As he watched it taxi up to the hangar, it dawned on him just how much he had depended on Holland's return. Tolver had breathed a sigh of relief when he saw Holland step from the plane. He had never been wholly convinced that Holland would return. He had not been sure what he might have done if faced with the same decision Holland had been faced with.

CHAPTER 17

WARD WATCHED AS THE CREW maneuvered equipment closer to the sunken river craft. He still did not know for certain what was secreted in those crates that rested in the hull of the rotting boat. But one thing he was certain of, those crates were very valuable to a lot of very rich people, and if they turned to dust while being removed from the rotting boat, or if the whole area around them suddenly began to cave or slide, Ward could well imagine the consequences.

A large portion of his own crew would be devastated if those crates were destroyed—even though none of them had any idea what the crates contained. The men might have tangled emotions about the whole project, but none of them would want the destruction of something they had put so many years of their lives into unearthing, unless they planned it.

Dr. Singly knew what was in those crates. He knew that they held records and samples of a rare discovery. A discovery made several years ago by a Dr. Cedrick Grinzak, a medical scientist. Dr. Singly knew that Dr. Grinzak, along with his discoveries, had been lost to the world when the boat he was fleeing the jungle in had been sunk by angry natives.

The fact that the sunken river craft also held the remains of two of the doctor's cohorts from the states, along with the boat's captain and two crew members, was of little concern to Dr. Singly. As far as he was concerned, their demise was of little importance to the world.

But from the day he learned of the boat's fate, some twelve years after the fact, Dr. Singly had been a principal element in pushing for the recovery of that boat.

Dr. Singly had discovered that the boat had been attacked and sunk by a group of angry natives who would have stopped at nothing to prevent Dr. Grinzak from escaping the jungle.

Dr. Singly, along with others of his noted reputation, had been convinced that if that much had been recorded about the fate of the boat, surely there was more information to be found. Maybe there was information about the exact location where the boat had gone down. Someone in that jungle must have knowledge of that boat.

When the story, with the help of the late Dr. Grinzak's former aid, Zonia Gilez, finally reached the attention of Cedrick Grinzak Jr., the only son of the brilliant but strange doctor, it had been a red-letter day.

Cedrick had been elated. He had, at last, learned the details of his father's demise, and those details had included an explanation of his father's discoveries.

Cedrick literally took his father's office apart trying to locate every available note concerning his work. Fortunately, his father had left everything in reasonably neat order when he departed from the family home and fled to the jungles of South America.

His father's original office/lab was a part of the family home. Cedrick had been able to decipher some of the notes, and was now certain he had found the reason for his father's sudden departure from the states.

Aside from his father's own notes, Cedrick discovered many pages of scientific text and relevant information, that had been usurped from other scientific manuals, dating back to the early 1950s.

Among the first pages Cedrick discovered were pages of information on the discoveries of Nobel Prize winners George W. Beadle, Edward L. Tatum, Joshua Lederburg, and Max Delbruck, all of whom were prominent in early genetic research and attempts to decipher the molecular codes of DNA and RNA.

When research on the genetic significance of nucleic acids was intensified, many scientists became accomplished cryptographers. Cedrick's father, Dr. Grinzak, was no exception. However, Dr. Grinzak had taken the earlier pioneer's discoveries to a whole new level; he had managed to decipher the genetic code.

After extensive research, Dr. Grinzak had discovered the means, by using RNA messengers, to trick specific genes of small animals into believing they had not completed their work, or had failed to complete it accurately. By this method, Cedrick theorized, his father had found a way to alter or repair the animal's structure. He could remove parts from the animals and within weeks the animals would re-grow the missing parts. Cedrick was convinced that, at that point in time, his father was in dire need of human subjects to test his discoveries on. A further search revealed records indicating his father had departed for South America. He even pinpointed a specific location.

After weeks of searching and questioning hundreds of people in the jungle area where his father had reestablished his headquarters, young Cedrick's efforts began to pay off. He learned as nearly as possible where the river craft had gone down. While searching for an exact location, Cedrick had by chance stumbled across the remains of his father's lab that had been erected in a remote sector of the jungle some twelve years past.

The lab was all but buried in tons of tangled growth and rotting debris that had become trapped in the growth. Cedrick, along with his crew, had managed to chop and hack their way into the main lab portion of the building. It was then that Cedrick discovered that his father had actually lived in his jungle lab, and had made it his home.

Cedrick's mother had lied to him about his father. She had led him to believe that his father was a brilliant scientist that was involved in the government's affairs to the extent that it kept him away from home against his will, and that given a choice, he would have preferred to be home with his family.

But this lab, from all indication, had doubled as living quarters. This lab had been his father's home; a home he had willingly chosen over his family.

Young Cedrick was feeling almost sick, and at the same time, awe struck and elated at this discovery. His father had spent the last years of his life in this lab, working on the most awesome and frightening discovery since the beginning of time.

CHAPTER 18

DECIDING NOT TO DELAY HIS query any longer, Ward Holland went in search of Dr. Singly. He wanted information about the contents of those crates. He felt he had a right to know what he was dealing with here. His men had a right to know. But if the contents were indeed, of some highly classified materials, he would withhold the information from the crew for a while, but there should not be a problem with him knowing about their content.

Ward was primed to force answers from Dr. Singly if necessary. However, it never became necessary.

Ward found Dr. Singly looking through some papers that Cedrick Grinzak Jr. had given to him before he entered the jungle. Ward stepped noisily up to the doctor and asked, "Dr. Singly, what can you tell me about this Doctor Grinzak? And I already know that the doctor and his crew went down in that Piranha infested river three decades ago. I know their boat was attacked and sunk by jungle natives. I know the crates that went down on that boat contain something very valuable. Now I want to know exactly what's in those crates, I want to know what the problem was between the doctor and the natives, and why all the interest in those crates after so many years?"

Dr. Singly looked up at Ward as if he had just discovered something about him that might be worthy of his interest. The doctor carefully laid the papers aside, cleared his throat and said: "The late Dr. Grinzak was a noted research scientist... as I'm sure you already know. He worked virtually alone in the U.S. for many years. Then he made some fantastic discoveries and realized he needed more freedom to advance his discoveries than the laws in the states would permit. He chose this area because it gave him the freedom he needed to go forth with his experiments. He had access to actual human subjects without fear of retribution."

Ward looked toward the spot where the river craft was buried and said to nobody in particular, "Pardon me all to hell for my assumption, but that looks a lot like retribution to me."

Ignoring Ward's comment, Dr. Singly said calmly, "In the beginning, there were any number of sick and crippled natives who were willing to offer themselves as subjects for the advancement of the doctors work in return for the pay the doctor offered them. And of course, there was the hope of being cured of whatever ailed them."

Dr. Singly cleared his throat, glance at Holland to see if he still had his attention then continued, "Substantial pay was also offered to older family members and caregivers, or if the handicapped subject happened to be a minor child or dependent."

"And this was all legal, of course," Holland said sarcastically.

Again, Singly ignored him, saying, "A short time after the doctor began his experimental testing on humans, he discovered the missing ingredient he had so greatly needed for success. When he set out to use his newfound discovery to its fullest potential, he had more volunteers than he could handle; and all for free."

"What a surprise!" Holland said without looking at the doctor.

Singly gave Holland a contemptuous look and continued with, "Dr. Grinzak could now, with his new discovery, practically rebuild a human body from a corpse. With his discovery he could change the human body at will, everything from the color of one's eyes to the color of the skin. He could control the height, or even the bone structure of an individual. He could cure the incurable; he could wipe out cancer and viruses; he believed he would eventually be able to bring the dead back to life."

"You sure this guy wasn't nailed to a cross instead of being eaten by piranhas?" Holland asked.

By now, Singly was talking more to himself than to Ward, so rambled on: "The last year of Dr. Grinzak's life, he had used his own body as a subject for an experiment. Dr. Grinzak was almost sixty years old chronologically, when he made his monumental discovery. However, he could have been a man in his mid twenties when he boarded the riverboat to depart from the jungle. When the people of the jungle learned, the doctor was planning to leave them after they had offered up so many of their children and family members to his experiments, they were a very unhappy lot. They had witnessed the doctor's magic as he cured their people of every affliction from blindness to mindless. They had stood in awe as they watched new fingers, sometimes whole new hands, feet, arms and legs re-grow on family members. They watched as their old men and women regained their health and their youth. The people of the jungle had accepted Dr. Grinzak into their realm as a permanent fixture; and they had no intentions of letting him escape from them. The doctor owed them his life; and even if he wasn't willing to see things their way, they fully intended to collect…

"How did this story ever get out of the jungle? How did Dr. Grinzak's son learn about all of this?" Ward asked.

"He learned of his father's discoveries and his tragic death, through his father's former aid, a Ms. Zonia Gilez," said Singly. "The lady is still living in the jungle today. Zonia, herself, is living proof of the doctor's success. She is over sixty years old and looks like a woman in her mid twenties. She has the zest of a teenager…without the teen-age intellect. She helped Cedrick Grinzak piece together the complete story, from the time his father entered the jungle up to his fatal attempt to escape."

"What went wrong with his escape efforts?" Ward asked "According to Zonia, Doctor Grinzak, after contacting a trusted friend in the states, managed to convince his friend that it would be to the world's best interest if the friend were to visit the jungle lab and see, first hand, what he had accomplished. Dr. Grinzak's friend, along with another medical scientist, did visit Dr. Grinzak's jungle lab, and with proof of the doctor's accomplishments, the two men returned to the states and immediately began planning to move of Dr. Grinzak from the jungle lab to a very private lab in the US. Of course, the doctor was to bring from the jungle all of his records of discovery as well as samples of a very precious vaccine that was an extremely vital part of his procedures."

Doctor Singly stopped talking for a few seconds as if his thoughts had turned inward, then he continued, "At this point, one can only imagine where the world might be today, physically and scientifically, if the doctor had succeeded in reaching the states with his discovery. Fortunately for the world, there was a sympathizer left behind in the jungle. One who was wise enough to understand the importance of the doctor's work, and was willing to put her ultimate effort into seeing that the world would have a chance to benefit from his genius. Cedrick Jr was easily convinced that his father's discoveries were priceless, and if they could be retrieved from that river, the world could be controlled by whoever held those discoveries. You Mr. Holland have unearthed the proof we needed to convince the world that we were not mad when we decided to pursue this endeavor, at whatever the cost. Now, we have proof that the story was factual and that no matter what it has cost the world, in money or human life, it will prove to be worth every last penny and every drop of blood that has gone into this historical milestone. We, the people who have sponsored this fantastic recovery, now have the means of controlling not only our own futures, but the future of the world. Now, Mr. Holland, do you understand the importance of this mission you have accomplished?"

"Yes Doctor, I understand fully—and I'm sorry I can't share your enthusiasm," said Ward.

"And I suppose you could explain why." Said Singly

"Easily," Ward told him bluntly, "Grinzak's endeavor cost me something that can never be replaced—my wife—my daughter's mother—and seventeen years of our lives, to say nothing of the dozens of lives that were lost working this project. And Dr. Grinzak's snake medicine can't give any of it back. And frankly I feel that somehow there are going to be more consequences... that something else will prevent you from using Grinzak's discoveries."

"That is pure ignorance and superstition talking, Holland." Singly said. Looking as if he'd like nothing better than to lay Ward Holland out cold with his bare hands. "I don't suppose you're trying to tell me something I need to know, are you Holland?"

"Nope!" Ward said with emphasis. "I just have an inherent belief that there are some things that should be left alone—this is one of them."

"You *are* an ignorant man, Mr. Holland," said Singly. "In my opinion, there could never be a more meritorious way to die than to give up one's life for such a great cause, and as for the lives of the men who were lost here, that applies two-fold."

"I might agree with you," said Ward, "if those men had had a choice in that decision, but none of them even knew what they were dying for; they were prisoners here with no choices at all."

"As I said before, Mr. Holland, you just do not understand. If any of you had been permitted choices, this great event would never have happened. If any of you had been given choices, most of you would never have remained here long enough to finish this project."

"You're probably right about that." Ward said grimly. Unless we were given a better reason than we had, to stay."

The ones who were managing this project from the states could not have anyone leaving until those crates were retrieved." Singly said adamantly. "Once word got out about what we were doing here, there would have been too many curiosity seekers, objectors, reporters, and what-have-you, flying into the jungle. Those people would have caused any number of problems for the project and most likely it would have been delayed indefinitely, if not abandoned completely. You know how those religious freaks are, to say nothing of a competing industry or some of those environmental freaks. Any number of them could have halted the project, or tried to take over the operation by what ever means available to them. No Mr. Holland, we would never have been permitted to finish this project in peace if any of you had had been given an opportunity to spread the word around about what we were doing here. There was too much possibility that one of you might encountered someone who remembered Dr. Grinzak's work here in the jungle put it all together. We couldn't take the chance. It had to be done the way we did it."

"No, Singly, it didn't have to be done the way you did it. It's just that you all chose to do it that way, and it was wrong from the beginning, and I still believe you'll all pay for it eventually."

"Okay, Mr. holier than thou, is this really any different than being forced to fight a war on some distant continent? Millions of people have died fighting wars they did not instigate, against people they had no quarrel with, for a much less worthy cause than will be realized here. No matter which side wins a war, after a while it just begins all over again, and people fight and die. The ultimate end being death. What we offer is life, at least for the deserving. And if you can't, or simply refuse to see the whole picture, then I can only stand firm with my earlier assessment; you are ignorant, Mr. Holland. You are totally blinded to all except the pettiness of your day-to-day existence. Great men have always known that people of your scope were expendable for the betterment of intelligent, intellectual mankind. Your reluctance to accept greatness above pettiness definitely separates you from the greatness."

"Maybe so," said Ward, looking more fed-up than impressed with Singly's spiel, "but sometimes I'm right too."

Ward heard footsteps coming up behind him and recognized the sound of Keil's boots, even before he spoke.

"Mr. Holland," Keil said, sounding anxious. "We need you at the dredge site. There's a big problem—Mr. Tolver asked me to find you. Could you come right away?"

"What in hell happened here?" Ward asked when he reached the dredge site. But even as he asked the question, he already knew the answer. Someone had dropped a crane's boom across a working bulldozer. The crane was sitting at an angle and was sinking into the earth. As the crane sank farther into the mire its boom was applying more pressure on the trapped dozer and the dozer was sitting way too close to the west end of the sunken riverboat.

It was obvious to Ward that the dozer was also sinking, but not at the rate the crane was going down because the dozer was on higher and dryer ground. But the dozer was presenting more of a problem at the moment than the sinking crane. If the earth continued to soften from the surrounding inflow of slush, and the dozer continued to sink it would rip the old boat apart or take the boat with it as it made its decent into the sinking earth.

Ward knew that if the sunken boat was ripped apart or turned onto its side, it might cause the crates to shift since so much of the sand had been shoveled out of it in order to locate the crates. Although, there was no way of determining at the moment what condition the crates were in, or if they were stabilized with other material that had settled into the boat over the years.

Ward didn't want anything left to chance. He wanted the problem taken care of immediately. The crane, as it tilted farther onto its left side continued to apply pressure to the trapped dozer, and it would continue to do so until the boom could be lifted.

Ward didn't even bother to ask how this had happened, because it was obvious. The left side of the crane had reached a spot of soft earth and had tilted. The operator couldn't have controlled the crane, or prevented it from tilting onto its side any more than he could have known that the sinkhole was developing.

The mysterious sink holes had, from the beginning, just popped up from nowhere and always without warning. Within minutes the slush could turn formerly stable looking earth into a sucking monster. Ward believed that the sinkholes developed from beneath the earth's surface, most likely from underground streams that managed to find the vulnerable, silty soils, then push their way to the surface.

For the most part, they were not visible until something or somebody applied pressure to their surface. This one was spreading, weakening the more stable soil farther out around the sinking crane. It was too late to even try a last-ditch effort to remove the crates even without the safety measures they wished to apply. His men couldn't work in the rapidly developing sink holes without being sucked into the mire.

Ward's jaw set into a hard line when he saw the crane jerk and tilt even farther onto its side as the monster mud sucked at its bulk.

"Oh man! This is about a bitch-n-a-half!" Keil groused. "And it's a miracle nobody was badly hurt."

"I'm happy nobody was injured," said Ward, "but I'd be even happier if this hadn't happened."

Ward heard Tolver yelling instructions to another crane operator and turned his attention to the method of operation that Tolver had begun. He felt disappointment nagging at his insides when he realized Tolver was launching the same action, he, himself would have. Then he felt a bilious anger at the cheap pettiness in himself that created that disappointment. After all, wasn't he the one who had insisted on Tolver taking over the operation while he was in Houston? But worse than his self-reproach, were the stinging words that Dr. Singly had flung at him, words that were still ringing in his ears. Ward was even angrier with himself when he realized that he had let the asinine doctor rile him. *But I guess I'm okay. If I were truly a petty-minded man, I could easily hate Dr. Singly.... Okay! So, I hate him!*

Ward straightened his shoulders and walked rapidly toward the approaching second crane. So far, the soil was remaining stable in its path. The soil had to remain stable if this was going to work at all, if any of this operation was to be salvaged. Ward directed the second crane to a spot as close to the sinking one as possible. Before the second crane had stopped moving, the men were there with pieces of timber, metal, and fiber siding, extension ladders and anything else that was solid and sturdy enough to walk on. Within minutes they had formed a bridge over the mucky surface and had reached the mired crane. The operator of the second crane began lowering a cable, which was equipped with two large hooks, down to the waiting men. The men were having a problem with footing as they moved around the sinking crane and all but two of them had decided to work on the side that offered the best footing.

The bridge they had formed with the timbers and other debris had permitted them to reach the crane but not to maneuver around it. None of them were anxious to use the sinking machine for support; none of them wanted to add to its descent. Ward tried to give instruction from the sideline and realized that the men couldn't hear him over the noisy commotion and the roar of the crane's engine. The only way to get his instructions across was to join the men at the sinking crane.

Ward asked Tolver to have some of the crewmen find and inflate as many spare inner tubes as possible, then tie them together and form a bridge around the mired crane with the inflated tubes. Ward removed his boots and walked to the crane, then he began giving instructions to the two men who were trying to reach the opposite side. The men were up to their waists in mud, but they had managed to make progress by half crawling and half pulling themselves through the mud with a swimming motion. Now they were waiting for the hooks to be lowered enough to reach them and hopefully find enough solid parts of the crane to attach the hooks to. Ward could see that the two men were sinking farther into the mud with each breath, and their lives were in danger. He asked them to use the crane for support and work themselves back to the more solid footing and wait for the inflated tubes. Neither of the men was anxious to leave the position that had been so hard to gain; at least not until they had the hooks secured. The hooks were close now and the crane operator was easing them into reaching hands. Ward decided to let the men try to fasten the hooks since they could use the crane for support once the hooks were in place.

Ward knew the crane could never be pulled from the mud by those hooks, because they were not the type that could be fastened to more stable parts of the crane, but the temporary measure would prevent it from slipping deeper into the tapioca textured mud, and give the men time to build a sling from cable and larger hooks. The temporary measure would also enable other operators to remove the toppled boom from the dozer.

The bulldozer had settled upon solid footing with most of its bulk still above ground. If the boom could be removed soon, the dozer could be easily removed form its present location, ending the danger that it presented to the sunken boat.

One of the men asked Ward if it were possible the dozer had settled upon the sunken boat, and if that was what was stopping its descent into the earth. But Ward knew that hadn't happened. The boat was at least five northwest of the dozer and, unless this sinkhole kept spreading, the dozer and the boat were safe for the moment.

Ward knew the area east of the crane was solid enough to support any of the equipment. All of the area around the sunken boat sloped sharply toward the west and the underground seepage was moving in that direction; and Ward wasn't at all comfortable with that knowledge. He knew the westward flow was creating a future problem for the second crane, unless they could work fast enough to keep ahead of the flow.

Ward knew from past experience that trying to keep ahead of sinkholes was equal to trying to hold back the wind. To prove his point, he heard men yelling and looked up in time to see the crane operator trying to extend the boom on his crane in order to keep the hooks in place while he backed his crane farther away from the spreading mire.

Clearly, the second crane was now in jeopardy as the earth began to soften near its base. Ward looked around to see how his two men were coming along with the hooks and noticed that one of the hooks had been fastened to the crane and only one man was visible. The second hook was dangling in the air and the lone man was fishing frantically around in the mud.

Ward knew without asking that the missing man had somehow stepped into a spot that had no immediate bottom and wondered how the other man had managed to avoid it. Ward yelled for someone to bring the tubes and was told that all of them were not ready yet.

"Bring the ones that are" he yelled, "and keep working on the others!" Somehow, he made himself heard above the noise of the machine and the clamor of the crew.

Without being aware of doing it, Ward had reached the man who was reaching deeper and deeper into the bubbling mud, trying to locate the lost man. Then someone arrived with the tubes and tossed them to Ward. He reached one ahead of himself to the frantic man who had just come up for air.

Holding onto his tube, Ward began his personal search and realized that there was no way they were going to find the man within arms reach. Holding onto the tube he began feeling with his bare feet, slipping deeper into the muck until only his head and one arm was visible. When he couldn't feel the man's body beneath him, he worked his way to the surface and moved the tube to another location, then began the same procedure again. Within seconds he felt the man's body, and tried to get his feet underneath him, hoping to bring him up by that method.

The thick mud and the man's weight was too much for him to hoist with just his feet, and the slimy texture of the mud prevented him from grasping the body even if he could have lifted the man's weight and pulled him through the mud. Ward had no choice; he had to go in after the man.

Other men had reached the area with more tubes and rope and were trying to assist in the recovery. Ward gave them quick instruction and then taking a length of heavy rope with him, he began working himself under the mud. "When you feel me yank on the rope, start pulling," he informed the men, and then he disappeared into the slime. Ward's last thought as he went under was, I've got about ninety seconds to get this man to the surface, get the mud from his lungs and start his breathing again. Otherwise, I might as well leave him in the mud, it would be a much kinder fate than the living hell he would have to cope with as a vegetable.

Ward cursed the slimy mud and his inability to fasten the rope with any sort of accuracy and speed. He worked frantically with the heavy rope that didn't want to yield to the operation. He could feel his lungs swelling and realized that he was losing his ability to concentrate. Everything was happening in slow motion now. He was getting close to the point of having to return to the surface for air or pass out.

Ward knew that he would never have time to return if he went up for air. He had to make this one trip count or forget it altogether.

When he finally got the rope tied securely enough to enable the crew to lift the man to the surface, he yanked hard on the rope and began pushing the man's body upward until he was sure that it was rising steadily, then holding onto the body with what strength he had left, he felt himself being slowly lifted just as his own consciousness began to falter. His fingers felt like useless hunks of Jell-O, and he could no longer determine if they were gripping the body. Ward knew that he still had at least five feet of mud above him and that thought created an instant of panic that boosted his adrenaline.

He grappled through the mud until he found the end of the rope that he had tied around the man's body, and somehow, he managed to hang on.

Ward felt hands tugging at him even before he reached the surface where life-giving oxygen awaited him. As his head appeared above the mud, his men were waiting with pails of water and the nearest one was emptied over his head while another one doused his face.

His men were clearing the mud from his mouth and nose as they dragged him to safety.

When his head had cleared and he could see again, Ward saw the man he had rescued had been laid upon a scaffold with his head at the lowest end, and his face down. The mud had been washed from his upper body and it looked as if his breathing passages had been cleared. The company medic was still working with him, but Ward couldn't determine anything from the old doctor's expression; he always looked pained.

On wobbly legs, Ward rose and walked toward the activity. As he drew near, he could hear the doctor talking to the ailing man and heard the man try to respond. It was obvious that he was alive and breathing, but his speech was garbled; the sound he made was more like a dying frog than a human voice.

Ward pulled the old doc aside and asked in a hushed voice, "Does this man have a chance to recover as a normal human being doctor?"

"Yes," answered the doctor. "He will be as normal as he was before he inhaled all that mud. I have cleared his lungs as well as possible with the equipment I have to work with. His good health and time will have to do the rest. He's breathing better now, but after coughing up all that crap he sucked into his lungs, his throat and lungs are going to be very sore for a while. I'm going to insist on him resting for a day or two and not talking unless absolutely necessary."

Ward looked at the three men who had been watching the doctor. None of them had said a word, but Ward could see the sheer relief in their faces as the company medic spoke those encouraging words.

Then Dr. Singly stepped up to the medic and asked, "Did I hear you say the man was going to be normal after this, Doctor?"

"Yes, you heard me say that!" Answered the old medic, pointedly.

Ward couldn't help but wonder what Dr. Singly's interest was in the man. After all, at this point in time the man's welfare had nothing to do with the success of this operation and Ward knew that Dr. Singly was fully aware of that fact.

"Well, if almost suffocating in slimy mud makes these people normal maybe you should consider that treatment for the larger portion of this crew, Doctor!" Singly said in a serious and somber voice, and then he turned sharply and walked away.

"Damn you, Singly!" Ward said through clenched teeth, "I really wish you were worth killing!"

Even the old company medic was looking at Singly's back with a venomous hostility that was rare for a doctor whose entire lifetime had been spent trying to save lives.

The bulldozer had been removed from its precarious position and was sitting on solid ground. The crew had returned their total attention to the problem of the, now stabilized, but still mired crane. The operator had found solid footing for the second crane and it looked as though the softening soil was still moving west, away from the equipment

Ward watched and listened as Tolver gave instructions to the men. Again, Ward was feeling a grudging respect for Tolver's knowledge. He knew the man had not spent all of his time behind a desk in the city because what he was asking for came from experience—Tolver actually knew what he was doing.

Ward walked with the men to the hangar's repair shop and removed a roll of heavy steel cable from a wheel rack. The men would need at least a hundred feet or more of the cable to construct a sling that would be attached to the sunken crane. After the sling had been securely attached to the crane, it would be fastened to the second crane's boom for the final removal. This procedure would be a first for his men. None of them had removed a large piece of equipment from a sinkhole by this method. The last episode of sinking equipment that Ward's crew had encountered was back during the early years of dredging a newly drained riverbed. At that time, they did not have the second crane to rely on. This should be easier, but Ward knew he wouldn't bet his next meal ticket on it—nothing in this damned jungle was ever easy. If he were one to believed in evil spirits, he would swear this friggin' jungle possessed one—one that was putting a lot of effort into keeping him here.

CHAPTER 19

IT TOOK THE REMAINDER OF that day and most of the following morning to remove the crane from the sinkhole. It took an additional day to clean the silt from the engine, to repair the damage to the boom where it had struck the bulldozer and put everything back together again.

Both Ward and Tolver were spending more hours than either of them wanted to in trying to determine a shortcut to the recovery of the sunken boat. Neither of them wanted a repeat of the last episode.

They had to find a way to get the equipment near the boat without destroying the equipment or the boat. At the very best they could only remove a portion of the tons of earth that still held the lower half of the old boat beneath the earth. The rest, most likely additional tons, would have to be removed by the crew with shovels. Even the portion of the boat that had once been uncovered by the dozer, some ten feet down, had since been covered over again by shifting soil.

The Cessna was landing almost daily now, bringing in new supplies. Ward's feeling of freedom was renewed with each landing.

Tolver was becoming more disgruntled by the hour. He could understand why the men who had been here for years were ready to skyjack one of the cargo planes to escape from this hell.

Tolver was sure that Holland could handle any part of this operation and that his own presence here was a joke—not just a joke, but totally irrelevant to the end result. He wanted to leave...now! He never wanted to see another sink hole or listen to another mosquito's threatening buzz. He was certain could never have lasted as long in this stinking jungle as Holland had. He was not at all sure that he wouldn't have skyjacked one of the delivery planes years ago, leaving the others to fend for themselves. He was sure of only one thing at the moment, he would put in an immediate request to be removed from this assignment. He wanted the hell out of here. The sooner the better.

Holland could handle anything that needed to be handled here and he was conditioned to this sort of life—if one could call this life.

Tolver was ready to retire anyway. If his superiors wanted to stir up a stink over his leaving this project, then let them. He knew them a lot better than Ward Holland did, and he knew who they were—they wouldn't dare try to keep him here against his will.

Ward watched as Tolver talked to the pilot who had just landed with an unexpected supply of perishable foodstuff. The aircraft was loaded with assorted types of fresh fruits and vegetables that couldn't be purchased locally, and the few repair items that had been ordered several days ago.

Ward wondered why someone had decided to offer such an unexpected treat to a crew that, at this point in time, only wanted to finish this project and get the hell out of the jungle.

As Ward neared the small cargo plane, he could hear Tolver's raised voice, it was obvious he was pissed to the core, and not because the repair items were late in arriving at the site.

Ward continued to walk toward the plane and, as the voices grew louder, he busied himself by checking out a track on one of the dozers.

He could hear Tolver shouting his resentments to the pilot. Tolver was demanding to be removed from the jungle assignment, and his threats were volatile.

Ward could hardly conceal his satisfaction at Tolver's displeasure, but at the same time he was feeling sympathy for the man's dilemma. Ward was certain that Tolver had not asked for this assignment. Ward's guess would be that he had entered the jungle outpost with the intention of being gone before sundown. He could well understand Tolver's anger at how circumstances, and Ward Holland, had redirected his plans.

Ward had, in spite of himself, gained a great deal of respect for

Tolver, and was reasonably sure if he ever needed an ally in his corner that Tolver would be there for him—but where-in-hell was he seventeen years ago.

The one thing Ward couldn't understand was Dr. Singly's intrigue for the dredge site. The doctor was spending every minute of his daylight time and often, long after the sun had set, studying the dredge site. The man could have gone back to the states days ago if he had chosen to do so, but he had chosen instead to remain at the post. He seemed to be totally impervious of the mosquitoes, the humidity and the many loathsome critters, including the Anaconda, which normally would cause even the bravest to reconsider their position.

Ward's belief was that the doctor was blind to the jungle's hostility. That he had a special knack for removing everything from his consciousness except the ultimate goal, which in his case, was the retrieval of those crates. It must be nice, Ward thought, to be so totally devoted to a single cause that one could even cover up pain and discomfort with that devotion.

"Oh well, to each his own, and thank God I'll be rid of him soon," Ward mumbled to himself as he walked to the company truck that would take him to his quarters.

Mario had a hot dinner waiting for Ward when he entered his quarters. As he walked through the door, the aroma of the food was overwhelming. It had been three days since he had given any thought to how good food smelled. He had eaten his food on the run and out of sheer necessity. He would enjoy this meal.

When Ward finished his dinner he complimented Mario on his culinary skills, and even helped him clear the table and put the kitchen back in order.

Some daylight hours remained and Ward had no idea what he would do with them. He walked through his small quarters as if searching for some lost article... *My quarters*, he thought, as he looked around the small house. *Four rooms and a bath. A place I've spent seventeen years of my life trying to escape from.* The house felt empty; and it echoed its loneliness as if it knew it had already lost the only people who had ever cared.

Ward was feeling uncomfortable with the ominous quiet, and the placid mood that had engulfed him.

The sun had set and darkness was rapidly closing in on the humid night, but Ward was still feeling as if someone or something had captured his entire life and was running it past him in slow motion.

For the first time in seventeen years there was nothing he could to do to pass the time except re-read some old books or go to bed. He was too restless to read, and the idea of going to bed was met with total rejection.

He walked outside and meandered around the grounds for several minutes. Then as if a magnet were pulling him along, he strolled to the small, fenced parcel of earth that held the remains of his beloved Lydia.

He stood motionless, staring at the mound of earth that he had somehow managed to keep the unwanted and ever moving jungle growth from taking control of. His attention traveled to the headstone that Mario had carved from native stone. It looked as it did the day it was placed there—sixteen years ago.

As Ward gazed at the head stone, he wondered if what he was feeling now was what Harri had felt the day he informed her that they would be leaving the jungle. Now that he was free to make decisions, actually free to do whatever in hell he wanted to do, he realized that it was not this parcel of jungle earth he had hated, it had been the prison of his existence; the chains...

Ward stood, letting his tangled emotions run unchecked, and from his chaotic rationale, a new realization dawned: This place, this god-forsaken place, would remain forever in his daughter's memory as a hallowed spot-on earth. She had never felt those chains.

<hr />

CHAPTER 20

WARD WALKED FROM THE FENCED plot of earth to the company truck. He opened the door and seated himself behind the wheel. He sat for a while staring into the gathering darkness, then he started the engine and drove back toward the equipment compound—he didn't feel like sleeping, but maybe he could relieve one of the guards that needed a break. As he neared the compound an uneasy feeling settled over him. Something's wrong here, but he couldn't identify the problem.

Ward was certain that he no longer belonged here, not even for the sake of his crew. He was a fifth wheel now, and like Dr. Singly, his presence here was a waste of his and the company's time. Maybe he should find Tolver tonight and inform him that he was pulling out. He would say good-bye to his crew, and he and Mario would gather the remainder of their things and leave the jungle outpost on the next U.S. bound aircraft.

As Ward drove slowly toward the equipment compound, he heard sporadic bursts of rifle fire. He turned his lights off and drove on cautiously. He parked his truck in the shadows of a storage building and walked gingerly toward the compound.

The rifle fire increased and Ward was startled when he saw a large section of the compound light up with flame. He dashed for cover when metal fragments littered the sky after sticks of dynamite were tossed among the huge earth moving machines.

The post guards were firing continuously at a throng of crazed, zombie-like men who rushed head on into the compound, mindless of the guard's rifles.

Ward was trying to maneuver himself into a position that would enable him to get at the spare weapons that were stored in an underground bunker near the compound. That same bunker housed their generators and fuel supplies. The generators supplied lights to the landing strip, the hangars, the crew's housing, and this acre of fenced storage area.

The whole area was now in total darkness except for the flashes of light from rifles in the battle zone, and one small fire that had survive the guard's extinguishers.

Ward wondered if one of his crew had turned the compound's lights off, or if the generators had been knocked out by the invaders. Either way, the darkness was presently a blessing. As he inched his way closer to the bunker, thick smoke from the burning chemicals and oils filled the air, burned his eyes and left an acrid taste in his mouth. His lungs felt as if they were being torn from his chest with each breath.

Ward knew he had to get at the weapons if they were still available. He couldn't believe that invaders could have found the underground storage area so soon, but if they had, he could forget about going home, at least for a while. If some one had found the bunker and destroyed its contents, it would take every available man present and all the company could send in to finish this project before the heavy rains began. Just thinking about how he would handle such a problem made him sick.

This was the first raid that had reached the compound where the equipment was presently secured. After the eight-foot high, heavy steel fence had been erected, and around-the-clock guards had been posted at the new site, the crew had been lulled into believing that their efforts had actually discouraged the jungle looters.

The steel fence had been built to protect the equipment from just such an invasion as this. Now it looked as if it had been a total waste of effort and money. It obviously hadn't even slowed the assailants, much less stopped them.

How did those dirty mongrels get close enough to destroy that fence without the guards seeing them—and why hadn't someone noticed that the fence was being overgrown in the past few weeks. With the end in sight, everyone had gotten a little careless, and now some of his crew could die because of it.

Ward wondered why the raiders had hit them at this particular time. If it weren't for the fact that the equipment was being destroyed, he would believe that his own company had staged the assault in retaliation for the men's recent mutiny. But he was sure his company's supporters would not take chances on losing the, yet to be retrieved treasure, by destroying the very equipment that would be needed to retrieve it.

So why now? Did the raiders know the crew had uncovered something of value? But how could anyone know they had discovered the sunken river craft? Unless they had been informed. Who among his men would do this?

None of his crew knew what they had unearthed, or how valuable it was, but it didn't take a rocket scientist to guess that nobody would put so much money and effort into the project if there weren't something of great value there.

On hands and knees Ward crawled along in total darkness. He cursed the sharp pieces of debris that tore at his flesh. He was crawling through an area that must have been a landing place for most of the shrapnel. Ward reached out cautiously with his right hand and it came up wet and sticky from the unexpected contact with a still warm, but very dead body. The body was lying directly in his path a few feet from the bunker's entrance.

Ward pulled a cigarette lighter from his pocket. He would chanced a quick look at the obviously dead, man. He moved the lighter as close to the man's face as possible and thumbed the small switch. As the lighter flared into action, a barrage of bullets kicked up dirt and debris all around him. He heard the thudding sound of bullets hitting flesh as they struck the dead body that lay within inches of his own face. He quickly scampered away, and slid through the open door of the bunker.

The bunker was equipped with two sets of doors. The first was an oversized, airtight, waterproof door that prevented moisture from entering the bunker. Ten feet down a flight of steps and a few feet farther ahead, along a wide, eight-foot-high corridor, was another large door of the same structure. Both doors stood open now, which caused Ward to step even more cautiously through the second door. These doors were never to be left open for any reason, and Ward was sure that all of his crew knew that.

He closed the door cautiously behind him and flipped a switch that lighted the interior of the bunker. Everything looked in place and Ward breathed a sigh of relief; the generators had not been destroyed and all the fuel tanks were intact. Ward knew it was possible, even likely, that one of his crew had shut off the outside lights to protect the crew from enemy bullets, but he knew it was also possible the cables had been severed between the bunker and the compound. If the cable had been severed by the enemy, that too, would have been initiated by someone from his own crew, nobody outside the crew knew where the cables were buried—and it would also explain how the invaders managed to cut through the fence so easily; they not only had coverage from jungle growth, they had coverage from the almost total darkness.

Ward walked cautiously around the inside of the bunker looking for intruders. Nothing moved and nothing appeared to be out of place. But there were areas inside the bunker that were so dimly lighted that it would be difficult to determine if someone were hiding there. But none of their vital equipment was stored in the darkened areas, so nobody had bothered to add light there. Ward walked into a dark corner, still believing it possible that somebody was inside the bunker. If nobody was, he wondered who had opened the doors. And why? Something here didn't make sense. That dead body outside the bunker's door didn't make sense.

Ward still didn't want to believe what he had seen, and was hoping he had made a mistake. He hoped that on further inspection he would learn that the body was not that of J.C Mathson, Young Brent Mathson's father.

Ward knew he wasn't wrong, though. Even in that quick flash of light from the small lighter he had recognized the face. Mathson knew about this bunker. If he were here with the raiders, he could have led them directly to it. Possibly without raising suspicion from the posts' guards.

Mathson could have emptied the bunker of its equipment without anybody knowing he was in the area. Or he could have destroyed the bunker and its contents with one carefully planted explosion. Mathson knew enough about this installation and its operation, and was smart enough, to have practically taken it over with only a few men. So why was Mathson laying dead at the bunker's door and nobody else was near the place.

After a more thorough search of the bunker, Ward was convinced that there was nobody inside and nothing seemed to be missing.

This whole scene was out of kilter, and Ward knew that the news about Mathson would never set well with Harri. It would take a lot of convincing to bring her around to believing that Mathson had anything to do with this raid. But why else would he be here? And who had killed him? Ward was wondering if Brent was also here among the raiders.

Would Mathson have brought his son along to help launch such an attack on people he had once cared for? Ward doubted it. He picked up an assault rifle and two hundred rounds of ammunition, turned out the lights, walked up the short flight of steps, closed and locked the bunkers door and crept cautiously into the shadows, but after the bright lights of the bunker, the night seemed even darker and the whole area was just one big, black shadow.

The battle was still ongoing but it had died down to an occasional burst of gunfire, as if both sides were now trying to seek out definite targets and conserve ammunition. When Ward moved away from the bunker's entrance, he moved in the opposite direction from the body of J.C. Mathson. His mind was not on the dead body now, and he wasn't trying to avoid it, he was trying to get his bearing in the darkness, hoping to give his crew a hand in this battle without killing some of his own men or being killed.

Ward had no idea where any of his own crew was at the moment and had no desire to open fire on just anything that moved, and if he was lucky maybe his crew was thinking along the same lines.

About ten feet from the bunker's entrance, he stumbled across another body. He hesitated to use his lighter again; he didn't want another barrage of bullets raining on his spot of turf. He could only be lucky so many times, and his luck was bound to be wearing thin.

He knelt down and began feeling around the man's body. He found the man's rifle, lying as he had dropped it. The man had not moved after he had fallen, and he wouldn't be moving again, not on his own volition. Ward decided to leave him be for the moment.

If he had been an enemy, he wasn't going to do any further harm. If he was a part of Ward's crew nothing could be done for him now.

He stepped away from the body and began his cautious inspection of the battle arena. Suddenly everything around him went deathly still. No shots were being fired. The rifles were silenced in all directions. Then from a distance he could hear the sound of more gunfire. Another battle had taken place near the dredge site; he could hear yelling above the rifle fire.

"What the hell is going on?" Ward asked himself.

In answer to his question, the battle at the dredge site seemed to rage with increased velocity; the whole area sounded as if a full-fledged war was taking place. He didn't have enough men to initiate such an attack on enemy forces. As far as he knew, all of his men were here at the compound, being held down by guerrilla soldiers—or whoever in hell they were!

Suddenly the compound came alive with gunfire. Once more bullets were whining from every direction, splattering the walls of nearby buildings and ricocheting off the heavy equipment. Some of the shrapnel was pelting him and he could feel warm blood running down his neck and seeping into his collar. Another stray bullet ripped a gash through the soft flesh of his upper right shoulder.

He quickly stepped behind a metal building, removing himself from the line of fire. He shouldered his rifle and looked around, still not knowing where his own men were located and reluctant to fire until he was sure of his target.

Just as Ward was working himself into a position where he could join in the battle without killing his own men, the compounds lights came back on, and he could see his men chasing shadowy bodies into the darkness, firing as they ran.

Fifty yards from the compound his men entered an area of shadows where the compound lights did not reach. They slowed their pace and began to pull back. There was no sense in being foolhardy just because they had the enemy on the run.

Ward's crew was still firing but only at targets that were visible. None of the men were anxious to follow the guerrillas into the jungle on a moonless night. They all knew the possibility of ending up in a sinkhole was a greater reality than getting shot—let the enemy find the sinkholes.

Ward's crew was returning to the compound when another fierce round of gunfire broke out near the dredge site. They turned sharply to re-enter the battle, only to discover that the enemy was now engaged with another party who was firing on them.

Ward smiled—they were firing on each other now. They must have been firing on each other at the dredge site earlier; none of his men were there.

All of the heavy equipment had been secured inside the compound for the night, and the guards that would normally have been at the dredge site were at the compound when the raid began. Ward was wondering if every rotten man of them would be wiped out before one of them discovered they were killing each other. He could hope…

The battle at the dredge site was still raging. Ward's men returned from the shadows to the compound and began discussing that battle. They were convinced the raiders were firing upon their own group. Ward felt no sympathy for the murdering raiders who were killing each other, but all of his crew were a little bewildered at the fact that it could happen so easily; that it wasn't beyond belief that it could happen to their own men.

Inside the compound the men were feeling uneasy and a little confused as they looked for casualties among the fallen. Ward was happy but amazed when he realized he had not lost a single man, and only a few had been injured, and most of the injuries were minor.

The damage to the equipment was mind-boggling. Only three of the machines that were stored inside the compound were still in operating order; most had been blown to scrap metal fragments. Ward turned slowly, dread making him tense when he heard a commotion coming from near the bunker's entrance. Some of his crew had discovered the dead bodies.

Ward wished fervently he could have removed the body of Mathson before it was discovered. He knew some of his men would recognize Mathson and would jump to the most obvious conclusion, just as he had. "Damn it to hell!" He swore, as he kicked at the cement base of a metal building. "I just can't believe Mathson was involved in this! But what else can I believe?"

Ward headed toward the bunker, anxiety nagging at his insides. He wasn't at all sure he wanted to learn the identity of the second body. If it were young Brent Mathson lying there, well... he would rather someone else identify the body.

Ward was sure if it were Brent, he would never be able to tell Harri. He would ask Keil not to mention the nauseating facts surrounding his death. It would tear her up to know Brent could ever become involved in such a vile act as this one had been.

"Mr. Holland!" Ward heard the muffled voice calling to him just seconds before he stepped into a lighted area. He held back and listened; he couldn't make out the direction the voice came from.

"Mr. Holland! It's Keil...Is that you?"

From Keil's tone of voice Ward knew he didn't want the other men to hear his call.

"Yes, Keil. It's me. What's up?" Ward asked, softly.

Keil slipped quickly into the shadows and moved silently until he stood beside Ward. Then he said in a hushed tone, "Mr. Holland, I really hate to do this to you but I'm going to ask you to trust me to do something that I believe is right. I'm sure you won't approve, and you may not give me permission to do it, but if you don't, I'll try to do it anyway even without your permission."

"What are you talking about, Keil?" Ward asked, inching farther into the shadows.

"Brent's out there!" Keil told him. "He's waiting for me to return to him...to tell him he has permission to take his father's body. Brent knows his father is dead. He wants me to help him remove the body from the bunker site. I'm asking you for permission to let me help him.

Brent realizes this is a touchy situation for him and his crew. He knows that his presence here would be hard to explain and that some of his men could even be killed if they tried..."

"You're damned right they could…!"

Mr. Holland," Keil interrupted. "I know what this looks like, but right now Brent just wants to remove his father's body, then he and his troupes will leave the installation. He says he will contact me when there's more time; when the situation isn't so volatile, and explain the whole thing."

Ward felt a flooding of relief wash over him at the realization that the second dead body was not that of Brent Mathson. After a few seconds of reveling in his relief, Ward was struck with an intense anger at the young rebel. How dare he come into this camp with a horde of raiders. How dare he have enough nerve to ask for help after his bloody invasion failed.

"No!" said Ward, sharply. "I won't be a party to helping someone who just tried to kill us. I'm surprised that you would consider it Keil… unless you know something that I don't. If there's another reason, they're here…"

"I don't know, Mr. Holland!" Keil said stiffly. "I honestly don't know why they're here. I only know that Brent was my friend, and I believe he's still my friend, and before you ask me, the answer is no, I have no reason to believe that he's still my friend either. It's just a feeling."

"How did he contact you, Keil?" Ward asked.

"Well…he…this is a little embarrassing Mr. Holland, but when we were kids, we had a secret signal we used to call to each other in the darkness. Brent, Harri and I were the only three who ever used the signal. I heard him call to me a little while ago—he saw me in the light while I was talking with the men at the bunker where his father's body was. When I heard the call, I went looking for him. He wants me to lead the men away from the bunker long enough for him to remove the body; he doesn't want to cause any trouble."

Ward was struck with a moment of indecisiveness which added to his anger. He knew he had to say something soon. Keil's request couldn't wait until morning for an answer. He had to make a decision now. Why was he hesitating? He had made quick decisions before. They were usually right, and hadn't he, just a short while ago wanted to remove Mathson's body before it could be discovered? Didn't Keil have a right to the same feelings?

"I'm not going to give you permission to help Brent, Keil," Ward told him. "I don't have to give you permission to do something that you personally feel is right. You're a man now. You can be responsible for your own actions. If you can live with what you're doing, I won't interfere, but don't ask me to help!"

"Thanks Ward!" Keil said quickly as he slipped silently into the darkness. Ward smiled. It was the first time Keil had ever called him Ward.

Five minutes later, the compound light went dark again and a small fire had been rekindled near one of the heavy machines in a dark corner of the fenced equipment yard.

All of the men who were still milling about the compound, convened on the area where the fire was blazing out of control. Within five minutes, the fire was out and the lights were turned on again. The men were all searching the compound and other nearby areas for whoever was responsible for the fire and the black-out. When they found no one but their own men inside the compound, they searched through the bunker.

They found nothing out of place or missing in or near the bunker—except the body of J.C. Mathson—it was missing. For several minutes nobody even noticed the body was missing and even then no great importance was placed on its absence. Each man believing some of their own crew had taken it and added it to the other dead bodies gathered from in and around the compound.

As Ward walked back to his truck, he looked at his watch. It was two in the morning. Things at the compound were so quiet he could hear gas bubbles exploding in a nearby sinkhole. When he reached his truck, Keil was waiting for him. "Thanks again Ward," said Keil. "We couldn't have taken care of that task so quickly without your help—and likely me and Brent would have been killed!"

"I don't know what you're thanking me for," said Ward. What makes you think I helped you?"

"Sorry sir! My mistake!" said Keel "I suppose it was just a lucky break for us that the lights went out in the compound and that fire rekindled itself. Good night, sir. I'll see you in the morning."

Ward slept well for the remainder of the night. He felt good; at peace with himself for the first time in a long while.

Until he said good night to Keil, the only feelings Ward had experienced recently had been those of fear or anger. Last night he had made a decision—a decision based on nothing but a feeling—a feeling that could be dead wrong, but it felt right. Today he still believed he had made the right decision. Likely, he would never know, but Keil would remember—and that mattered to him.

CHAPTER 21

THE FOLLOWING MORNING WHEN WARD reached the compound area, his crew was clearing the debris from the battle scene and putting things back into order. There was a large portion of it that could never be put back in order, but Ward knew that enough of the equipment would still operate to finish the project—if nothing more went wrong before the project's end.

In the cold light of day, the compound looked sadly like the aftermath of a major twister. Tangled bits of burned and warped scrap metal were being collected and piled into an unused corner of the fenced yard. It would be left there to rot into the black earth. The equipment that had managed to escape the invader's assault had been move to the dredge site and had been in operation since early morning.

Ward listened as the men discussed the events of the night before. Some of them had finally begun to wonder what had happened to one of the dead bodies that had been discovered near the bunker. "Who cares?" said David Winters, one of the youngest of the crew. "There were dead bodies all over and none of them were ours; that's all that matters."

"You're right Dave," Bob said looking puzzled, "but when I was checking to see if I recognized any of them…I though I had recognized the one that was missing."

"Maybe you were mistaken," said Dave, "maybe you just thought you recognized it. If it was dead, it didn't walk off during the night, that's for sure."

"I suppose you're right again," said Bob. "It's just strange that…"

Ward walked on, leaving the men to ponder the mystery.

He spoke briefly to a few of the crew about the attack of the night before and asked about the condition of the remaining equipment.

Ward was leaving the compound area and heading for the dredge site when he saw a pickup truck speeding toward the compound. The truck hardly slowed until it neared the enclosure. It came to an abrupt halt just inside the gate. Ward decided to stick around for a few minutes—see if there was another problem. Most likely one of the young men was just feeling his oats and taking his exuberance out on the beat-up truck.

"Mr. Holland, I'm glad we caught up with you," said the driver, stepping from the vehicle before it stopped rocking. "We found something that you'll be interested in…I think!"

"What might that be?" Ward asked.

"Well…actually we found more than one thing you'll want to see right away, I suppose. First, those crates are being removed from the sunken boat. They were bringing them up to the surface when I left the dredge site. Mr. Tolver and Dr. Singly were both there. It seems the equipment operator had a streak of good luck riding with him this morning. A little while ago he accidentally opened up an area along side the boat that permitted one of the men to enter the old boat and locate the crates. Mr. Tolver went in with the man to supervise the removal. The man and Tolver repackaged the crates to protect them, and managed to remove both crates from the old boat before the soil began to cave in around the opening. Tolver was happy as hell that the crew was spared having to remove tons of dirt with shovels."

"You said there was two things I might want to see…"

"Oh yes! Almost forgot… One of our men found four of last night's raiders still alive. They were near the dredge site. They're in pretty bad shape, but one of them is talking. We thought maybe you'd want to know what he's saying."

The two raiders who were still able to talk were telling a strange story about an army of ghost like men who had obviously followed them here and set upon them with guns and machetes—for no apparent reason.

"Ghost, my ass!" said one the other raider, a burly man that was obviously in bad shape, "Twern't no ghost that attacked us! That was that bunch a' scalawags we tried to do some dealin' with a few days ago— 'guess they thought we took something they wanted to keep." He tried to laugh at his private joke, but cut the laugh short when he realized it hurt too much.

The man slumped back against the tree trunk that held him in an up-right position, and went quiet again.

Ward asked the other man who seemed to be in better shape, if he knew anything about the group that had attacked their party, and if he knew the reason for the attack.

"No, not really," said the man, "but Hank could be right. It might be that a party we ran across a few days ago has been followin' us. Guess they though they had a reason to attack us!"

"And why would they think that?" Ward asked.

"Well...we sort of came upon their camp in the middle of the night, and I guess some of our troops got a little carried away when they realized that bunch were sittin' ducks. Actually, it sorts of served them right for bein' so stupid. They only had one guard on duty. We just marched right in and practically took over their operation. We took all the guns and food we could find. Some of them got down right nasty, and we had to shut them up. But I guess they had some stuff we didn't find, they sure pulled together in a hurry—did a number on our outfit last night—wiped us out. Far's I know we're the only four left. You gonna' shoot us now?" He glanced at the other three members of his party as he asked the question.

"I don't know just yet what I'll do with you," Ward told him. "It may depend on what you were doing here. Why you were raiding my camp. Why you were trying to kill my men. And please don't tell me it was all just a big mistake; I already know that!"

"No, it wern't no mistake," said the speaker. "We been plannin' this for a while now. Someone told us weeks ago that you all were pullin' out. That just a clean-up crew was left here. We were plannin' on takin' over here, even takin' the airplanes when they come in. If we had of done what we were plannin' on doin' we would have been rulin' the whole country in no time at all. You understand there was nothin' personal 'bout what we planned. It's just the way things are here—ever body does it. Now…are you gonna' shoot us?"

"No, I won't shoot you," said Ward. "I'm going to have some of my men haul your worthless asses to Villa Guano and turn you over to the authorities there."

"I'd rather you just shoot us," said the man, looking to the other three members of his crew for confirmation as he spoke.

"I'm sure you would!" Ward said grimly, "and I'm sorry, but it's just not going to be that easy for you."

The Cessna 310 left the runway with Tolver, Dr. Singly and the pilot, along with the treasured crates at approximately four in the afternoon.

The last few hours had gone so smoothly that it had taken on a sense of unreality. Ward kept waiting for something to go wrong and it never did. The day had been cooler than usual; the sun was shining brightly; there was less humidity in the air.

Things were too quiet…too sane…

As Ward walked away from the dredge site, he detected a slight ringing in his ears. An uneasy feeling settled over him like a shroud. He stopped, turned slowly around, and placing a hand above his eyes to block the glare of the late afternoon sun, he stared solemnly at the Cessna as it began a slow turn into a heading that would take it to its planned destination. Everything appeared to be working fine for a change and all was on schedule, why couldn't he accept that?

Ward walked on toward his truck wondering what the hell was wrong with him.

The following day, Ward stood in the doorway of the large, steel framed hanger and watched as the giant cargo plane landed. The remainder of the crew, along with the two wives that had stayed behind with their husbands, and all of the crew's personal belongings were inside the hangar, waiting to be loaded into the giant aircraft. The last thing to be loaded into the huge plane was the remainder of the heavy equipment—the remainder being the only three pieces that had survived the raid two nights before.

By nightfall this place would be void of all human life. Ward was sure that would not be an existing condition. The natives and other jungle scavengers would be fighting for the empty storage buildings and anything else left behind that wasn't nailed down or beyond removal. But that was not his problem. When he left this jungle, his problems would be over.

✦ ✦ ✦✦✦ ✦ ✦

CHAPTER 22

WHEN THE CESSNA 310 LIFTED off the runway at the dredge site, Ted Tolver was seated in a front seat beside the pilot. Dr. Singly was strapped in a seat behind the pilot. The doctor had chosen that seat because from there he could keep an eye on the treasured crates; he could even reach back and touch them as often as he felt the need to do so. Tolver glanced back at Dr. Singly to inquired if he were comfortable with the seating arrangement, but Singly never heard Tolver's inquiry.

The doctor was totally oblivious to everything that was happening around him. He now had his hand resting on one of the crates. On his face was a look of pure ecstasy. Tolver couldn't help but smile at the serene scene.

Tolver himself was feeling almost giddy with relief. He and Dr. Singly were finally leaving this hostile, animal infested steam bath and soon the remaining crew would follow. After they were gone, if the damned place disappeared from the map, well…at least one of his prayers would have been answered.

The Cessna had reached its designated altitude and was leveling off for the trip to the next fuel station; the only stop before reaching its destination in the U.S., where a number of impatient men and women anxiously awaited its arrival.

Tolver watched as the pilot tinkered with the plane's control panel. He was hoping that tinkering with the gadgets was nothing more than a means the pilot used to while away the airtime. There was no reason to believe that anything was wrong with the plane, it seemed to be flying just fine. Even the pilot didn't seem to be overly concerned, but Tolver could tell that the man wasn't altogether happy with the craft's performance.

"What is that strange smell?" Dr. Singly asked from the rear seat. The instant the doctor asked the question, Tolver also noticed the odor, and it was rapidly filling the cabin of the Cessna.

Now, the pilot did look concerned, he had recognized the odor instantly, it was the smell of burning electrical wiring.

The engine suddenly began to sputter and the plane was losing altitude. Within a few seconds the plane's engine had stopped running altogether as if the master switch had been turned off. The pilot worked frantically trying to restart the plane's engine. When he realized he was wasting his time, he began to search for a place to make an emergency landing. After searching the terrain below, he realized that the very idea of making a landing in that tangled mess below was a joke. He tried calling in a 'May Day' but the radio was dead also. Then his heart skipped a beat when he saw in the distance a villa, and possibly a place to land the plane. If only he could hold his altitude for a few more minutes. He set the plane on the least possible descent, and tried again to restart the engine. He was still working frantically with the ignition when he felt the plane jerk. It was clipping the tops from the jungle's tallest trees in its path.

Below, a small group of men watched as the plane made its rapid descent into the jungle. When they could no longer see the plane, they smiled—then they began the two-mile trek through the jungle to the plane's crash site; the plane was practically on time and right on target. This unexpected landing had been well planned.

<hr />

CHAPTER 23

HARRI HAD FINALLY DRIFTED OFF to sleep on Senior Manillo's screened-in patio, but not before she had re-lived her former life in the jungle. She had awakened several times during the night as small creatures called to each other in the darkness. She had no fear of the creatures, she was just naturally a light sleeper.

Each time she roused from sleep her thoughts wandered to Keil, and her anxiety for his safety caused her to want to push time ahead, to rush toward that terrorist village and the bastards that held Keil's life in their evil clutches.

At three in the morning, Señor Manillo stepped quietly onto the patio and spoke softly, "Señor Holland, it is time to travel."

Harri had been awake for five minutes or more. She answered immediately, "Si, Señor Manillo, I am awake."

Señor Manillo had steaming coffee, hot tortillas and chili gravy waiting for her. The two ate silently in the dimly lighted kitchen. There was only one light in the house now, and it came from a kerosene lamp that hung from the kitchen's ceiling on a metal hook. As the lamp flickered softly, it cast eerie shadows on the surrounding walls.

The cool dampness of the early morning hours, teamed up with the flickering shadows, lent an uncanny feeling to the atmosphere.

When they finished their breakfast, Harri quietly loaded her duffel bag the truck while Senior Manillo checked the truck's tires and its radiator. Then excused himself he returned to the house. He wanted to leave a final message with his nephew, Mando.

Senior Manillo was not at all pleased about leaving the boy behind for the six or eight hours that it would take for the round trip, but he wanted to help the young hombre who had already given him five thousand pesos and had promised the same amount again if he would return to the drop off point in six days. He and Mando needed the money too badly to refuse this assignment.

And above all, he was convinced this young, foolish one had a very good reason to go into Villa Sangre De Lobo. He would pray for his safe return.

When they reached the drop off point, Señor Manillo asked Harri, "Do you have a...a...como se llama? You know, the little thing that will keep your directions straight while in the jungle?"

When his question finally registered, Harri smiled and said, "Oh, you mean a compass! Yes, I have one."

Harry felt like hugging the man, but under the circumstances she thought better of it, it could be misunderstood. She didn't want him think of her as anything less than all male, so she shook his hand warmly and said, "Mucho gracias Señor Manillo, and I'll see you in six days." Then she picked up her duffel bag and began her journey to Villa Sangre De Lobo. Which translated into 'Blood of the Wolf Village.'

✦ ✦ ✦ ✦ ✦ ✦

CHAPTER 24

For over an hour Harri fought her way through masses of thick, tangled growth. She found herself stopping often now, studying her surroundings, hoping to find a break in the tangled growth. The weight of her duffel bag, along with the jungle's heat, which normally would not have caused her a problem, were now taking their toll on her strength. It had dawned on her shortly after she left the beat-up road where Señor Manillo had dropped her off, that Maybe she was not as physically fit as she once was.

Harri could vividly remember trekking through this type of jungle, and due to that memory, she couldn't be comforted by any hopes of it getting better. Compared to what she might encounter before she reached her destination, she knew this could well be the creampuff portion of her trip.

She pushed on, trying not to think about anything except reaching that damned villa and seeing to getting Keil out of there.

By ten in the morning, there wasn't a dry stitch of clothing on her body. So far though, she had managed to keep moving without having to use her heavy machete; but she was wasting too much time.

Again, as she stopped to observe her surroundings, she was keenly aware that she might have lost some of her natural senses along with along with her physical ability.

Harri could remember a time when she could have traveled three miles in one hour even through such tangled mess as she had encountered here, and nothing would have escaped her vision, not a bird, not a lizard, much less something as large as a human body.

Now she didn't trust herself to travel at a normal pace and still accurately observe her surroundings. Her frustration at herself and this whole crazy idea was mounting. The jungle's tangled obstructions were tearing at her clothing, slowing her to a snail's pace, and jungle's heat was melting her skin.

Finally, out of sheer frustration she stopped long enough to remove her machete from her pack. Within minutes she was using the blade like a pro. She discovered that swinging a machete was not one of her lost arts. She could clear a path with a single chop and her confidence began to return. She knew she was getting her second wind, and that her old jungle skills were returning.

Her sense of direction was clear and she no longer needed her compass. She was on the right path; she could feel it.

And like the jungle creatures that survive by instinct and cunning, she could feel something else, there was danger lurking nearby. Her senses had been alerted by the sudden hush that had fallen over the jungle. She moved on cautiously, keeping a constant eye out for any movement from any direction.

As the day wore on, the uncomfortable feeling that she was being stalked clung to her like a second skin. She tried to ignore the feeling, telling herself she needed to reach the villa as soon as possible. She was aware that her anxiety over Keil's situation was pushing her, creating a potent need to move on.

To keep herself in check, she kept reminding herself that while time was important, getting there was a priority. She would be useless to Keil if she too were taken captive or worse.

The sun was hanging low in the west, and Harri's endurance was wearing thin. Once again, she stopped for a breather. She carefully scanned the area, hoping her continued feeling of being stalked was due to anxiety and being unfamiliar with the area.

For over an hour she hadn't noticed any lull in the jungle's activity as would be normal if someone was out there prowling around. Everything in her own path either fled or took cover as she passed through their dominion. But in the distance, things moved normally without a hitch.

When Harry spotted the aged moss-covered tree trunk that was twisted almost beyond belief, she decided it would be a good place to rest for a while. She propped her bag against the tree and sat herself on a huge moss-covered root. Behind the gigantic root was a spongy bowl-shaped hollow large enough to curl up in. It was a perfect spot to conceal her presence from human or beast.

Harry removed her cap and ran her fingers through her soggy and thoroughly matted hair. She fanned herself with the cap. The cool air moving against her skin felt like a short visit to paradise, but it did little to relieve her anxiety. In the short five minutes she had been resting, the whole area around, as far as she could see or hear, had become wrapped in silence. Nothing was moving. The jungle around her held its breath.

All of Harri's senses had leaped to high alert. She knew she was not the only human in the area. She hadn't actually seen anything that would lead her to that conclusion, it was what she hadn't seen that had alerted her instincts. Every indicator told her somebody other than herself was moving stealthily through the jungle. Was that person watching her at this very moment?

That thought didn't worry Harri as much as it might have if she wasn't so sure of her own ability to observe the movement of all life in the jungle around her. Harri was certain that even if she were a bit rusty, she would spot the movement of any person close enough to see her as she sat concealed in her present shelter.

Yes, there was somebody out there, somebody as familiar with the jungle as she was; somebody she hadn't been able to locate as of yet. But that somebody hadn't located her yet either. But she would bet that person knew she was here; the person could sense her presence as she sensed his. Harri almost laughed out loud at the thought that it might be a female stalking her.

"No female in her right mind would be caught dead in this freakin' jungle." Harri said, with a note of conviction.

Darkness was falling rapidly, and she hesitated to move from her present shelter. She was more than half way to her destination, maybe she should just stay here, eat a small snack and catch a few winks.

Harry sat perfectly still for over ten minutes, observing the surrounding landscape. All was quiet. She moved cautiously to another position and scanned the area that had been concealed from her view. Everything looked natural. Small jungle creatures had resumed their normal activity. For the moment the danger seemed to have passed. Was it behind her now? Or was it in the lead? Would it be waiting for her at some point up ahead?

After eating a light snack, Harri convinced herself that her present spot of turf was the best of all possible places to spend the night. She rolled out her sleeping bag, unzipped it and crawled into the soft padding. But even as tired as she was, she lay listening to the night sounds until utter fatigue robbed her of all consciousness.

Harri awoke suddenly with a start. The night was dark as pitch. She looked at the luminous dial on her wristwatch, it was three in the morning. "What the he...! I don't wake up at three in the morning!"

Then she heard it!

Harri knew the unusual noise must have been what woke her. The noise was not a natural jungle sound. Somebody...some human...was out there. She lay still, listening. The night was dark. Nothing was visible to her, but she was sure she had heard voices, human voices.

Harry eased herself up on one elbow. She heard footsteps... close by. Harri eased back quietly on her sleeping bag and listened without breathing for a few seconds. Then she heard a loud grunt as if someone had been punched or slugged. Then she heard the voice again: "Move, sucker! You can stop when we reach your permanent resting place."

The speaker wasn't ten feet from her sleeping bag. She lay still, her body tense, ready to spring into action if the party spotted her.

Her eyes were adjusted to the darkness now. She saw two shadowy forms moving past her secluded spot. If she breathed, they would hear it.

One of the shadowy forms was holding a weapon close to the other's back. Occasionally the one with the weapon gave the other a shove, trying to encourage the person to move faster. Harri watched the eerie performance, thinking maybe she was dreaming. What would anyone in their right mind be doing out here at three in the morning? Playing cops and robbers? She doubted it.

She lay still until the two moved well beyond her bed, then she let the air escape from her lungs in a potent rush, and breathed heavily to replace the oxygen that had gone stale in her head.

Harry couldn't go back to sleep. She wondered what was going on out there. She might even have been worried about the scene she had just witnessed if she had believed for a split second that either of the people involved could have been Keil. But that had not been a concern. One of the night prowlers had been short and heavy; the other a little taller and very skinny. Keil was much taller than either of them, and had a body some men might kill for.

She lay for several minutes, listening to the jungle's eerie, night sounds. The endless drone of a thousand small creatures came through the night, muffled only by the dense foliage of her sheltered niche, but Harri was listening for another sound. A sound that was no longer there.

When nothing around her moved for several minutes, Harri felt her eyelids growing heavy and slowly drifted back to sleep and dreamed she, Brent and Keil were playing games of hide-and-seek among tangled vines and jungle foliage. Sheer contentment created a smile enhanced by the soft glow of a waning moon.

Harri woke early, feeling relaxed and refreshed, anxious to began her day. She had slept soundly after the early morning episode.

The morning broke bright and clear, and so far, it was cooler than the day before. She ate a few sticks of beef jerky and a granola bar, which she washed down with a jungle-temperature, canned soda.

After several hours of pushing herself harder than was necessary, Harri checked her compass and her watch. She was still on course and apparently making good time.

Harri stopped short when she came upon a well-used trail. Everywhere she looked were signs of recent human activity. She turned slowly around, checking out the area and listening. All she could hear was the very welcome sound of running water. She left the trail and headed north, listening as she walked. She wanted to keep the sound of water within earshot, and at the same time move as far as possible from the well-established trail. A trail that had been used frequently and recently.

Harri knew she was still five miles or so from the dreaded Sangre De Lobo, and if Señor Manillo was correct, this particular section of the jungle shouldn't be overly populated with terrorist, but everything could have changed since he traveled through the area. Senior Manillo made that journey several years ago.

Harri walked at least two hundred yards north of the well-trod trail for twenty minutes before she began her new heading toward the villa. She crossed the small stream of crystal-clear water, then followed it for a short distance until she found a spot where she could fill her canteen and drink from the stream.

The spot where she knelt down to drink was fairly well concealed from view, except from one direction, and that was the direction the bullet came from.

The small, plastic, accordion type cup she was drinking from went flying from her hand when the bullet smashed it to plastic splinters. Harri dropped her duffel bag and reached for the Glock inside her shirt. Her action was off by a split second, and before she cleared the holster with the weapon the gunman spoke sharply, "Don't try it pal."

When the shooter stepped into view, Harri became sick with disgust; the tall, skinny creep from the airport was holding a rifle on her with one hand and motioning to her with the other to step away from her duffel bag. He walked to the bag, then while keeping her covered he reached down and pulled the strap loose with his free hand. The container that held the AK-47 was the first thing visible to him as he opened the bag. He pulled the container from the bag, then opened it with his free hand. When it dawned on him what he held, he actually drooled.

While he was rejoicing over his discovery, Harri chanced an attack on the creep. Again, she was too slow. He had her covered with his rifle and this time she knew she had made a mistake in getting his attention. She could tell by the look in his beady eyes that he had decided it would be easier to shoot her than to keep her covered while he ransacked her duffel bag.

As he raised the rifle higher in order to get a clear bead on his target, Harri knew that any action she took now wouldn't be wasted or foolish. It had become a life and death situation with no time to make shrewd decisions. When he brought the rifle up, she lunged at him. He tried to avoid the collision but this time he wasn't swift enough. She hit him solidly, causing him to stagger. Before he could regain his balance, she managed to land a staggering blow to his head. The blow stunned him momentarily, slowing him down; giving her a chance to grab his rifle.

While the two wrestled for the rifle, it accidentally fired, sending a bullet whining into the treetops, barely missing Harri's head. The rifle was an older model, lever action and needed the use of both hands to work another bullet into its chamber. He tried pushing Harri away long enough to chamber another round, but she had managed to get a grip on him that surprised even her. She rammed her knee into his groin. He let out a wounded animal scream and dropped the rifle as he grabbed for his privates.

Harri tried to slug him, but he skidded away and went for the rifle. She grabbed him from behind and tried to break his back with her knee. As she increased the pressure of her knee, she felt her grip slipping again. To retain control of the situation she gave him a violent shove that sent him face first into the stream of water. When he came out spluttering, she kicked him squarely in the face with her steel-toed boot. He made one futile attempt to rise, then sank slowly back to the sodden earth.

Harri pulled her Glock from its holster and aimed it carefully at the man's head. She had taken the slack from the trigger, thus removing the safety setting, and the creep was only a split second from hell, but she couldn't pull the trigger. She held the gun aimed at his head, cursing herself for not doing what she knew was the right thing to do under the circumstances.

"Pull the trigger you idiot! Kill him!" She whispered furiously to herself. *"You'll meet him again! Next time you might not be so lucky!"*

Angrily, Harri turned away. She gathered her things, returned them to the bag and walked away quickly; cursing herself for being a lily-livered milksop.

Harri wasn't at all happy about her judgment call, but as her anger began to settled down and a semblance of sanity began to return, she was happy to know she couldn't kill a defenseless being, even a murdering animal like that creep. But her common sense told her that her moral hang-up could very well cost her life before this mission was over.

Harri changed her direction once more, moving carefully away from the stream of water. She knew it was possible the creep was not alone, or that one of the terrorist guards could have heard the rifle shots. Either of those possibilities were enough to convince her that her present location was no place for a picnic.

As she moved farther away from the stream, walking became easier due to the more open space, and more dangerous for the same reason. She changed her course slightly and then began to move back into the direction of the villa. Her new course slowed her progress but offered more cover. With the security of the added cover, she became more confident and let her mind wander as she tore her way through the heavy growth.

A sudden noise startled Harri from her reverie, but she instantly recognized the noise as the flight of a frightened animal. Then it dawned on her that the animal was fleeing toward her, not away from her. Something other than her presence had frightened the animal.

Harri backed into a dense growth of large leafy plants, and scanned the area for movement. Nothing was visible to her from that spot. Moving cautiously, trying to keep herself concealed from view she tried for a different view.

Moving cautiously away from the sheltered spot, this time taking no chances, she removed her Glock from its holster and held it in her hand while she investigated the spot the animal had fled from.

As she moved in that direction, she detected a faint but putrid odor. At times the odor grew heavier, then it would fade away. She walked a few more yards and the smell became obvious again. After walking another hundred yards, the stench became constant and totally disgusting. There was something dismal and frightening about the foul smell.

Except for her eternal curiosity, she would have fled the area like a scared rabbit. Moving on stealthily she came suddenly into a small clearing. She stopped, rooted to the spot, horrified by the scene before her. In a clearing some fifty feet in diameter were a dozen or more, very dead, human bodies. All the bodies were in different stages of decomposition. Some of the bodies had been torn apart by jungle scavengers, and some looked as if they had been dead only a few hours.

All of the bodies that were still intact were dressed in combat fatigues, boots and caps. Judging from their clothing, the dead men could well have been terrorist guerrillas from the nearby villa.

Harri wasn't so much concerned about their history as she was about their present condition, and who had killed them...and why!

Maybe this is the dumping ground for the bodies of the prisoners that the terrorists are executing.

Holding one hand over her nose to keep from retching, Harri started to turn when she heard: "Not a pretty sight, huh?"

She recognized the voice instantly. She had her Glock in her hand and wanted desperately to turn and fire. While the thought played through her head the man said, "Drop the gun, buddy! Then you can turn around if you wish, but shooting you in the back won't cause me to lose any sleep." Harri lowered her arm, the Glock dangling from one finger as she turned around. She came to a complete stop just in time to see a bullet split the skull of the creep who had his rifle aimed at her chest.

The creep had obviously recovered from the near-lethal kick she had given him earlier, but she seriously doubted he would be recovering from this—not in the near future anyway.

If the bullet that removed that sucker had actually been meant for her, she could only be thankful that the shooter's aim was off by several feet. Somehow, she didn't believe the shot was meant for her; but she wasn't taking any chances. She tightened her grip on her Glock and headed for cover.

Another bullet whistled past her head as she made a dive into the nearest shelter, an alcove of tangled vines and undergrowth...and landed squarely on top of a dead...or dying body.

In spite of her steady nerves and her years of jungle training, she let out a startled yelp. This body's heart was still beating; blood was gushing from his chest; he still clutched an assault rifle in his hands.

Harri watched in horror as his hands relaxed their hold on the weapon, he was dressed as the other dead men were, in combat fatigues. The man's rifle held an almost full clip of ammo and there was a spare clip on his belt.

Harri eased herself away from the body, pulling his rifle along as she went. Then on impulse she reached back, took the spare clip of ammo and fastened it to her own belt. She needed all the help she could get now, and this rifle and ammo might come in handy.

She sat very still, trying to become as invisible as possible while her tension grew. She had to get out of here, but where was the second shooter?

That second shooter had obviously just killed this man. Possibly with that bullet that had whistled past her head. *He must know I'm still here. But maybe not! Maybe he thinks I've managed to get away from him. And maybe I could....*

Harri eased herself from the ground, checking the area as she turned slowly around. Nothing had moved or made a sound. Maybe she *could* break away now.

She had to get away from that dead body whose unblinking eyes were staring at her accusingly. And she had to get to Sangre De Lobo, if she planned to reach Keil before he ended up here in this stinking graveyard.

Harri stepped cautiously from the shelter of the jungle recess and found herself looking down the barrel of another assault rifle. On the other end of the rifle was the other ape from the airport—the one with the handlebar mustache.

For the first time in her life Harri felt totally defeated. Hopeless and helpless. She stood and waited for the man to blow her away—and wondered what he was waiting for. As she stood waiting for a bullet to rip through her body, she could feel the hair raising on the back of her neck. This ape must be one of those kinky bastards that loved to play with his food before eating it. Harri's anger began to build, and she knew she would force his hand before she would let him torment her. She would force him to kill her instantly.

All she had to do was attempt to kill him. Just raise her Glock and fire. She was a very good shot. Just raise her Glock and pull the trigger. As the seconds ticked off, she felt her arm rising...

"You're one lucky bastard," the man said to her, speaking in perfect English. "That sucker there had a bead on you and was pulling the trigger. You can be thankful that I'm an excellent shot, because that one—he wouldn't have missed!"

"Who are you?" asked Harri, trying not to show her fear. "And what in hell is going on here?"

"Are you referring to the dead terrorists back there? Or, to these two suckers I just killed, or all of them?" He asked, while squinting at her as if demanding an answer.

"All of them," she answered, trying to keep her voice steady as she glanced from the two, he had just shot, then beyond him to the graveyard.

"I killed those murdering terrorists, including this one," he told her, looking as if he dared her to object, "and I shot that skinny jackass over there too...not particularly because he was going to kill you. I just got tired of seeing him around. He was always in my face. I hated the bastard! He was working for the terrorists!"

"Then I suppose I should thank you for saving my life," Harri said quietly, wishing she knew what this maniac had in mind for her.

"It's not necessary, he told her with an impatient air. "Frankly, I don't believe that skinny freak could have killed you. He couldn't shoot straight enough to hit the ground. He was going to try to kill you, but you could have handled him easily—like you did back there by the stream of water. That shot he fired at you back there was the best shot he ever made in his life, and I can guarantee you he wasn't aiming at your cup. You should have shot him when you had the chance. You were a fool to walk away, leaving him to come after you again. Why didn't you shoot him?"

"I don't find it easy to shoot defenseless people," she said cautiously, trying not to rile that fragile, trigger-happy portion of his brain.

"Defenseless my ass," he made a choking sound as he spit out the words. "A damned cut-throat spy, that's what he was. He worked for that bunch of murdering dogs at Sangre De Lobo. None of them have a right to live. They have no right to inhale other people's air!"

I was right about him, thought Harri. *He would slit a person's throat for breathing his air.* But for some reason not clear to her, he had saved her life, and she was thankful, but she doubted he did it out of a love for humanity.

I sure hope he doesn't discover I'm a female, thought Harri, while betting a few pages of her favorite bedtime story that he didn't like women.

"My name is Harri Holland," she said, holding out her hand to the man.

"So, it is!" he said, refusing to shake her hand. "We're not friends. Won't ever be. Won't ever see each other again."

"You did save my life," said Harri. "That means something to me."

"Well, it doesn't mean a damned thing to me," he said, sharply. "I just hate to see people get killed that haven't harmed me, and as far as I know, you haven't. And just for the record, I already know who you are. I knew who you were when I saw you at the airport. You're Ward Holland's kid!"

Oh, shit! Thought Harri, wishing she had split the scene instead of trying to be sociable. *I wonder if he knew me as Ward Holland's boy—or his girl?* Then she said, "Well thanks anyway sir. And if you have no problem with me leaving now, I'll be on my way. I still hope to reach Sangre De Lobo before midnight."

"You're a damned fool Harri!" He told her, shaking his head. "But if you want to get yourself killed, why should I try to stop you? Go on! Leave me to my rat killing! I have a few more to scare out of their nest before I call it a day. If I should happen to see your pop, I'll tell him what happened to you!"

Sweet man! Harri thought as she gathered her bag, and without bothering to adjust it, she removed herself from his presence as subtly as possible. Trying not to appear ungrateful in her haste.

She was grateful to the man for saving her life, and for not shooting her, but from where she stood, her observation of the man's activities here had done little to change her earlier opinion of him. The man was totally nuts, and she didn't even want to know the reason behind his insane, private war on the terrorists.

This strange man may be doing the world a favor by wiping out the terrorists in Sangre De Lobo, but she would wager a guess that anybody who differed from his own ideas or plans would end up with the terrorist soldiers—rotting away in his private graveyard.

CHAPTER 25

A SHIVER OF SHEER RELIEF RAN down Harri's spine as she reentered the seclusion of the jungle's lush, thick growth. She wanted to pull it around herself like a protective blanket. Nobody had to tell her how lucky she'd been to escape that nut case's presence without provoking his killer instincts. Which, if she were guessing, wouldn't be a difficult chore.

An hour later Harri was miles from the graveyard and had almost managed to put the grisly incident out of her mind as she concentrate on her present plans. It was getting late. The sun would be setting soon and she was still two or more miles from the infamous villa.

Harri suddenly felt her senses sharpening and knew she was. nearing her destination. She stopped for a quick check on her surroundings and listened to the multiple hushed sounds all around her; distant cries of jungle birds that were unaware of her presence; a bird feeding its young in a tree over a hundred yards away. And now she felt the presence of people not yet visible to her. She smelled body odor. It smelled dirty and evil.

The going would be tricky from this point on. She had to keep out of sight, remain alert every second. Harri had no doubts that guards would be watching for intruders.

Harri searched for a suitable place to stash her duffel bag and the bundles of money that were taped to her body. She would travel as lightly as possible from this point on. The bag would be a burden if she should encounter a problem that required freedom of movement.

It didn't take long to secure the bag and the bundles of cash after finding a perfect place to stash the stuff. She placed her possessions, along with the dead terrorist's rifle, into a hollowed-out spot among a heavy growth of vines and leaves, then carefully replaced the disrupted foliage over her stash and mentally marked the spot.

Harri assembled the AK-47 she had taken from the duffel bag, shoved a .9mm Glock in a pocket inside her jacket, then dropped several clips of ammo into another pocket.

She began working her way carefully around as much of the undergrowth as possible, which seemed to offer less cover than before. She kept the AK-47 in her hands and moved on quietly, stopping every few minutes to listen and study her surroundings. The whole area was ominously quiet.

Five minutes later, Harri knew she was nearing the villa and should be hearing noises; barking dogs; motor vehicles. Some indication of life. She could feel the presence of human types all around her; and she could smell them.

The sun was setting, but there was still enough light to see clearly for a while. Then she heard the trucks. Their engines were grinding as if pulling a heavy load, they were moving along in low gear.

Walking in deep shadow, Harri headed toward the sound. When muffled human voices became audible, she stopped and listened, trying to make out the conversation, but she was still over a hundred yards from the activity, and all but the sharpest sounds were absorbed by the jungle's lush growth.

She wouldn't chance going near the activity, but she wanted to know where she was in relation to the actual villa. She could see the place the voices came from. Several structures were visible through the trees. This place was not Villa Sangre De Lobo.

She scanned the area for a suitable tree she could use to elevate herself above the jungle's floor. She wanted a better view of this action. She spotted a tree with a huge trunk and a number of large branches.

Harri climbed cautiously from branch to branch, hoping the uniformed men who were milling around the compound would not detect her movement.

The installation looked like a small military base. From her perch she had a bird's eye view of the place. Trying not to make any sudden moves, she reached slowly into a zippered pocket and removed a pair of binoculars. She carefully trained her sights on the operation. A long, low, bamboo structure, with more than ample parking space, seemed to be the center of activity. At least two dozen small huts, arranged in rows of six, were located thirty yards in back of the larger structure. The huts were completely enclosed by an eight-foot-high stockade wall constructed of hundreds of needle-sharp bamboo poles. Above the poles, several strands of razor wire had been interwoven and strung along securely to steel rods set about eight feet apart.

The huts all looked the same. The small buildings could be sleeping quarters for terrorist soldiers. The huts could even be storage units, but why so securely protected from outsiders? What could be valuable enough to require such measures?

Another long, low, nondescript building, located just fifty feet west of the stockade wall, looked as though it could be a mess hall, or a large classroom...and this foul-smelling place could be a prison.

The two trucks that had just entered the parking area appeared to be military vehicles with tarp covered beds. The tarps were supported by a series of bows, creating an oval shelter, most likely for hauling troops and firearms to combat zones.

Suddenly she heard a sharp, startled yell and saw three uniformed men go tearing after something not visible to her. The men ran behind the parked trucks and were out of her sight for a few seconds.

Then she saw a single man making a dash between the two trucks. He was obviously trying to escape. His hands were tied behind his back and he was running fast, headed in her direction. Suddenly, nobody was paying him any attention and Harri wondered why.

Then she saw one of the soldiers open the door of a separate enclosure and release a huge dog. The animal made several rapid trips around the grounds, sniffing as he ran, then set after the fleeing man, alone.

The soldiers were laughing. None of them seemed particularly worried that the animal would fail its mission.

I'll bet their lack of concern is justified, thought Harri. *I'll bet that creature has never failed a mission.* The fleeing man ran past her without looking back, and the dog was less than a hundred yards behind him. *Well—there's always a first time for everything,* Harri told herself as she reached into another pocket and removed the silencer that had been hand crafted for her Glock. She quickly adjusted the silencer and waited until the dog was well past where she sat perched on her branch. Then she pulled the trigger. The animal stumbled without making a sound, for which she was grateful. The dog tried once to rise and she fired again, this time putting a bullet through its head. The dog lay still and the fleeing man was well out of her sight now, hopefully headed toward the safety of the outside world and freedom. She would guess that nobody would bother to look for him until the dog failed to return.

She returned her attention to the large bamboo structure. Harri decided the place was a roadhouse of sorts, a very popular hangout for local terrorists—or any other vermin that made up the overall population of the area.

No human types were visible inside the stockade wall, and all of the hut's doors were closed. Outside, near the roadhouse, soldiers with rifles were milling about.

While Harri watched, one of the trucks backed up to the stockade wall. Something was being unloaded into the enclosure. When the men finished their chore they entered their trucks, two men per truck, and the slow-moving vehicles pulled away from the wall heading back in the direction they came from. Harri watched them out of sight, wondering what their mission had been.

There was still a few trucks and four military type Jeeps in the parking lot. Harri decided to just observe the place for a few minutes longer. If nothing happened, she could gain information from before complete darkness set in, she would skirt the joint and head directly for the villa. Which couldn't be far from this installation if she had judged correctly.

It was getting too dark to linger near the roadhouse. Harri decided to move on. Lights were being turned on throughout the place and she could see a faint glow emitting from some of the huts behind the stockade wall.

As she drew near the roadhouse, she could hear loud singing and guitar music coming from inside the structure. A few people were milling around the building but nothing was happening that gave her any clue for a next move.

As Harri walked away, the music stopped and the patrons cheered. She wondered if the cheering was for the musicians' talent or for the fact that they had stopped playing. Harri's vote was for the latter. She adjusted her duffel bag and set out once again for Sangre De Lobo.

As Harri walked away from the roadhouse, she turned to look back; an involuntary shudder played along her spine. Somehow, she knew she hadn't seen the last of this dive.

By the time she reached the villa, total darkness had settled upon her path. She had fully expected to encounter at least one guard along the way, and wondered why she hadn't. Maybe there hadn't been enough outside activity in the area recently to justify keeping guards on duty except in the most likely points of entry. She was not entering the villa from the most likely point.

+ +++++ +

CHAPTER 26

HARRI COULD SMELL FOOD COOKING even before she saw the lights of the villa. The food smelled scrumptious. It suddenly dawned on her how long it had been since she had eaten a meal, other than the few dry snacks she had taken from her duffel bag. Her stomach rumbled offensively as the smells grew stronger.

Trying to ignore her hunger pangs, Harri concentrated on entering the villa without arousing attention. A dog was barking in the distance but she was sure that it was not her presence that had riled it. She entered the villa from the east, or rear, depending on how one looked at it. The faint glow of candle and lamplight was visible through nearby windows.

Harri stopped some fifty feet from the nearest structure; an animal shelter. She listened for a while to the many different sounds that wafted through the night. In the rear of the animal shelter was a large heap of composting refuse that smelled almost as bad as the graveyard back in the jungle. The smell helped to ease her hunger pangs.

Somewhere nearby someone was strumming a love song on an out of tune guitar.

Harri moved away from the smelly heap, inching closer to the villa's alley. The food smells grew stronger as she drew closer to the poorly constructed hovels that made up this eastern section of the villa.

Before entering the alley, Harri stopped and disassembled her AK-47. She concealed it in the two large, double pockets inside her fatigue jacket. She slipped a full clip of ammo into her Glock, returned it to another inside pocket, then continues to moved cautiously down the littered alley. A hundred feet into the alley, she saw the well used break between two huts that would take her into the villa's dirty street.

Reaching the street, she stopped again to study her position. She really needed a plan, but in order to make plans she needed information, and trying to get the information would be risky and take up too much time. She also needed food and someone to ask questions of. There were children and dogs in the street, so there must be someone here she could talk to. *Anybody who'd tolerates children and dogs can't be all bad.*

Three men pushed through a swinging door that Harri was standing in front of. She stepped aside in time to avoid being knocked into the street. She had forgotten that doors swing both ways in these villas, and that it's best not to stand in front of them. The men who came through the door hardly noticed her and walked on down the street. She heard voices approaching from the opposite direction and stepped back into the shadows between two crumbling adobe buildings.

Harri was hoping to avoid an encounter with anyone until she had gotten the feel of the place. As the voices drew near, she stepped farther back into the shadows and stumbled over a sleeping pig. The pig jumped and squealed. Startled by the sudden action, Harri fell against a wall of the building on her right. Someone looked into the darkened space and yelled in Spanish, "What in hell is going on in there?"

"I'm taking a piss," Harri yelled back, also in Spanish.

"Don't piss on the pig!" Someone yelled back, then laughed as if the statement was gut splitting, hilarious.

Harri waited until the voices disappeared, then stepped back into the street.

The activity in the villa, such as it was, was slow paced. Nobody seemed to be going anywhere in particular, and Harri came to the conclusion that the people, mostly teen-agers, were walking the streets just so they wouldn't have to go home and go to bed…or whatever it was they did when they could no longer walked the streets. Harri guessed the small adobe huts had no type of air conditioning and would hot as hell at night. A good reason to walk the streets.

Harri walked two blocks or more and nobody was paying any attention to her, other than curious stares from youngsters. She was beginning to feel a little more relaxed except for a gnawing hunger that was steadily growing. Did she dare ask questions? None of the people she had seen so far looked particularly violent, and she wondered where the bad guys were hanging out.

This was beginning to feel a little strange, and a nagging doubt was working it way to the fore. Was she even in the right villa? This place looked too peaceful to be a terrorist den of iniquity. Maybe she had taken a wrong turn somewhere along the way.

Without jeopardizing her position, she needed to find someone she could question, but the first thing she needed to do was find food. She was starving.

It must be dinnertime around here, she thought hopefully. The smell of food was coming from everywhere. A little late for dinner, she supposed, but it hadn't been dark all that long.

Harri passed a small, dimly lighted cafe that had strong food odors emitting from the doorway. She couldn't stand it any longer. She stepped inside and walked casually to a small table for two.

The table was covered with a worn, faded oil cloth that hadn't been thoroughly cleaned in months. She could see dried bits of food along the edges of the overhang.

She looked closely at the two wooden chairs and then seated herself in the cleanest one. She glanced quickly around the small room: Ratty curtains, dirty windows, dirt floor. The dirt floor had been packed down over the years to a glass like finish. At some time in a distant past, the floor had been covered with clay tiles. A few still remained in protected corners.

Someone had picked up a bit of trash from the floor and piled it in one of those corners. Harri's intellect was objecting to everything about the place, but nothing could discourage her stomach. It just didn't care where the food was being prepared—or how.

A cute, chubby faced young girl that looked as if she had worn the same outfit for the better part of her fourteen or fifteen years, walked to her table, smiling broadly. The girl asked Harri if she wanted food and something to drink.

No menu. No frills. Just a smile, and if she were lucky, something to eat.

"What do you have?" Harri asked in Spanish.

"Menudo, tamales, tortillas—cervaza tambien," The girl said, still smiling.

"Bring me a double order of everything, por favor," Harri told her, studying the girl's face, appreciating the genuine friendliness that the girl was extending to her.

As she waited for her food, Harri watched the street in front of the small cafe. The traffic was still very light, and mostly teenagers. Occasionally one would poke a head into the cafe and look her over curiously before walking on down the street.

All the people here appeared to be so…normal. So non-violent. So, unlike what she had expected. Something was wrong, but she wasn't ready yet to believe she had made such a gross error in her directions.

When Harri saw the young girl bringing her food, she moved her chair back out of the way. The plates looked hot, and while the girl seemed to have complete control of them, she wasn't taking any chances.

Still smiling, the girl carefully placed the hot plates and two beers in front of Harri. Then without asking permission she seated herself in the chair on the opposite side of Harri's table.

Harri smiled at the girl encouragingly, thinking that this was working out better than she had expected. The girl placed her elbows on the table, rested her chin in her open palms and watched Harri eat.

After Harri had finished her food, which was surprisingly good, she asked the girl, in Spanish, "How long have you lived in this villa?"

"Fourteen-and-a-half years. I was born here," the girl answered.

"Do you like it here?" Harri asked.

The girl darted a quick glance toward the kitchen, then leaned closer to Harri and said in a low voice, "I hate it here. It is a pig sty, and all the people here are pigs—except mama."

"Do you really know all the people here?" Harri asked.

"Yes…No…" she stammered, then continued, "I know all the people who have lived in this villa since I was born. But many people come here—people who do not live here—people such as yourself. Most of them do not stay long. I do not know them."

"Where do all the people, such as myself, lodge when they come here?"

"Where they choose to, I suppose. I am not sure," the girl answered.

"Does the villa have a hotel, or a place where one could rent a room?" Harri asked.

"The girl smiled shyly, looking uncomfortable. She looked again toward the kitchen, then began picking at the grease and dirt under her fingernails. Harri could see the hurt and disappointment in the girl's face, and knew she would leave the table unless the air was cleared soon. Harri was sure that she had somehow garbled a word, or poorly phrased a sentence the girl had totally misunderstood and had drawn the wrong conclusion.

I must remember at all times that these people believe me to be a male. Since I planned it that way, I'm glad it's working, but if I keep forgetting I'll be in over my head before the sun rises tomorrow. Worse still, for me the sun might not rise tomorrow.

"I am alone," Harri told the girl quickly, hoping to avoid any further misunderstanding. "I wish to remain alone. I will be here for only a short while, and I need a place to sleep. That is all—just sleep!"

Now, the girl smiled brightly. Her eyes sparkled with hope. "Oh! Si!" she said happily. "I will speak to mama. Sometimes, mama will let others sleep in our spare room, if she likes the way you look. Mama has…what some in the villa call, the magic eye. Her eye can see inside others. She knows if one is bad; and she is always right. Maybe she will like you. I will ask her."

The girl rose from her chair and started to rush away. Harri placed a restraining hand on the girl's arm and said, "Not so fast. I want to relax for a while before making any decisions. I like you. I want to just sit here and talk to you for a while."

Harri felt almost guilty when she saw the radiant glow on the girl's face. Here was a young girl that loved attention and most likely received very little from anyone in this dump. If she did, it would be the wrong sort of attention.

The girl was obviously a true innocent, and Harri hated deceiving her, but she needed information. She needed it quickly.

"My name is Harri," she said to the girl. "What do the people here call you?"

"My name is Stella and that is what the people here call me."

"Well Stella, do you think you and I could be friends?" Harri asked. Again, the girl smiled shyly at her, then turned to look toward the kitchen, as if someone back there was making her decisions by means of telepathic signals.

"If you really want me to be your friend, and if it is all right with Mama, I would like to have a friend," said Stella.

After chatting for a few minutes, Stella fell silent. Harri watched her without speaking, wondering if once again, she had said something to offended the girl.

Stella sat quietly, a distant look on her face, a slight slump to her young shoulders. She began cleaning her nails again.

Harri had an almost overwhelming urge to prod Stella, to keep her talking, but she didn't want to scare her off, so she waited.

Suddenly, Stella looked up. She looked directly into Harri's eyes with a thoughtful expression on her cute, round face. Harri waited for her to speak.

"You are different, Señor Harri!" She spoke the words so quietly that Harri almost missed them.

"Different?" Harri asked. "Why do you think I am different, Stella?"

"I do not know—you are just—different," said Stella, looking at Harri as if she was trying to determine what was different about her.

"Different from what?" Harri asked, smiling softly at the girl who was obviously not sure of where this conversation was going and not really sure if she wanted to continue with it.

"You are different from the other men that come here." Stella told her. And again, she glanced toward the kitchen. "The men that come here," she continued, "mostly they look like filthy pigs!"

"Come now Stella," said Harri, "surely all the men who come here do not look like pigs. There must be someone special…"

But Stella had fallen silent again, and from the look on her face it was obvious that her thoughts had turned inward. When she finally looked up, her face held a strangely sad expression.

Harri waited.

"There is…was…one man. He was not a pig. He looked nice…like you," said Stella, softly.

Harri's heart skipped a beat, did she dare to hope? She looked at Stella and smiled. If there was only some way to get this girl to describe the man, she was speaking of without letting her know she was trying to get information from her. The one thing Harri could remember well from past experience, was that the people from these villas had an uncanny ability of knowing when they were being pumped for information. Even the slow-witted among them could usually sense a ploy, and she seriously doubted that Stella was slow witted.

Harri reached across the table and squeezed Stella's hand. "I know how you feel, Stella," she told the girl quietly. "I have a friend—one that I miss very much. This man and I, we grew up together in a place not far from here, but I haven't seen him in a long time. I carry pictures of him though, and when I get to missing him a lot, I look at the pictures."

Harri was hoping that Stella would ask to see the pictures, but she just looked more forlorn than ever and then said sadly, "I do not even have pictures. I do not have a friend."

"Oh! I must have misunderstood," said Harri. "I thought the man you spoke of was your friend."

"No, he was not my friend," said Stella. "He was just someone that I liked very much—but I guess he did not like me. He went away. He did not even say good-bye. If he were truly my friend, he would have said good-bye."

Harri took her wallet from her pocket and pulled a few pesos from its fold. She closed the wallet carefully, then as if on second thought, she reopened it and turned to the photo section. She pulled the pictures of Keil from the wallet and placed them in front of Stella. "Those are pictures of my friend," Harri said softly. "I wish you had a picture of you friend. I would like to see a picture of him."

Harri watched Stella closely as she gazed at the two pictures of

Keil. There was not the slightest indication that she recognized the man in those photos.

Harri felt disappointment settle over body like a wet blanket. She was sure that Stella had never laid eyes on Keil. Stella would have remembered Keil. Harri was sure of that.

She returned the pictures to her wallet and handed the pesos to Stella. "I need to pay for my food and find a room for the night. If your offer is still good, I would like to talk to your mama about her spare room now."

Stella took the bills and started toward the kitchen. She stopped short as the front door opened and two uniformed policemen came into the cafe. Stella looked startled, then hurried away from the table with the pesos.

The two policemen seated themselves in the back of the small cafe, both facing the door. They obviously wanted to keep an eye on the customers. Harri looked around, she was the only customer in the place.

Stella was gone for several minutes. When she returned with Harri's change she placed it quickly on the table and mumbled a small "gracias, Señor," and hurried away. Harri took that action to mean the bedroom was not available.

Not wanting the sullen looking policemen to think she was scared, or in a hurry to leave, Harri sipped slowly on the last dregs of her warm beer. She was sorely tempted to order another, but decided not to press her luck. She stood up slowly, checked her pockets to be sure everything was in place, and walked casually out the door.

She headed back up the street in the direction she had walked from earlier. Just in case the two policemen were watching her she decided to make the pig route her way out.

She entered the small space between the two buildings, stepped over the pig this time and walked on into the filthy alley. She lost herself among the chicken coops, wrecked autos and other debris that littered the alley as far in both directions as she could see, which wasn't far, the night was dark. The only light came from the faint glow of small, dirty windows.

Harri turned left down the alley, following along behind a row of haphazardly constructed buildings: bars, cafes and what-have-you. She walked slowly, hugging closely to the rear walls of the buildings.

As she moved along, she studied the structures. Any that had lights glowing inside received special attention. She noticed that most of the buildings were constructed of more than one type of material. Many were several types, even rusty, corrugated metal.

Harri had noticed earlier that some of the fronts were faced with old brick, and from the street side they didn't look half bad. Some of the walls were constructed from poles; their roofs were covered with thatch.

Harri tried to sort out which were places of business and which were private homes. It was difficult to determine one from the other, most likely many of the structures served as both. *Why couldn't one of them be a rooming house?* She really needed a bed for the night, and nothing in this villa, that she had seen so far, looked even remotely like a hotel.

Also, nothing had fully convinced her that this was a terrorist villa. She wanted to believe that it was, because she didn't have enough time to go searching all over the damned jungle for a single villa that would look like every other villa in the freakin' jungle. None of them would have their villa's name hanging from tall poles and lighted in neon.

This has to be the right villa, she told herself. "But where in hell are all the terrorists? Two evil looking policemen do not a terrorist villa make," she philosophized.

✦✦✦✦✦

CHAPTER 27

HARRI WONDERED IF SHE HAD somehow wandered off course in the darkness. Then suddenly she heard loud voices coming from one of the nearby buildings. She eased herself closer to the window of the building. The windows were too dirty to get a good look at anything inside, but she could see she had worked her way back to the spot where she had left Stella and the two policemen.

She was directly behind the little cafe now. One of the policemen was yelling at Stella and an older woman. The older woman looked enough like Stella to be her mother.

Harri stood fuming as she watched the scene through the widow. She could hear every word the foul-mouthed policemen were saying.

"…. we will watch this place every minute if we have to." He yelled at the woman. "If we find that you are harboring gringo spies here again, you can say good-bye to your cafe and your home. The only reason you are still here, after we discovered that last gringo had been hiding here, is because your old man was my mother's cousin. My mother has mushrooms for brains because she believes family should be protected. But the family bloodline means nothing to me. Do you hear old woman? Nothing!"

"Stella was right! They are pigs!" Harri hissed the words into the darkness, her anger building to a boiling point.

Stella sat at a table near the older woman, silently weeping, trying to hide her tears from the policemen. As the men were leaving, one of them placed a hand on the older woman's throat and glared into her face. "Do not forget what I have said," he sneered, then slammed the woman toward the nearest wall. Stella cried out when the older woman struck a rough support beam. The man grabbed Stella by her long hair and yanked her around to face him. "That goes for you too female dog," he yelled into her face, before shoving her against the wall.

With a jerky motion, the policeman who had been yelling tried to tuck his shirt into his pants. When the shirt didn't work to suit him, he yanked at the gun belt that hung loosely around his waist. Realizing that he wasn't making any progress with the belt either, he stormed from the room, his partner followed him through the door.

"I should follow those mongrels and break their freakin' necks!" Harri whispered the words harshly, feeling a bitter bile seeping into her throat. She stood rigidly, trying to bring her anger under control; trying to allay her badly wounded sense of justice.

But even as her anger raged, she knew that breaking their evil necks would only create more trouble for Stella and her mother. The only way to deal with this problem would be to find all of them and wipe them out—like flies. As her rage ran uncontrolled, she kicked at the solid foundation of the stone structure. "I wish I could...I wish I had the time to hunt down every last one of those bastards: I wish I had the power to wipe them off the earth!"

Her anger settled slowly as she walked along the cluttered alley, picking her way through the debris. When she began to think rationally again, she knew she had to get back to her immediate problem, which was finding Keil. And before she could find Keil, she had to find the prison or stockade where he was being held. After she found that, she had to learn as much as possible about the place and determine what method she would use to get him released. She needed a clear head to think with, and only sleep would fix that problem. This had been a long and tiring day and it must be nearing ten.

To Harri that was not a late hour; but the time would pass quickly and she needed to find a room. If she couldn't find a room, she would be forced to return to the jungle and once again, find a place to sleep among the jungle's creatures—it wasn't an appealing thought, but then, neither was the idea of sleeping in this villa.

Until she had worked her way back to Stella's little café, Harri had been looking for an exit from the ally back into the street. So far, she hadn't found one. She would walk to the end of the alley, then re-enter the street from there. Maybe the two policemen had crawled back under their rocks by now and she could look more closely at the villa from the front side. Maybe she would get lucky and find a hotel or some place with a bed. Surely there was one bed available somewhere in the villa.

If what she had heard about this place was correct, it got a lot of traffic. *Where does that traffic sleep?*

Maybe it doesn't sleep!

She picked up her pace while making plans for the following morning. She would re-visit Stella's Cafe and try to strike a deal with Stella's mother. She would offer so many pesos in exchange for information that the woman wouldn't consider refusing her. And if Stella's mother didn't have the information she needed, she would pay her for a name of someone who did. If what she had heard from that deplorable policeman was correct, Stella's mother had found sympathy for at least one gringo in the past. If the price was right, maybe she could find a little sympathy for one more.

Harri was working her way around a pile of rubbish when an alley cat let out an angry screech and dashed across her path. The sudden action of the animal thoroughly unnerved Harri. She stood silently wondering if anybody had heard the noise. Deciding that such a noise in this alley would be a common occurrence, she moved on, confident that she had not drawn any attention.

Harri could see a lighted opening between the buildings less than fifty feet ahead of her. She would enter the street there. She was well away from the little café and those two vile policemen. At this late hour there shouldn't be much traffic in the streets.

Harri had forgotten all caution while pondering the possibility of finding lodging for the night. Too late she felt the presence of the shadowy form that leaped from the darkness. The man grabbed her from behind with a chokehold and held her fast with one arm locked securely around her neck. With his free hand, the man pinned her left arm behind her back. Harri was sure her arm was being torn from its socket. With her free hand she began pulling at the arm that was choking her. Realizing that she was making no progress, and her lungs were bursting, she made a last-ditch effort to free herself. She surprised the man by reaching up with her free hand to catch a handful of his hair. Bringing his head downward as she bent forward, she easily hauled the man over her shoulder. The action broke his chokehold and he landed solidly on his back, his head within inches of her steel-toed boots. She was sorely tempted to kick his brains out but decided to question him first. Maybe he knew something she needed to know. Before he could regain his senses, Harri removed her Glock from an inside pocket and worked a bullet into its chamber. She aimed the Glock at his head, then asked him in Spanish why he had attacked her.

The man knew that the person standing over him held a gun. Cautiously he asked, "What were you doing in the alley at this hour?"

"I'm a stranger here," Harri told him. "I'm not familiar with this villa. I was looking for a room—a place to sleep tonight. Is there a law against walking through an alley?"

The man lay quietly, realizing he had made a mistake. This person was not from this villa. He needed to think fast, to say something that would help to determine how much trouble he was in…and if there was a way out. This person holding him at gunpoint was obviously not one of the pigs that patrol the streets and alleys at night terrorizing the owners of the small businesses. But who was he?

"How did you get here?" He asked. "I would have known if an automobile, or even a horse, came into this villa."

"I walked!" Harri told him. The man was silent for a moment, trying to digest that bit of information. "If you are not lying, then you must be loco. Nobody walks into this villa."

"I did!" Harri said. "So, you can change 'Nobody does' to 'One did!'" Cautiously Harri stepped away from the man. She held her Glock steady, ready to fire if he so much as moved a muscle. He must have sensed her intentions because he didn't move. But he didn't want to stay on the stinking ground in the filthy alley either. He had to do something; the smell was making him sick.

Convinced that his chance of never growing old was better than average, he said calmly, "May I get up from the ground and face you while we talk?"

"Yes," Harri told him, "But keep in mind, buddy, any sudden moves could result in your sudden extinction!"

Harri asked the man a few more questions. He answered them calmly and quietly. The man was thoroughly convinced now that he had made a big mistake. This person who could have shot him was definitely not one of the uniformed dogs who terrorized the local people at night. But allowing for that mistake, he still wanted to know who this man was, and why he was prowling around in the alley so late at night. The man's story about looking for a room, or a place to spend the night, was obviously a crock of frijoles. Nobody looked for a bed or a place to sleep in an alley—especially not in this alley where even the villa's dogs refused to sleep.

"Why did you attack me?" Harri asked, again.

"Why were you lurking in the alley?" The man asked, quietly.

"It is my business why I am here," Harri snapped. "You have no reason to attack me for walking through an alley."

"I believe we both realize that I made a mistake," the man said quietly. "But that mistake cannot be changed. So, what will you do? As you must have already determined, your choices are few. You could shoot me, but why would you? You have no justification. You must know, if you are a morally just man, that I have a right to protect my property from intruders, and you are the intruder here. If you have a mission in this villa, I could possibly find sympathy with your cause, but if you are not one of them, you are a fool to come here."

Harri stood mute, trying to decide if she should trust this man and wondering who "them" were.

Her options were few and she had to trust somebody. While she pondered the situation, the man spoke again. "If we could talk freely, it is possible, I might help you. However, I must know what it is that you expect to accomplish here before I could make such a decision. You are obviously not one of us, or the others. You are not of this villa."

"How can you tell who, or what, I am, in the darkness?" Harri asked. "You can't see my face. You only hear my voice."

"If you were of this villa, there would be only one reason for you to be in this alley at this hour. You would be harassing the merchants. If that were the case, you, or perhaps I, would be dead now. One from the hateful villa would not be standing here conversing with me. Not after my attack upon him. If there is something you would ask of me, you should ask now, or shoot me, because very soon the one I mistook you for will be along and we might both be dead. I would rather die by the hand of a total stranger than by a terrorist dog."

"We can't talk in the alley. Not if you're expecting an unfriendly party to arrive." *I'll have to trust this man if I expect to get information from him.* Harri sensed that the man was not her enemy, even if he wasn't her friend. She would trust him.

"I know of a place where we can talk," the man told her, sounding anxious to move along.

"Okay, you lead the way," Harri said. "And you're right—I do need help. I need help from someone who knows everything there is to know about this villa.

Harri walked close behind the obviously young man. He walked with a straight back and a proud stance. She kept her Glock in her hand as they meandered around one obstacle after another until they reached what appeared to be an ancient warehouse, or storage building.

The windows of the old building were covered with severely warped and weathered, wooden boards. Weeds and shrubs growing along the walls of the structure reached above most of the boarded up windows.

Harri and the young man waded through the tangled growth, sometimes hugging the wall closely, on a barely visible path. That path led them to a spot where the weeds had been thoroughly trampled down, exposing a tall, narrow window also covered with aging boards.

The window had been hidden from view by vines clinging to a rotting trellis until they were practically standing in front of it.

Quickly and quietly the man pulled the boards aside. Harri was a bit surprised to learn the window was actually a door, of sorts.

The man stepped through the opening and then motioned for Harri to follow. Directly behind the loosened boards, just inside the building, was a small space that permitted both of them to stand, but only because neither of them carried an extra pound of flesh on their bodies.

The place smelled musty and old. From the looks of the junk that filled the room, most of it could have been sitting in the same position for a century. Harri was thankful that she was not the typical, finicky female. She was sure the place was full of spiders and mice, to say nothing of snakes and other creeping critters.

Harri watched with interest as the man moved large, heavy crates from their path. She was mystified at the ease with which the crates moved. Common sense told her those were not normal storage boxes; they were, in fact, doors. Not doors in the normal sense that opened on hinges, but doors that rolled on wheels. When the crates were removed from their path, a narrow hallway opened up allowing them entry into another part of the building. At that point, the man pulled the crates back into place then raised and locked their wheels. He removed a small flashlight from a pocket, and lighted a path that led to a trap door. The man stooped over and pulled a metal lever. The lever released a latch with a metallic click. He lifted the heavy door, revealing a set of old but very sturdy wooden steps that led into a darkened basement.

As Harri looked into the black hole, something tripped a warning signal in her brain. Once again she wondered if she was being a damned fool. She was trusting a total stranger with her life. A stranger who had just tried to kill her. How did she know what was lurking in that dungeon? Maybe a room-full of terrorists. Or a prison that nobody had ever escaped from.

But her instincts were telling her to trust this man, and if she were to ever find Keil she had to start somewhere and trust somebody. She didn't have time to place an ad in the local paper asking for qualified and trustworthy people she could enlist in her cause. Even before she left Houston, Harri knew this trip was not going to be a picnic. She knew that every turn could, and most likely would, be hazardous. But somehow, she doubted that any danger would come from this young man. She honestly believed that if her life was in danger, so was his. Which was not an altogether consoling thought.

When they reached the bottom of the steps, the man turned his flashlight to the center of the cavernous, foul-smelling room. The ventilation system, if there ever had been one, was obviously not working. The room smelled like stale cigarettes and urine. The man lighted several candles that were placed randomly on wooden tables that were pulled together in a U-shape. Many mismatched chairs, and a few wooden benches were placed around the outside of the U.

This basement was being used for a council room, or a secret meeting place for people who would rather not meet in the open. Harri wondered why. Were there dissidents among the villa's residents who were weary of the current regime?

Obviously, there were. This knowledge lifted her spirits a few notches. She sincerely hoped that she had stumbled onto the side that could further her own cause—if such a side existed. She had only two days to find Keil, she needed all the help she could get, as soon as she could get it.

She had given herself only six days total, to complete this mission and return to the spot where Señor Manillo would pick her up. She had used up two of her days trekking through the jungle. It would take another two days to return to the pick-up spot after she had found Keil.

"Amigo, you may be seated now...unless you prefer to stand," said the man as he seated himself at the nearest table on the inside of the U-shaped arrangement. Harri seated herself across from him.

For the first time since they met in the alley, she really looked at the man. The candlelight was sufficient to see every feature of that young face. Harri felt a momentary shock as she gazed steadily into a face that could easily have been her brother Mario's face five years ago. The ice blue eyes that looked steadily into her own were waiting for an opening statement from her. But Harri hadn't recovered from the shock. How could two people who were not even related look so much alike?

"You look surprised," said the young man. "Are you disappointed? Or just surprised to see a blue-eyed native in this part of the jungle?"

"You must realize that your appearance is not common for this area," said Harri. "I suppose I am a little surprised. Do you have a name amigo?"

He held out his hand and said, "Alberto Ekio, and you . . . do you have a name?"

Harri took his hand, held it for a few seconds as she continued to search his face. "Harri Holland," she said, no longer wondering about the resemblance between this man and her foster brother, Mario Ekio. She was convinced that they were brothers. She couldn't begin to guess how or why fate had connected her to Mario's brother here in Sangre De Lobo, but she was sure that it had.

"Yes, amigo," said Alberto, "my people—and myself, we always surprise those who expect us to look like the natives, especially those who are not from our villas. Alberto smiled at Harri and her heart softened. There sat a portrait of Mario, a portrait that was created a few years back, but one she remembered so well.

"There is a story behind the reason we have the eyes of ice," said Alberto, smiling impishly. "According to a legend, one that many of my people believe to be true, our eyes were created by a strange doctor that lived among my people long before I was born. To my sorrow, the story must wait. I'm afraid it would be a long story for which neither of us have the time at the moment."

Being forced to think about her shortage of time sent a jolt of alarm through Harri. She sat up sharply in her chair. "That's a fact Alberto, I have very little time to spend in this villa, and I must trust you with details of my mission because there is nobody else. I am looking for a friend who came into this villa. I'm not sure when he came here, or exactly how long he's been here—but I must find him soon."

After Harri had explained her reason for being in the villa, she sat rigidly, waiting Alberto's response.

Alberto absently tapped his fingers on the tabletop while he searched his brain for an answer to Harri's problem. He hesitated to voice his fears to this person who could possibly be an ally to his own cause. He and his people needed an ally from the outside. Alberto knew that this man's friend could very well be dead. However, it was possible the friend was being held by the terrorist pigs who rule the villa with machine guns, grenades and those horrible dogs. Alberto knew he must level with this man if he were to gain his trust enough to ask his help for his own people.

"If your friend is still alive," said Alberto, looking doubtful that such a possibility should even be considered, "my fear is, that he would be better off if he were dead. I fear he will be in the Sangre De Lobo stockade. If he is, there is no way that you, or anyone else can help him. It would take an army to get near the place."

"Who should I contact to learn if my friend is being held in that prison, who would know?" Harri asked.

Again, Alberto thought carefully before answering the question, then he said, "Trying to gain such information would be unwise."

"Why do you feel it would be unwise to ask for information about my friend? Surely there are others here in the villa that would help me if I paid them well."

"No amigo. There are none here that could help you with this information. None who would trust you enough to answer your question. The ones that would gladly help you, even without pay, would not have the information. Possibly they would guess at your friend's fate, just as I have. They would advise you not get involved. On the other hand, it would not be wise to trust those that might have the information you need. They would offer you information for your money, but the risk to your life would be much greater than your chance of freeing your friend."

"Where is this prison located?" Harri asked.

"It is less than two miles east of this villa if one had wings, but the road to the prison is a winding road. It is possibly . . . three miles. The prison is a part of a large complex. At that same location is a public gathering room, you might call it a "joint", or perhaps a "dive". Or maybe even a hang out for the 'low-life'. Many guards live there; they eat and sleep there. The place is open twenty-four-hours a day. Each day, half of them is drunk while the other half keep watch over the stockade. That is standard procedure for that dreadful place. Also, there is a new Sangre De Lobo. It is located just two miles south of the prison. Most of the terrorists live in the new villa. We, here in the old villa do not want to be a part of the terrorist operation and would change the name of our villa if it were permitted. Also, if it were permitted, many of the people here would gladly go elsewhere to live. Most of us who remain in the old villa are not terrorists, and do not approve of the murdering dogs who still rule our villa with violence. Many of this villa's people would join our efforts if they were sure who they could trust. Some of the people have trusted the wrong men and have had their families murdered for their efforts."

"Why have you so readily trusted me? Or have you?" Harri asked.

"As I said previously, you are not of this villa. I have no reason not to trust you. Although I must believe, if you persist in following through with your plan to locate and free your friend, that you are not sane—also, that you should not make plans to become an old man. There are few places in this villa that are safe from the terrorists, even for the people who make their homes here. For strangers there are none."

"Is that why we are here, at this particular place now?"

"Yes. It is the safest place in the villa," said Alberto. "You can feel privileged that I brought you here. There was no chance that I would ask one of the villa's men to enter this room without first having put him through every conceivable test to determine his loyalty. Even some of the people that I consider friends, I would not trust. They have too much to lose not to cave in to pressure from the terrorists. There are a few—less than twenty of us—who do not have families in this villa to worry about; these few I trust completely. Our lack of ties has put us in a better position to undermine the terrorists' operations. However, we have little in the way of weapons to stage a war against the evil ones."

"Are you telling me that less than twenty men are trying to undermine the operations of the terrorists?" Harri asked. "How many people live in the old villa anyway?"

"In the old villa," he answered, "there are about four hundred people and the majority of them are not terrorists. Many of the families who live here are just normal people, trying to live normal lives, but it is impossible as long as they are ruled by violence. They are afraid to choose sides because they have learned from experience that it does not pay to cross the ones who rule."

"How about the new villa?" Harri asked. "How many terrorists live in that villa?"

"Two hundred. Maybe more. It is hard to say. They come and they go. . ."

"Of the four hundred here in the old villa, how many do you believe would help you if they knew for sure which side you were on, if they were sure they could trust you?" Harri asked.

"Even if they could trust me completely, and most of them do, they would still be afraid," said Alberto. "Very few of the people here would endanger the lives of their families to assist in such a cause. We have no weapons to fight a war. We have nothing to offer the people that would convince them they have a chance to survive such an effort. The men with families, they wait and pray for an opportunity to get their families out safely. Under the present rule, there is no way for us to remove the old ones, or the children, they would all be murdered!"

"The ones of you who are working against the terrorists, if you have no weapons at all, how do you hope to win freedom for your people?" Harri asked angrily.

Alberto rose from his chair and motioned for Harri to follow him. He walked to a closed door on an opposite wall. He opened the door and lit a candle. The interior of the small room was filled with old weapons, along with several new assault rifles. Harri moved to the shelf that held the new rifles and ran her hand over one of the shiny surfaces. "What is wrong with the weapons here?" "Nothing that a few thousand rounds of ammunition wouldn't cure," Alberto answered.

"You have no ammunition for the weapons?" Harri asked in disbelief.

"That is correct," Alberto said wearily. "The men who sold us the rifles took all of our money then disappeared. We do not know if the men were killed by the terrorists for selling us the rifles, or if they were the terrorists. You must admit, it would be a clever plan; take all of our money, leaving us broke and with weapons that were useless to us. Not one of us who is working to rid the area of the terrorists would dare bring ammunition into the villa. We have to hope for an outside contact who would dare to enter the villa with such items. We have yet to located such a person. Any man in the villa who is trusted by the terrorists enough to get the ammunition past the many guards posted around the area would never be trusted by any of us. So, you see amigo, that is why we have no ammunition and why we cannot protect our people from the evil ones."

Harri filed that information in the back of her head as another worthy cause she would consider giving some serious thought to if she managed to escape this villa with her own skin intact. At the moment she already had more to worry about than she could handle. If she had heard Alberto correctly there were more terrorists' guards at the stockade than she had first thought, and even more vicious dogs guarding the place. As if just a few dozen murdering drunks were not enough to discourage any sane person.

Well, I don't recall anybody ever accusing me of being sane, and I will get Keil out of that stinking prison. I know he's still alive . . ..

Harri looked again at the row of rifles and the many empty clips placed alongside the weapons. She shook her head. What a damned shame. Then she noticed something that caused her to take a second look. A 30 round ammunition drum for an AK-47! She needed that clip and she should have purchased one before coming into the villa. She had not had time to look for one in Houston and no time to locate a dealer in Villa Guano. Now, here was the clip she needed and maybe Alberto would consider selling it to her.

✦ ✦ ✦ ✦ ✦ ✦ ✦

CHAPTER 28

"Amigo! Amigo, wake up! It is one o'clock in the morning! You asked me to wake you!"

Harri sat up slowly. "It can't be!" She groaned. "I just fell asleep five minutes ago."

Two hours earlier, Alberto had found a cot and a thin pad among the many items that were stored in the old warehouse. He had assured Harri that he would wake her in time to reach her destination before three in the morning. He handed her a cup of hot coffee. After taking one swallow of the black liquid, she decided that it could rouse the dead. She finished the coffee quickly and thanked him, but refused a second cup. If strong coffee did indeed keep a person alert, she would be on her feet, fully awake, a week from now.

Alberto had packed the items she had requested in a heavy canvas bag. The bag was the size of a small backpack, but it was sufficient to carry the things she needed for the night. Among the items in the bag was the 30 round ammo drum for her AK-47. Alberto gave her the clip, firmly refusing to take pay for it. He argued that it was useless to him without ammunition. Harri refused to see it his way and while his attention was elsewhere, she had managed to slip a packet of pesos into his back pocket.

He followed Harri up the steps to the ground floor of the warehouse. As they walked, he cautioned again about the danger of her idiotic plan. He insisted that if she were determined to go through with it, she should at least remember to watch out for the pitfalls he had pointed out. He pushed a container of the strong black coffee into her bag just before she stepped through the tall, narrow window and blended like a shadow into the night. An hour later Harri looked at the luminous dial of her watch and cursed softly. She had planned to be at the stockade no later than three. It was almost three and she wasn't even sure where in the damned jungle she was at the moment. How could she have gotten off course? She looked again at the small compass. She couldn't possibly be off course by more than a few hundred yards.

She heard the grinding sound of the truck's engine at the same time she sighted the flickering headlights through the trees. The truck must be leaving the roadhouse she thought, most likely in route to the new villa. She stepped back into a sheltered spot and waited until the vehicle passed her by, then she stepped into the road the truck had just passed over, and headed for the prison compound. She knew where she was now and she had already wasted too much time.

Harri followed the road until she caught sight of the stockade complex. At that point she left the main road and came in from the south end of the building.

She had noticed when she was observing the place from her perch in the tree last evening that most of the action was from the west and north side of the complex. She hoped there was nothing she had missed in her earlier observation that could be crucial to her succeeding on this first try. She seriously doubted she would get a second chance.

After talking with Alberto for over an hour, it had become clear to her that this was the only place that Keil was likely to be if he were still alive. This *was* the terrorist prison. The two dozen or more huts inside the stockade were where prisoners were held until they were executed, or until they could offer something very valuable in exchange for their freedom.

Harri had also learned from Alberto that three in the morning was possibly the best time to strike the place. Most everybody would have gone to their respective quarters by that time. Even the guards would not be expecting trouble at that hour and would be more apt to be careless.

She wished now that she had known as much about the terrorist's operations a week ago. She might could have arranged for Keil to be released, but she hadn't known, and now it was too late. What ever she could do had to be done now.

Harri walked stealthily toward the roadhouse, watching everything that moved. She carried the AK-47 in a ready position and surprisingly enough her hands were steady. She was thirty feet from the roadhouse now, and inching closer with acute caution. Walking on the toes of her boots, she lifted her feet carefully and placed them on solid ground even more carefully. She couldn't hear her own footsteps. Bending low, she tried to blend with the night. There was nothing to protect her from being seen now. Nothing between her and the roadhouse...and a guard that was walking straight toward her. Harri watched and held her breath. When he reached the end of the building, he turned east along the wall. He walked half way to the end of the building and stopped. Turning his body to the wall, he unzipped his pants and proceeded to take a leak. Fate had arranged her next move and Harri took full advantage of it. With a few long, silent strides, she was behind the guard. With the butt of her rifle, she came down on the back of his skull. He never knew what hit him. She removed a piece of rope from her bag and tied him securely, hands and feet, then taped his mouth. She didn't want the sucker to wake up yelling. She moved on cautiously, but stopped again when she spotted another guard coming around the corner. Not seeing the first guard anywhere, he called out.

Muffling her voice, Harri called back, "over here, I've found something." Three minutes later the second guard was sharing the fate of the first one.

Harri moved silently toward the front door of the roadhouse, confident that she had taken out the last of the guards that were operating on the outside of the dive. Slowly she pulled deep breaths of oxygen into her lungs, preparing her body for its next action. Then she saw them, moving on swift and silent legs, their teeth bared and ready to rip her to shreds. Harri quickly backed up against the wall and waited. Fortunately, she had anticipated a meeting with these beasts. Actually, she was surprised—and thankful—that she had not met them sooner. When they were five feet from her, they bared their fangs and lifted from the earth in a mighty leap; their goal her throat. The beast was met with a face full of mace—not just ordinary mace, but the container held a powerful substance that also paralyzed the vocal cords of those monsters and blinded them. They would be out for at least thirty minutes and maybe forever. Harri knew the huge animals might never regain consciousness, and couldn't bring herself to feel a great deal of sympathy for them, even though she knew the dogs were not responsible for what they had been trained to do. A missile wasn't responsible for it had been programmed to do. Nonetheless, it was a potential killer when aimed at a target. Harri walked away from the creatures with one goal in mind, free Keil, then get the hell out of there.

Walking gingerly up to the door of the roadhouse Harri took one more deep breath and held it for several seconds. "I really hate this!" she whispered to herself. "Damn, how I hate this!" She took another step, straightened her shoulders and whispered to the night, "But I'll hate it even more if I don't do it." And with that certainty established, she raised her foot waist high and slammed a steel-toed combat boot through the flimsy wooden door. Within seconds, thirty rounds of hollow points were blazing from her AK-47. She quickly removed the larger clip and replaced it with fifteen round clips, then raised the rifle, ready for a second assault. Nothing moved inside the large, smoke-filled room. A large portion of the interior of the bamboo dive had been re-arranged and Harri could still hear things falling from bullet torn walls. She stepped inside and looked cautiously around. The place smelled like a brewery. The contents of broken bottles of whiskey and wine were pouring into the dirty floor. The fumes were stifling. This place that had long been a heaven for gunrunners, drug traffickers, and marauding thugs was suddenly very quiet and lifeless. She looked around at the demolished room, trying to adjust her eyes to the darkness. She had to find keys to the stockade. Alberto had told her the roadhouse was also the headquarters for the prison's operation. The keys must be here somewhere. She walked around the huge room listening for sound, watching for movement. There could be more guards hiding inside the place. As she walked slowly through the darkened room, she poked her rifle barrel behind objects that could have concealed a body. She kept her rifle positioned and ready when nearing dark corners. After making a complete round of the room she was convinced that there were no living bodies in the place. She headed for a door located behind the bar; the only door she had seen except the one she came through when entering the place.

Harri almost lost her balance when she stepped in something liquid, which was flowing across the floor behind the bar. She held onto the bar and moved on toward the closed door. Just as she let go her hold on the bar, she almost stumbled over a body that lay sprawled near the closed door she tried to reach. She stepped back quickly, almost yelling out at the sight of blood and booze running together near her feet. She looked again at the closed door and hoped the room behind it was an office. She pushed the door open. It was an office. There was even a light burning inside it. A large desk sat in the middle of the room facing the door she had just walked through. She searched through the desk and found no keys. She looked quickly through other shelves and drawers and when she still hadn't found the keys she turned to leave, deciding the keys were not in that room. She moved back toward the door that would take her back into the main bar area, wondering which lifeless body might have the keys in his pocket. Suddenly a nerve jarring, noise startled her senseless for a second. She pushed herself against the wall near the door and held her breath, rifle at the ready. Seconds passed before she decided the noise was caused by things giving away from bullet riddled walls, due to her earlier razing of the room.

As Harri stepped away from the wall she bumped her elbow on the doorframe and heard keys rattling. Dozens of them were hanging on a pegboard just behind the door where she was standing. Not knowing which one she needed, she took them all, pushing them into her pocket as she headed through the door and back into the main bar area. Her eyes had become accustomed to the dark now and she was moving around with a little more ease. She wished there were an exit to the outside from the rear of the roadhouse. A rear door would be closer to the stockade, but she hadn't seen another door earlier as she walked through the place. She didn't want to waste any more time looking for one. She stepped over two more bodies and almost ran toward the front door. She had already spent more time in this place than she had planned on. As she reached the door another loud clanking noise brought her to a sudden stop. She turned back toward the bar. Rifle raised, she searched for the source of the noise. In the dim light she could see liquid spreading across the floor. Another shelf of bottles had collapsed. The aromatic liquid emitting from the bottles could set one's senses to reeling. She needed fresh air. Before she had made a complete turn, she froze. A sound that she recognized all too well reverberated like thunder echoing through a canyon wall. A steel plunger had fallen on an empty chamber of a .357 Magnum that was pressed firmly against her skull. At warp speed, she reached inside her jacket, coming out with her Glock; praying that fate had really dealt her another ace; praying that the .357 magnum was really empty of all ammunition, not just that one chamber. With the Glock in her hand, she spun around. She had the gun aimed at the man's chest and was pulling the slack from the trigger. She raised her eyes to the man's face and gasped, "Brent!" A split second later a powerful fist slammed into the side of her head, sending shock waves to her toes and her senses into another dimension.

✦ ✦ ✦✦✦ ✦ ✦

CHAPTER 29

LIKE WATCHING FUZZY PUZZLE PIECES fall into place, Harri's consciousness was returning, one small click at a time. Her muddled thoughts were slowly coming together, and she could almost think rationally again. "If I'm not dreaming, I must be blind, or dead." Harri wasn't sure if she had actually spoken those words, or if just thinking them had set off the jack hammers in her head. "I couldn't be dead," she moaned, "death couldn't possibly hurt this much." She tried to raise her hand to examine her head only to discover that she couldn't move her hands; they were tied behind her back. "What in hell is going on?" Her question sounded flat as if it had been completely absorbed by the thick, deep silence and the pitch-black darkness that covered her.

Confused and disoriented, her body stiff and sore, Harri settled back on the hard surface of what must be a small cot. She tried to sort through the questions that hammered at her brain, but the effort of thinking was too much. Harri lost her tug of war with the black hole that pulled at her consciousness.

Two hours later Harri was fully awake, but fully awake was the only thing that had changed in two hours. Her hands were still tied and the jackhammers were still working on her brain. This time Harri didn't even try to think, she just lay perfectly still, using as little effort as possible to breathe. But after a while, in spite of her resolve to not think, bits and pieces of the past few hours began to return. She was mentally tracing her thoughts from Alberto's warehouse to the roadhouse. Her heart began to beat faster. Something had happened at the roadhouse—something strange—and horrible. *I though the man who hit me was Brent. I really have lost my mind if I could even imagine that Brent would . . ..* "It was Brent! Damn it! It was Brent!" she said aloud, rising quickly from the narrow cot. She fell back just as quickly when a wave of nausea hit her. Dizzy and unable to see, she wondered if she might be more seriously injured than she had at first believed—her head felt like huge slab of hammered hell.

Why would Brent hit me? Harry wondered. *Most likely he didn't recognize me.* She told herself. Fighting to hold onto a lifelong loyalty, a loyalty to a boy she had once loved with all her heart, a boy she would have died for not so long ago. Even Harri's vivid recollection of the incident at the roadhouse couldn't force her to accept what she knew was a fact. Not with total conviction; not yet...

Harri was certain that the boy she had loved for so long would not have hit her, but Brent was no longer a boy. Brent was a man, and she hadn't even spoken to him in years. He could be anything . . . even a terrorist. "No!" she said aloud. 'There has to be another answer." Harri groaned at the pain that stabbed her head each time she forgot and raised her voice. She wouldn't do it again—not even to defend Brent, because if she had him in her sights right now, she would most likely shoot him. But Harri's heart was still staging a valiant battle in his defense.

But all loyalty aside, she knew what she had seen, and common sense was putting it all together. Sure, it was possible that Brent didn't recognize her, but why was he there? Why was he working with the terrorists? "Oh God," she groaned aloud, "why would Brent be working with the terrorists?" Her head was splitting again.

Harri tried turning her head from side to side. Checking to see if any of her parts from her shoulders up were operating properly. She decided that something inside her head, or maybe her neck, was broken.

Harri lay perfectly still on the hard cot, searching for answers to her multiple questions. Why is it so dark? Why can't I see? If I'm not blind surely there would be a spark of light from some source, but there's only darkness. There's not even a ghost of light glowing through a window and I can't get at my watch with the luminous dial. Frantically, she began working at the thongs that bound her hands. Harri knew she was tearing the skin on her wrist and she didn't even care. She could feel the texture of the thongs that bound her wrists together and was certain that they were leather. Harri also knew that if they were leather, and if she could tear the skin on her wrist, that her blood would soak into the thin straps causing them to stretch and she would be free in no time at all. Toward that goal she was working when she heard a doorknob turning. She stiffened, and suddenly her pain had disappeared. Her only feeling was tension and fear. She heard heavy, labored breathing. Somebody was inside the room with her now. She heard a sharp scraping sound and a low grumbling as a body moved clumsily along, as if searching for something. Again, she heard the grumbling sound that could have been a protest or a profanity. Then without warning a brilliant glare lit the small room and sent spikes of fire through her head. Harri turned her head away from the light, shielding her eyes from the brightness. Happy to learn that she wasn't blind, but wanting to scream at whoever had turned on the light.

Whoever had entered the room walked to her cot and stood looking down at her. An awful odor permeated her nostrils as she lay with her head turned toward the wall. Harri knew she had to open her eyes and dreaded the pain that would follow. She had to know what she was dealing with here, not that it would do her any good as long as her hands were bound behind her back, but her basic nature wouldn't permit her to die without knowing who was killing her—or, as to that matter, who could smell so horrible. Whoever, or whatever had entered this room smelled like something from one of the gaseous sinkholes she used to throw things into when she was a child. She could well remember holding her nose as she watched the bubbles rise and pop after tossing sticks and rocks into the slimy, foul-smelling pools.

"Get up!" Said a thick, guttural voice from behind her.

Harri turned slowly toward the voice, squinting the eye that wasn't swollen closed, against the brilliant light. She glared at the ape-like creature that stood by her cot. The overweight being was still breathing heavily and was having a problem setting a tray on a wooden chair that had been pulled along side the cot. Harri was watching his face, trying to determine if this creature that had brought food had any intentions of doing anything but feeding her. *He must not be planning on killing me right away or he wouldn't be wasting food on me—unless the food is meant to kill me.* Harri reasoned that if the food was the means of her demise, this person had surely not prepared it. She had never seen a face so totally blank; so completely lacking in expression.

The slow-witted mortal finally got the food arranged on the chair then turned and started back toward the door, moving as if each step was causing him great pain. In spite of her splitting headache, Harri tried to yell at him before he reached the door.

"How do you expect me to eat with my hands tied behind my back?"

Her angry question would hardly suffice as a yell, but the man stopped in his tracks.

"Nobody told me to untie you." The man spoke in a deep, guttural voice. "I was told to feed you—that was all!"

"Do you always follow orders to the letter?" Harri asked, wincing from the pain that speaking caused.

"If I didn't, I wouldn't have my job," the man said slowly.

Then I suppose you had better come and feed me, or at least untie me and let me feed myself," Harri snapped,

Without turning around to look at her, he said, "I never thought about that. Guess you do need your hands to eat with."

Harri shook her head. The man not only looked like an ape; he had the same IQ. *Outwitting him will be a breeze,* she thought. *Wish I could be so sure of anything else around here.*

Harri wanted to ask him where she was and how long she had been here. Maybe she should even ask him how long he planned on keeping her here, and if he planned on killing her. The ape would tell her the truth—if he knew the truth—he couldn't think fast enough to lie. Harri was beginning to feel an unwilling sympathy for this creature, and she hated herself for it.

This poor sucker's job was to keep her alive, thought Harri; keep her alive so whoever was in charge here could kill her whenever it was convenient to do so. Meanwhile, that person would get his kicks from knowing how much she was suffering. She had to use this simpleton to get out of here.

The small room was not a typical jail cell. Its walls were solid and there were no windows or bars. The ceiling light didn't come from a candle or a gas lamp. The fixture was fitted with a regular light bulb, and the light switch was by the door, the light bulb was powered with electricity from some source. Maybe a generator. There was obviously a ventilation system because the air was fresh—or had been until this creature entered the room.

"Well! Which will it be?" Asked Harri. "Are you going to untie me or feed me?"

The man turned slowly and walked back to where she set. He stepped behind her. With fumbling fingers, he loosened the leather thongs that bound her wrist together. When the ties were removed, she rubbed her wrist to relieve the itching and restore circulation to her fingers.

After the guard had untied her hands, he stepped outside the door and waited until she finished eating, then he came in and re-tied her wrist. She talked him into leaving enough slack for circulation this time. After he had left the room with the empty tray, it took her all of five seconds to remove the ties from her wrist.

Harri walked barefoot to the door. She stood quietly, listening for noise. She heard nothing. She tried the doorknob. Surprisingly it was unlocked. She walked out into a hallway. The hallway was empty. No guard. Not a living soul was present. She saw three additional doors along the hallway and a fourth at the very end of the hall, she would check them out.

Harri stepped back into the small room and quickly pulled her boots on, then she searched the inside pocket of her fatigues for aspirin. The small bottle was still there—she had no water to wash them down with so she chewed four of them, then almost choked trying to swallow them. If the aspirin didn't kill her first there was a chance, they would relieve some of the pain in her head—at least enough to permit her to think—and she really needed to think—she had to get out of there.

Harri walked to the nearest door and turned the knob, the door opened—a bathroom—a bathroom with no window. After using the toilet, which was the cleanest one she had found in all of Columbia, she stepped back into the hallway, pulling the door closed behind her. She tried the next door she came to along the hall—then the next—both were locked. "Damnit!" She kicked at the locked door. "I have to get out of here. I have to learn what day it is, and I have to find Keil, and I'm running out of time."

—If the clock hasn't already stopped!

The two locked doors looked the same as the bathroom door and the one she had been imprisoned behind, but there was another door at the end of the dark hall—it was different. "That must be the way out." She said aloud, thankful that her head was feeling better—the aspirin was working. She walked to the end of the hall and checked the door. It was locked also. She pulled on the doorknob, checking it for slack—there was none. The door was solid as a rock.

The doors and the walls looked old, and not too well kept, but after kicking them a few times, she decided they were solid—she wouldn't break through one with anything less than an ax. Her bag of supplies, her rifle and her Glock were all gone, but she still had the knife that Mario had made for her. It was in her boot.

Harri removed the knife from its scabbard and began working on the set screws that held the door handle in place. In less than three minutes the screws were out and she pulled the handle loose from the door; but the door still wouldn't open. Harri began working on the internal parts of the lock with her knife blade. In another minute the door popped open an inch. She replaced her knife in its boot sheath and pulled the door open. On the other side of the door was a narrow staircase; its row of steps went almost straight up. The staircase was dark. She mounted the steps cautiously, checking them for solidity. When she reached the top of the stairs she found another door—an overhead door. She pushed on the door with her shoulder. Something was holding it, keeping it from opening enough to work her body through.

After ten minutes of hammering on the heavy door, using her shoulder as a ramrod, she had the door open enough to squeeze through, but before she attempted it she eased the door down on its framework and stood for several seconds, working oxygen into her lungs. Her head injury, along with the exertion of hammering the door loose from its metal latches had taken its toll on her strength. After she had stopped trembling from the intense exertion, she reached up to push the door open and then jumped back, catching her breath sharply. Somebody was opening the door from the other side. Harri flattened herself against the darkened wall just beneath the door and waited. When she caught sight of the first leg extending through the door, she grabbed the leg with both hands and wrenched the body into the stairway. As the heavy body came wobbling past her, she gave it an additional shove that sent it hurling on down the stairs. She didn't wait to see it land at the bottom, she just lifted herself through the opening.

Standing on solid ground, Harri breathed deeply. She was free! The night air was cool and damp and the sky above her was overcast. Her visibility was hampered by the closely-knit shrubbery and trees, as well as the starless night and the heavy mist that covered the area like a blanket. She had no idea where she was.

Harri peered into the darkness, seeing little. There were two lights in the distance, barely visible through the fog. A road ran past the spot where she stood. It meandered off toward the lights. The same road also went to her left and disappeared into the night. Harri's anxiety was deepening as she tried desperately to make a decision about her next move. She had no way of knowing where she was or how she would find her way out of the place, but somehow, she had to do it. There was no moon or stars to guide her, she would have to rely on intuition and luck.

This will never do, Harri thought frantically as she tried to collect known information about her position—realizing quickly there was none.

The mist was moving ghostlike across the jungle floor, but it cleared slightly at intervals. Harri could see objects in the distance that hadn't been visible a minute before. The two lights were clearly visible now. They were glowing from the windows of two almost obscure buildings several hundred feet to the south. To the northwest the road wound out of sight in just a short distance. Barely thirty feet away was a Jeep, just sitting there as if it were waiting for her. *Transportation! But to where?*

Indecision was shattering her effort to think rationally and causing an increased anger to build. She didn't need the anger, she needed to remain calm and think clearly. An idea began to form and before it could fully materialize, she turned and stepped back through the still open, trap door and headed back down the staircase, taking the steps two at a time. Before she reached the bottom of the stairs she slowed and removed her knife from her boot again. When she landed at the bottom of the steps, she leaned over the body that lay crumpled at the foot of the stairs and felt for a pulse. There was none; the man was dead; he was not the ape man who had brought food to her. She felt a moment's satisfaction for that knowledge, then she began searching the body for keys. She found a large ring of them. She returned her knife to her boot and ran down the hallway. She tried key after key in the first door she came to until she found one that unlocked the door. She pushed the door open. Inside, the room looked like the one she had woke up in earlier—except it was totally bare. One locked door remained and she was dreading opening it. Dreading to learn that it was also empty. She fumbled with the keys until the door unlocked. She pushed it open. Bingo! There was junk everywhere. She searched through the clutter until she found a flashlight and a few other items that might come in handy. Then she spotted the bag that contained her personal items. The contents were intact except for the Ak-47. Her Glock and even the container of stale coffee were still inside the bag. She pushed the flashlight and other items into the bag

As she searched through the chaotic mess in the room, she felt another rise of panic. Time was not on her side, here, and that knowledge was tearing at her nervous system. She wanted to get out of there, but she still needed to know where she was. She kept riffling through the junk in the room, searching for something—anything that would give her a clue as to her location. There was a map on the wall, but after searching it over it held no clues . . .. Unless . . . She stepped to the map again and studied it closely. It was a hand drawn map. It showed the old, and the new, Sangre De Lobo. The prison site was also marked, along with several other areas, none of which she recognized. One of the spots, which she assumed was of some importance to whoever had created the map, was circled in red, and if things were scaled properly and the map's directions were correct, that circled area was south and east of the prison compound by fifteen miles or so. Another spot, circled in blue, lay some fifteen or twenty miles north and west of old Villa Sangre De Lobo. Harri assumed that she was now at one or the other of those prominently marked places. But which one?

She would have to take a chance and trust to luck. Committing the map to memory she departed the small room and headed for the stairway. She still had her compass, and now she had her Glock and several rounds of ammunition.

Outside, nobody would ever suspect the underground compartments were there. Harri glanced again toward the two buildings in the distance. They were, completely shrouded by the ghostly mist, now. She wondered if there were guards sleeping there, or had her movement here alerted them? Most likely the Jeep had belonged to the guard that lay dead at the foot of the stairs. Harri stepped cautiously to the vehicle and quickly checked it over. Hot wiring this Jeep would be a piece of cake. Then she noticed that the keys were in the ignition. She wasn't sure she trusted her sudden good luck, but she wasn't questioning it either. She threw her bag into the Jeep and seated herself behind the wheel. She looked at her watch, it was ten p.m. She started the engine and drove the vehicle slowly around the area, checking out the road. As far as she could determine the road south dead-ended among the buildings. She considered that a plus—she didn't have to make a decision about which way to go now. She headed in the opposite direction and what she hoped was the direction of the prison compound. If she had guessed correctly, she was at the spot circled in red on the map. She reached into her pocket and felt for the keys to the stockade's gate. They were gone. The only thing she found in her pocket was the small can of mace—or what was left of it. She searched the bag and found a few of her supplies that might come in handy later, but nothing that would help her in a confrontation with the terrorists.

Harri drove as fast as possible over the narrow dirt road, wishing the Jeep had wings. Wanting to rush and at the same time dreading to reach the stockade. She had no idea how she would go about freeing Keil now that these goons were onto her. There would be added guards at the prison, now. The guards would not be overly concerned about her returning to the stockade, they knew she was securely stashed in her underground prison, but none of them would ever believe she came here alone. They would be out in force, looking for her accomplices and the guards at the stockade would be on red alert.

Harri had four full clips of ammo and the can of mace. Her only hope of getting behind those stockade walls now was to climb over a wall. She still had her wire cutters in her bag—and she still had those murdering guards and those horrible dogs waiting for her . . ..

◆ ◆ ◆ ◆ ◆ ◆

CHAPTER 30

WHEN HARRI REACHED THE STOCKADE—OR rather, what once had been the stockade—she sat in the Jeep staring, horror stricken, disbelief flooding her brain. The only thing left of the prison was smoldering ashes. Everything lay in a heap of charred rubble, even the prison huts were burned to the ground. She stepped from the Jeep and walked around the place in a daze, wondering what had happened here, wondering if any of the prisoners had managed to escape this burning hell. Somehow, she believed they had; she believed she would find Keil. He was still in Sangre De Lobo, and he was alive. He had to be alive!

Harri searched her mind for possible clues to where the prisoners might have escaped to. Somehow, she was sure they had escaped. Her feelings were strong and positive—they were still alive and they were still in this area somewhere.

Harri had that map from the dungeon memorized and she believed she could locate the place that had been circled in blue on the map. That place had to hold some significance for somebody linked to this smoldering hell. Her intuition was strong and that place circled in blue was pulling at her like a magnet. Harri was sure she could find the place, but she was also sure that it might take a while and time was a commodity she was short of.

Harri walked back to the Jeep and seated herself behind the wheel. Before starting the engine, she looked out over the destruction of the prison site with mixed emotions. That was the exact end she had planned for the stockade... and New Sangre De Lobo, but she had intended to release the prisoners first.

With grim determination Harri started the Jeep and pulled away from the devastated site. She drove northeast from the charred stockade for one half mile. From that point there was not even a trail that she could travel with the Jeep. She parked the vehicle in a secluded spot and removed her belongings, placing them under the nearest clump of foliage. "If someone finds the Jeep before I return, at least I'll have my personal things," she told herself.

With only a flashlight and her Glock, Harri walked through the jungle in route to where she had stashed her extra ammunition, her money, and the assault rifle she had taken from the dead terrorist soldier at the graveyard. She surprised herself by walking almost straight to the spot where she had hidden her supplies. Within an hour Harri was back to where she had left the Jeep. She gathered her personal things from their nearby stash and within seconds she was driving as fast as conditions would allow toward that spot that was circled in blue on the map.

Twice, Harri had to stop the Jeep and make a decision as to which way to go after coming to an intersection along the almost invisible road she was traveling. At the second stop, someone had deliberately tried to conceal the entry into the rutted road by overspreading it with vines and brambles. Later, another automobile had entered the juncture, disrupting the camouflage effort. Still following her hunch Harri turned into that branch road. Five minutes later she slowed the Jeep to a crawl as she watched a flicker of light through the trees up ahead. At times the light would vanish for several seconds then reappear. Harri drove around a sharp bend in the road and discovered the source of the lights. A six-passenger vehicle had been pulled as far off the battered road as possible and nosed into a perfect place of concealment. If her headlights had not caught the reflected glow of a taillight, she would have missed the vehicle altogether. She wondered if there were people in the vehicle. Maybe someone had spotted her headlights and was sitting there waiting for her. In spite of her caution, when nobody made any attempt to stop her, Harri guessed that the driver had abandoned the vehicle in order to reach a destination unannounced; as she too planned to do.

Harri drove on slowly for another hundred yards and again noticed lights flickering through the trees. At first, she believing she was overtaking a second vehicle. However, there were no more vehicles. The lights were glowing from the windows of a low, square building. The building was one of three. The other two were barely visible in the murky distance, and neither was lighted inside. None of the buildings appeared to have outdoor lights. Or if they did, none were turned on.

She pulled the Jeep off the road and parked it in a heavy growth of vines and shrubs. Harri left the Jeep and headed on foot toward the lighted building, then she stopped shortly, straining to see through the darkness. She had caught a glimpse of stealth movement off to her right. As her eyes adjusted to the darkness, she saw two shadowy forms moving toward the building.

Harri knew she would have to make every move by gut instinct now. She had no plan, and she didn't know who was her enemy or who might be an ally. She wasn't really sure where she was, but she was saying a silent prayer that her instincts had been correct, that this place was the one she was searching for—the place the prisoners from the stockade has escaped to. She couldn't begin to imagine why she believed so strongly that they were here. However, she had no other conclusions to draw from, so she would continue to follow her instincts until something more solid developed.

She watched the shadowy figures as they drew near the lighted building and wondered who they were and what interest the building held for them. If this place was their home or their headquarters, they surely wouldn't be sneaking up on it. The man nearest the lighted window stopped and conversed with the one who followed him. He was obviously giving instructions, but Harri wasn't close enough to hear what he was saying. She moved closer. The second man cut away and headed toward the rear of the building, the other stepped into the shadows on the north side.

Hoping she wouldn't be spotted, Harri made a silent dash toward a cluster of shrubbery near a lighted window on the south side of the building. "Hey!" Someone whispered loudly as she neared the shrubbery. Harri stood still, waiting for the person to speak again so she could locate his position. She peered into the shadows and saw the slight movement of large frame. The shadowy form appeared to be motioning to her to move on.

Realizing that her position here was shaky and that she had no idea who she was dealing with, she whispered huskily, "Que paso?"

"You're supposed to be covering the rear." A voice informed her roughly, in Spanish, "Move on! We have this side covered." She moved closer to the speaker, hoping to learn who 'we' were before she ventured any closer to the lighted window. As she drew near the speaker, he turned to her again and hissed, "Can't you understand simple instructions, you idiot? Move to the rear!" As the man spoke, she noticed a second human shadow a few feet beyond where the first was crouched. She took a step closer and the speaker exclaimed sharply, "What-in-hell? Who are you...?" Before he could finish the question, she raised her rifle and came down heavily on his head with the butt of the weapon. He fell at her feet. His fall slowed the action of the second man, who was not really sure what was happening but taking no chances. The man was not willing to fire his rifle until he learned what was going on, he lunged at her with the weapon raised. She stepped aside to avoid the impact and he sailed past her. Regaining his balance, he spun around just in time to meet the blow from her rifle butt. She had aimed for his head but the blow landed just below his jaw, crushing his collarbone. He cursed loudly and came at her again. She stumbled over the body of the man on the ground. As she fell, she tried to break the fall with her right arm and hand. She felt the flesh tear on her palm when she landed with all her weight on it. The man was at her side before she could move, kicking her with a heavy boot. He landed a solid kick to a spot just below her rib cage, knocking the breath from her lungs. He raised his foot and kicked again at her ribs. She turned sharply, and the kick landed on her shoulder, momentarily paralyzing her left arm.

Harri knew she was losing this battle in short order if she couldn't turn this action around. The man drew back a heavy boot and aimed it at her head. As his foot came forward, she grabbed at it with her right hand—the one she had torn open in the fall. She felt the flesh pulling apart on the injured hand, but she managed to hold on to the boot, causing the man to lose his balance. As he fell to the ground she rolled from his path, bounding to her feet at the end of the roll. She stood shakily, then aimed her steel-toed boot at the man's head. With all the effort she could put into the kick she brought the boot into solid contact with his skull... He fell back and lay still. She was sure he was not going anywhere for a while, but for added measure she brought the rifle butt down on his head. She had learned from experience that these suckers could recover from a kick; and that they had no particular compunctions about killing strangers.

She stepped away from the motionless body, checking the area for other movement. When she was convinced that she was alone, she stepped cautiously up to the nearest lighted window and looked inside. Cold fear gripped her body as she stared in disbelief at the scene inside. Keil was seated in a chair in the middle of the square room. His hands were tied behind him and his feet were bound tightly to the chair rungs. Three uniformed men, armed with assault weapons and knives were taking turns hitting Keil with their weapons and yelling at him, trying to make him talk. The men obviously wanted information that the battered Keil couldn't give them—or was unwilling to give them. If it was stubbornness that kept him from talking, that stubbornness was costing him his life. Harri could see at a glimpse that there wasn't much life left in him.

An animal rage took control of Harri's actions. Throwing all caution aside, and without a hint of a plan, she slipped a clip of ammo into the rifle she had taken from the dead terrorist back in the jungle and holding her breath in order to steady her hands, she aimed at the nearest uniform and fired. She quickly turned her rifle to the next man and fired again. The third man, caught by surprise at the assault was aiming at her as she fired the third round. At that moment, a barrage of bullets came through the north window. Harri aimed at the overhead lights and fired as she went through the south window. The sudden darkness was startling. She was pulling her knife from her boot as she ran toward Keil. Another round of bullets was fired wildly through the north window. She turned and fired again, hoping to slow the action of whoever was out there. She had Keil cut loose in seconds then while he was trying to stand, and not succeeding on his first try, she turned and fired another round at the north window. Keil finally managed to stand, by using one of the guard's rifles as a crutch. Harri steadied him with one arm while she kept firing with the other. She was thankful that Keil could still move, because she was nearing exhaustion herself; she didn't know how much longer she could support even a portion of his weight.

Suddenly Keil pushed her arm away. Harri looked at him quickly and realized that he must have gotten a run of adrenaline from somewhere, he was moving on his own power now. From the corner of her eye, she saw that Keil had raised the rifle he had been using for a crutch and was firing steadily at the north window as the two of them backed closer to the south one. Armed now with the rifle and a full clip of ammo he had yanked from a dead terrorists' belts, Keil followed Harri back through the south window. Outside, they backed against the nearest wall long enough to get a bearing on the situation. Bullets were whistling through the air and splattering against the wall all around them. Then it ended. In a heartbeat it was over.

The skirmish had lasted roughly one minute after Keil and Harri jumped through the window of the interrogation room. Harri glanced at Keil who was smiling now; and wondered what he found so damned amusing. Had the head injuries mangled his brain? Did he even know who or where he was? Alarmed, Harri asked, "Keil, are you still with me? Are you okay?"

"I'm fine now!" Keil answered, as he watched a group of men walking toward them with a buoyant air.

"I hope you know these men, Keil," Harri said, more than a little alarmed.

"Yes, I know them," Keil told her, wiping a rivulet of blood from his forehead. "They shared some time and space with me in Sangre De Lobo's stockade."

So, these men are the prisoners that had somehow escaped from the stockade with Keil. Harri wondered where they were while Keil was being worked over by the terrorists?

Harri was still confused about who the good and bad guys were, and how she would know the difference. However, for the moment she was more concerned about Keil's head and face than clearing up that picture. He was bleeding badly and needed medical attention. She had little in the way of medical supplies that could patch up wounds such as he had suffered at the hands of the terrorists. Her own head was splitting, not only from the abuse it had taken at the stockade, but from the noise and excitement of the past half hour, and the recent kick in her ribs hadn't added any medicinal procedures to her cause. But in spite of her headache and the questionable safety of their present quarters, she was thankful for what she did have. Keil was alive. And for the moment, except for his physical wounds, he was as safe as anybody present, which didn't lend a load of certainty to the moment.

Harri took her first aid kit from the Jeep and did the best she could to patch his head and facial wounds; some of the cuts had needed a few stitches.

When she was convinced that Keil was going to survive, in spite of his cuts and bruises, she began to pay attention to what was going on around her. She listened to the men talk until she had gained a fair idea of what had taken place after the stockade had been raided and then torched.

Harri learned that Keil and the other prisoners, after they had been released by a group of men unknown to them. The prisoners had been brought to this place known as "West Camp" in two large trucks. Keil and the other prisoners had been unloaded at a barracks building located a hundred yards or so northwest of the room where Keil was being interrogated when Harri arrived. Before the truck drivers departed from the barracks, they gave the prisoners two dozen rifles and a few hundred rounds of ammo, then said, "Keep a watch out for the terrorists. We'll be back for you as soon as we've made arrangements to get you guys safely out of Sangre De Lobo. But if anything goes wrong in the interim, you're on your own until we can regroup. Any of you that survive should head directly for Camp Rio Sombra," The speaker looked at Keil and said, "That's your old hangout, you can direct these men there. We'll meet you there as soon as possible and, hopefully, we will have made arrangements for your safe passage out of here. But there's always a chance that even we don't have all the answers. If somebody gets wise to us, you're really on you own. You'll just have to get out the same way you got in—whatever way that might have been."

Harri had asked as many questions as possible, trying to learn what had happened at the burned stockade and here at West Camp. Keil tried to explain:

"When we were brought here and unloaded, me and one of the other prisoners, a young Mexican, volunteered for first shift of guard duty. Just minutes before the designated shift change, the two of us were surprised by three of the terrorists. The young Mexican was killed on the spot, and I was taken prisoner. Somehow the terrorists had decided that I knew something about who had torched the stockade and removed the prisoners. They also wanted to know where Mathson was. He was supposed to be here in this camp."

It was comforting to know that her instincts were still working for her. It was also comforting to know that the prisoners who had escaped from that burning hell were still alive. Harri listened with interest as one of the prisoners gave his account of what had happened: When Keil and the young guard failed to return to the barracks after their shift as guard had ended, one of the other prisoners became alerted to a possible danger and went looking for them. He found the young guard dead, notified the others inside the barracks and went looking for Keil. When he reached the interrogation room, he knew something was wrong. He managed to surprise and overpower one of the guards and get close enough to a window to see that Keil was being pounded senseless by three terrorists. The man returned to the barracks where the others waited and informed them of Keil's situation. The prisoners gathered all the rifles and ammo and were advancing on the interrogation room when they heard rifle fire coming from the building where Keil was being hammered on. Not knowing exactly what was happening, the prisoners moved in closer before opening fire. When they saw the terrorists firing on the people inside the building they began firing on the terrorists.

After the battle had ended, the prisoners were surprised to learn that a single person, a female, had managed to enter the interrogation room and was well into freeing Keil when they joined the battle.

CHAPTER 31

AFTER THE STOCKADE HAD BEEN burned to the ground and the prisoners released, a half dozen terrorist soldiers had raced to West Camp in search of a man they knew only as Mathson. Mathson had been using West Camp as his headquarters for over a year, and had thoroughly established himself as a negotiator between the terrorists and the outside world. Mathson had, in a matter of a few months, enriched the terrorists' wealth by several million dollars. Recently, Mathson had been trying to free Keil West by soliciting ransom money from the states. However, he was having a problem meeting a deadline, and an execution was scheduled for West within the week. The terrorist soldiers were convinced now that Mathson had decided to initiate the release of West by using his own methods instead of waiting for the ransom money to arrive. The terrorist soldiers wanted to find and question Mathson about the destruction of the stockade and the roadhouse. When they failed to locate Mathson after searching through his private quarters two of the terrorist soldiers began checking around the campgrounds and spotted Keil and the young Mexican. One of the terrorists turned a high-powered light on them and had them covered before they could lift their rifles. The terrorists recognized Keil as the prisoners that Mathson has been dealing for. They shot the Mexican on the spot and took Keil captive, deciding to question him before killing him, since they couldn't locate Mathson.

The terrorists took Keil to Mathson's quarters, knowing that in time they would make him talk or kill him in the effort. Meanwhile, they expected that, in time, Mathson would return to his quarters and they would be waiting for him.

Keil had known the terrorists would keep him alive as long as possible in their effort to persuade him to talk. He also knew that many of the men these interrogators had worked over in the past had died before they talked; simply because they had no information to give. But with or without information, the end result was always the same; the men always died. Keil knew it mattered little whether or not he talked. He was glad he had no information for them.

The terrorists that had been advancing on the building when Harri arrived were from the camp she had escaped from. One of them had discovered she had escaped from her underground cell after killing a guard, but he had no idea she would be following him and the guard to Mathson's headquarters. They came to West Camp to have a talk with Mathson, to let him know that he would be held personally responsible for the death of the guard that Harri had killed before she escaped. One of the terrorists—the head honcho of Red Camp—had been suspicious from the beginning of what had gone down at the roadhouse where Harri had been taken prisoner. Mathson had seemed a little too anxious to keep the prisoner alive. Then when Mathson had left that half-wit, Jose Negis, in charge of the prisoner, the angry officer was even more convinced that something was amiss. When the prisoner escaped, killing one of the guards—a guard that he had personally sent to kill the prisoner—he was fully convinced that he had been right. Mathson wasn't working with them, or for them. Mathson was working for Mathson; playing his own game; making up his own rules.

The angry officer wanted to have a closer look at Mathson's rules. He located another guard and headed for Mathson's headquarters. After reaching West Camp, the two of them were surprised to learn that others officers had also become suspicious of Mathson after the prison had mysteriously burned to the ground and the prisoners had escaped.

During the final, short-lived skirmish at West Camp, that angry officer from Red Camp, had caught a bullet in the thickest part of his chest. His last and only consoling words, were, "I never trusted Mathson. I should have listened to my instincts."

CHAPTER 32

Harri sat with Keil in the cab of a slow-moving truck. Keil had refused to let her drive, insisting that he was just bruised up a bit and plenty capable of operating a vehicle. He rested his case with the fact that he was the only one who knew where they were going. He had to lead the other three drivers to their destination. Any driver unfamiliar with the bad roads would only slow things down for everyone. At this point, the whole crew was exhausted and needed food and sleep. Harri knew Keil was right.

The truck Harri was riding in was one of four that moved awkwardly through the night, over roads that were barely visible. Admittedly, she had no idea where they were going or what the plan was after they got there. She was too tired to ask him if he had any definite plans, or if he had any intentions of sharing them with her if he did.

For an hour Keil had been staring straight ahead without speaking. His silence was weighing heavy on Harri's nerves. In the darkness of the truck's cab his features looked grim. Suddenly Keil turned to her and said, in a not too pleasant voice, "Harri tell me, what in hell are you doing here in Sangre De Lobo? How did you get here? . . . . And it had better be a good story pal!"

"I came looking for you, pal!" she spat back at him. "And maybe you can tell me what you're doing here! How did you managed to get yourself into this damned mess?"

"It's a long story Harri." Keil sounded tired, and Harri could tell by the tone of his voice that he would rather she drop the subject. He didn't want any part of a discussion where he had to defend his position. "Maybe you would rather not hear it," he said quietly—hopefully, "at least not tonight." The effort of speaking was causing him a great deal of pain. The abuse his body had taken, and the strain of the past few hours were taking their toll on him. He was feeling sicker by the minute and was hours beyond tired.

"Yes, I do want to hear it!" Harri said, looking at him grimly. "Since I have risked my neck to rescue you, I believe I have a right to know why it was necessary for me to do something this dumb!"

"I really do appreciate what you've done, Harri," Keil told her, placing an arm around her shoulder. "You're right, you did save my ass—and you're also right about it being a dumb thing to do. I can't even imagine what made you do something this stupid. But I suppose you still deserve an explanation of why I'm here."

"Yes, I suppose I do!" Harri said, with a determined scowl.

"My reason for being here is simple, Harri—or it was in the beginning. I came here to locate those two crates that disappeared from our dredge site three years ago, but I encountered problems that I never planned on. Problems that I couldn't plan ahead for because I never knew they existed. I'm sure that you remember Dr. Singly and that engineer, Tolver. Although you weren't present at the time, you must have heard the story that followed their flight from the jungle post. The story that, with their pilot's help, the two of them flew out of the jungle with those two crates that a large portion of the earth's population would kill for. About a year ago I began hearing stories that triggered my interest big-time. The stories were coming out of Sangre De Lobo. It seemed that a group of the residents here, more commonly known as terrorists, had a super deal that was available to any interested party with enough money. Then, stories began to leak out about an aircraft that had crashed near the villa three years ago. I began putting things together and came up with the idea that Sangre De Lobo was where those very valuable crates were stashed and that someone in that villa was itching to deal. But I couldn't be sure until I found someone who could verify my suspicions. When I came into Sangre De Lobo, I managed to meet a select few of the right people.

I was actually making some progress. I had convinced one important person that I could make him rich beyond his wildest dreams if he could help me with a few simple details. I was really looking forward to getting my hands on those crates, I was already counting my millions, planning my retirement . . ."

Harri saw a look of disgust settle over Keil's face as he pushed himself back farther against the truck seat and looking as if he had decided to drop the subject and get comfortable.

"Well?" Harri snapped. "What happened?"

"What happened," said Keil wearily, "was that someone else had gotten the same idea. It seems that the people who sponsored the project from the beginning had managed to put together a small army to search the Sangre De Lobo area for the aircraft. They had also heard the rumors about the plane going down in this area. They found the airplane and the remains of the crew, but the crates were missing—which shouldn't have been a big surprise to them. Their biggest surprise was that the terrorists were waiting for them. Many of the men were killed on the spot and some were captured. The ones that were taken alive were men the terrorists had some personal knowledge of and knew they were worth more alive than dead. One of the men who was captured was a friend of mine. I was trying to negotiate for his release by contacting a party in the states, but it turns out that someone else was already negotiating for his release, and all my efforts did was to get my butt thrown into the stockade. My friend was released, but they needed someone to take his place I guess. My only hope was, that since he knew I had replaced him in the stockade, that he would try to arrange for my release. I have had little contact with the outside world since then—until last night. You know the story from that point on. Now, tell me, how did you learn that I was being held prisoner at Sangre De Lobo?"

"Someone threw a rock through Dad's office window. The rock had a note pinned to it. The note said you were here. I didn't want Dad to even see that note—you can guess the rest. I still wonder who threw that rock through the window. But I suppose it's not important. Anyway, it hasn't been up to now . . ."

Suddenly Harri was too tired to continue with the conversation. She knew she wasn't making sense anymore—even to herself.

The trucks were grinding to a halt. Keil was still driving the lead truck. Harri wondered why they were stopping. "What are we doing now?" She asked. Then before Keil could answer, she continued, "We need to keep moving Keil," she said groggily! "We need to be as far from Sangre De Lobo as possible when the sun comes up. I need to be in Villa Guano tomorrow. If I'm not, someone will come here looking for me. Someone that will wait for me in an area that I would rather not ever see again. The only way to get there is by trekking ten miles through a jungle—a very unpleasant trip. So, let's not waste any time by stopping. It can't be much farther to Villa Guano!"

"Harri, I hate to disappoint you," Keil said sternly, "but I'm not planning on leaving here until I have those crates. Or until I know for sure that they're not here. I learned last night that Brent Mathson is here in Sangre De Lobo. He's on the same mission as I am. He's after those crates. My plan now is to locate Brent and work with him as a team. You're welcome to stay on as part of that team if you want to, Harri. I can't think of anything that would make me happier than the three of working together as a team."

"Damn it, Keil!" Harri exclaimed, fully alert now. "What I wish is to get the hell out of here—for both of us to get out—and I wish you hadn't told me Brent is here.

"Why not?" Keil asked, surprised. "I honestly believed that information would make you very happy, Harri."

"Normally it would have, Keil." Harri said quietly, gazing straight ahead, seeing again that hard, stern face at the roadhouse, then the heavy fist coming at her head. Suddenly Harri was feeling sick again, and wishing she could put that horrible memory out of her mind, but it kept popping back like a tetherball.

"What do you mean by 'normally'," asked Keil, looking at her suspiciously.

"Well . . . .. a lot has changed in the past few hours, Keil; more than I care to even think about."

"What could have changed in a few hours that could change the way you feel about finding Brent Mathson again, Harri?" He asked her, still looking skeptical, not really believing she was serious.

"I got a good look at the man who tried to kill me at the stockade last night, Keil. I thought it was Brent. I've tried to talk myself out of believing what I saw. But now you tell me he's here. There's no longer room for doubt. I was right. It was Brent. I suppose I already knew it, but it was not an easy thing for me to believe. Brent took me captive after almost taking my head off with his fist. He put me in an underground confinement—not exactly a jail or prison, but definitely a confinement, and he placed guards at the site. That's why my head and face look as it does now. Brent did this to me, Keil. I broke out of his confinement, but I had to kill one of the guards to do it. I stole the guard's Jeep. That's how I managed to reach West Camp."

Keil sat staring at her as if she had gone mad. He reached over and placed gentle fingers on an ugly bruise, then said softly, "Harri, you have to be mistaken. I know Brent, he wouldn't do this to you—he wouldn't do this to any female. I would never call you a liar, but you have to be mistaken."

"I can appreciate your loyalty to Brent, but I'm not mistaken, Keil." She told him, solemnly.

Keil continued to search her face. He was having a tough time believing what he had just heard. Harri understood only too well. She too, still wanted to be wrong about Brent.

"Harri, I know how easy it is for someone to jump to the wrong conclusion about the actions of other people. There was another time when Brent was falsely accused of a vile act. Brent just happened to be present during an invasion of the jungle post where we all grew up. It could have been the worst and bloodiest of all invasions, but it wasn't because Brent and his father intervened. However, at the time it placed Brent in a very bad light for a while. Even your father believed that Brent was involved in that act of violence. Brent was innocent then and I believe you could be mistaken about him now. I know how much you cared for Brent, Harri, and it must be awful to feel so betrayed. I remember how relieved I was when I learned that Brent and his father were not working with our enemies but, instead, had followed them to our camp and saved our bacon. Actually, Brent's crew almost wiped out that bunch of marauders.

Harri sat quietly and listened until Keil had finished with his story. She was happy that Keil had those memories of Brent. She fully understood his loyalty to his friend. She could tell from the look on Keil's face that he wanted her to say she could have been mistaken, that it was dark, that it would have been easy to make such a mistake. She looked at Keil and shook her head, then said in a half whisper, "I wish you were right, Keil. God only knows how I wish you were right!"

Keil placed an arm around her shoulders and watched her weary expression. "You still love him don't you, Harri?"

She sat still, staring into the darkness, refusing to answer his question. She knew that Keil was feeling every ache in her own heart. She reached for his hand, giving it a small squeeze. Then she turned to him and smiled, thankful for his presence. "It'll be all right, Keil. It really will!" She knew Keil didn't believe her.

The large trucks pulled off the road into a clearing that had obviously been used before for vehicle parking. The men were stepping from their trucks and waiting for further orders from Keil. As Harri stepped from Keil's truck and saw all the men gathered around it, she was surprised at their number. She had only seen a dozen or so men back at West Camp. Each of these trucks must have held at least a dozen men.

Harri was still unhappy about stopping here, but arguing the point was useless. Also, she knew these men were tired and needed sleep. She could argue tomorrow. She would have a better chance of winning when her own head was clearer.

She could see a building in the distance but the structure was barely visible in the darkness. There were no lights on inside the building, which was nestled among a mass of heavy jungle growth.

Harri decided that for better or for worse she would stay with Keil—at least until he had made every effort to accomplish his mission here. Harri's greatest fear was that this stupid mission couldn't be accomplished. But she would stay anyway. She would stay until the end. If she survived it, she would get back with Señor Manillo at a later time and make sure that he was paid well for his return trip to the pick-up spot.

Harri could not leave Keil here. If she left him in Sangre De Lobo, all of the pain and fear she had suffered this past week would have been for nothing. If she abandoned him now, she would look even more an idiot than she already did.

Harri backed against the door of Keil's truck and shoved her hands into her pockets, waiting for the next move. Whatever that move might be she would be there. She had to be there. From the beginning there never had been another choice.

Harri and Keil, along with the other men from the stockade, were all trying to prepare food on a small two burner hot plate that Keil had managed to coax into action long enough to heat a few provisions. Harri noticed that some of the men were making cold sandwiches and drinking plain water instead of waiting for the huge pot of coffee to perk and the great tins of beans to heat. She helped two of the men to pull the wooden tables together. She couldn't understand why the tables had to be together until she saw the wooden benches. When the tables and benches were pulled together in long rows it gave them more seating space. This house, if it could be describes as such, had been Keil's camp for several weeks. All the furnishings, such as they were, had been left here when he had been imprisoned. Apparently, everything in the house was as he had left it. Even the tin plates and cups and the iron skillets and pots were still sitting in the long room that looked more like a boxcar than ordinary house. Harri walked through the long narrow building, inspecting walls that were bare studs on the inside, and pieces of metal siding on the outside. The almost flat roof seemed to be sufficient to shed water. The two windows had glass panes. The two doors had hinges and latches that worked. She couldn't say much for the decor but the men seemed to think it was great, and nobody would catch her complaining. However, there were no separate quarters where she could sleep. Just this one long room. There was a washroom, one that Keil himself had built onto the larger room after he had taken up residence here. There was no running water in the washroom and no commode. Just a big, metal tub for bathing, and a portable washbasin and a bucket of water with a rusty, metal dipper. Keil's guests, including herself, would be using the bushes out back a lot. Again, Harri was glad that she had learned early in life not to be squeamish about life's little flaws and uncertainties.

Harri sat and listened for a while as Keil outlined his plans for getting at the missing crates. Then the strain of the day—and the night—caught up with her and she drifted into a sound sleep.

+ + + ✦ + + +

CHAPTER 33

HARRI AWOKE NEAR DAYBREAK WITH a splitting headache. Someone had rolled out her sleeping bag and crammed a portion of it under her head, but it hadn't stopped the hammering in her brain. She needed a painkiller badly. She rummaged through her duffel bag until she found her first aid kit. She removed a bottle of aspirin, poured four of them into her palm and headed for the small room that had not quite sufficed as a bathroom last night. It did have a bucket of drinkable water though. The room was just an eight-by-eight cubicle with a large metal tub that sat off to one side. The previous night, she and one of the men had filled the tub twice with water from a nearby small river. They had taken turns bathing. After Harri's bath, the tub had been emptied by using a large siphon hose that ran from the tub to the outside, then it had been refilled. Harry didn't know how many men bathed after she slept. But If last night was an indicator, it was obvious that somebody was going to skip a bath or two. Harri's guess would be that many of the men would be bathing in the small river.

On an opposite wall from the tub was a wide, deep shelf that served as a dressing table. The shelf held a gallon of all-purpose water and a rusty washbasin. Above the shelf was a mirror that was covered with black splotches. Beside the mirror, Keil had driven a huge spike into the wall, and there he had hung a well-worn towel—several weeks ago. Last night Harri had washed the towel as best she could and re-hung it on the spike. Now as she drew a dipper of water from the pail to rinse her aspirin down, she almost gagged at the smell that emitted from the towel. Harri was certain that upon closer inspection the towel would reveal a tiny, green, living forest—complete with microscopic animals.

Harri was examining her face in the mirror while she waited for the aspirin to work its wonders. Her face looked as bad as her head felt, but there was little she could do for her face except hope that it would heal soon. If she were a good judge of bruises this one was going to hang around for a while; but she could see out of both eyes now. Harri placed a cool, damp cloth over her feverish face. It felt so good she decided to leave it there for a while. She turned to leave the small room. Still holding the cloth in place with one hand she opened the bathroom door—and stepped into Brent Mathson's open arms.

Harri was too confused to be alarmed by the encounter. She looked up at him, but her aching head would not cooperate with what her eyes were seeing. When the reality of Brent's presence began to sink in, Harri's first thoughts were: Was he here to avenge the guard she had killed?

Brent pulled her close and pushed his face into her hair. Harri tried to pull away but he held her firmly. Harri's heart was hammering through her shirt and she wasn't sure why. Yes, she was afraid of what Brent might do to her, but she knew the feel of his arms around her could have triggered her rapid heartbeat. She didn't know why Brent was here. She knew that Keil had intended to find him and join forces with him, but it looked as if Brent had found Keil, and she wondered how he knew where to look. There were so many miles of this jungle that accidentally finding a place like this one would take a lot of luck.

"Are you going to kill me now?" Harri asked quietly.

Brent loosened his hold and held her back, searching her face. He was surprised at her question, and couldn't believe she was really serious. Then he looked more closely at her bruised face and his thoughts whirled. *She had no way of knowing what had gone down at the roadhouse. She couldn't know that he hadn't intended to kill her. She had every reason to believe the worst about that whole scene. If only he could have had more time. If only there could have been another way to have handled that situation.*

Harri searched his face, hoping to find something of the Brent Mathson that she used to know—something that might erase that appalling scene at the roadhouse and ease the ache in her heart.

Harri was amazed at how little Brent had changed. He was taller and heavier. He had a few more lines in his face, but the eyes and square chin were the same. His cheeks and jaw line were a little more prominent, but she would have recognized him in the dark. The longer she looked, the less desire she had to leave his arms. She should yell, or try harder to free herself from his grasp but she didn't want to do anything but remain where she was, in his arms, throughout eternity. To Harri this moment was the culmination of a lifetime of dreams. This was Brent holding her close. This was the only male on earth that she had ever truly loved with all of her heart. He had haunted her dreams since childhood. She had loved him for so long she couldn't even remember a time when she didn't. And she could well remember how empty and lost she had been when he disappeared from her life. Harri had learned to survive without him. She had even learned to be happy without him. But she had never lost the memory of her first and only true love. She had never accepted the possibility that he might be dead, because he had always been so alive in her heart. Now here he was, very much alive, holding her in his arms just as if he hadn't tried to kill her a few hours ago.

"Harri, please! Try to understand," Brent was saying, trying to get her attention. "I had to keep you from talking for a while. That was the only way I could keep either of us alive even for few minutes. We're both lucky that those bastards who were with me had become distracted by the mangled door of the roadhouse and their comatose dogs. They didn't hear you call out my name. I knew when I entered the roadhouse that I was walking on thin ice; that my hours of being trusted by those goons were numbered. When I saw you, I had to make a good show of my loyalty to those butchering thugs."

"But you tried to kill me!" She interrupted. "You tried to blow my brains out even before you hit me—before you even saw my face. How do you explain that?"

I knew the gun was empty, Harri. One of those apes had emptied my pistol and dumped my ammo into his own pocket shortly after we began the trip to the stockade. He didn't know that I knew the gun was empty, which permitted me to make a good show for the suckers;

it didn't surprise me at all when the gun didn't fire; it only surprised me when you turned around and I recognized you. I had to follow through with my act in order to get either of us out of there alive, and to keep you from shooting me. Later I took the keys to the stockade from your pocket and left you with Jose. I knew Jose would follow my orders, that he would keep you safe as long as he had control of the situation. Jose is operating on less than a full charge, but he's really not a bad sort, and he was my only hope of saving you. I was afraid to tell Jose that you were my friend because I knew that if push came to shove, he would have told the other guards; in his mind he would have been doing me a favor. So, I just told him to guard you with his life and keep everyone away from you if possible. As soon as I could get away from those apes I headed for the stockade. After I released Keil and the other prisoners I asked two of the men I'm working with to take them to West Camp. Then I torched the stockade and the roadhouse and rushed back to get you. My intentions were to take you from that hole and join Keil at West Camp. When I found you gone and that damned guard dead, I almost went crazy. I went looking for Jose and he told me what happened—at least, as far as he knew. The only thing Jose was really sure of was that the guards had gone looking for you. So, did I. The one place that I never thought of looking was at West Camp. I still can't imagine how you knew to go there. Actually, I still can't imagine you being here. I was surprised when I found you at the roadhouse; and even more surprised when I didn't find your dad around. Keil has filled me in on most of what has happened with you since I last saw you, including the past few days."

"That must have taken a while," said Harri. "How long have you been here?"

"A while. I arrived just after you fell asleep last night. I was going to wake you, but Keil threatened my life if I did, so I just placed your sleeping bag under your head and let you sleep."

"How did you ever find this place?" Harri asked. "It took us forever to get here, and I still don't even know where we are."

When I discovered Keil and the other men had left West Camp, I went looking for them. I knew where to find the men who had taken

Keil and the other prisoners to West Camp. After talking to them I learned about the terrorist raid on the place. The two men told me they had set up a tentative meeting here at Rio Sombra in case West Camp was raided before they could return for the men. Rio Sombra wasn't hard to find. I've been here before. Actually, I spent a night or two here before Keil ever heard of this place. I knew when I found Keil that I could count on him to help me find you...Guess you can imagine my surprise when I found both of you. But there's no way you could ever know how happy I was to find you alive and well, Harri.

In response to Brent's emotional confession, Harri was at a loss for words. She placed her head on his chest, closed her eyes, cherishing the closeness and luxuriated in memories that flooded every connecting fiber of her mind and heart. Harri was feeling again the excitement of watching Brent move with animal like stealth through the jungle. She had thrilled at his closeness when they were hardly more than children. Harri hadn't understood her feelings back then, she had just accepted them. She was remembering the many times that she had walked proudly by his side, keeping up with him step by step, wishing that what they shared would never end. She hadn't understood that either. She wasn't even aware that it needed to be understood. Just being near Brent and living the moment was all that was important back then. Then she remembered the pain when it all began to fall apart. She remembered when she began losing control over her emotions and her life. She could remember vividly how scared she was when Brent began to change, and she had no control over that either. Then there was that bleak day when she awoke and discovered that she had lost him altogether. . .

"But now that we're all together again," Brent was saying, "we can get organized, regroup, and push on with our plans... and at the same time, see if we can clean up the act of these bloody terrorists who control most of this area."

With a start, Harri was suddenly hearing what Brent was saying, but she looked at him as if he was speaking Greek.

"What plans are you referring to, Brent?" Harri asked, angry at him for forcing her to think about something she really didn't want to be a part of just now.

"Maybe I misunderstood, Harri, but I thought Keil had talked to you about our plans. I thought you were....

"Keil has talked to me about his plans, "Harri interrupted. "But for the record, I fully intend to talk Keil out of this crazy scheme—at least, I fully intend to try."

"I doubt you could talk Keil out of pushing on with this plan any more than you could talk me out of it, Harri. I've been working on this for months now and so has Keil. With his help and his knowledge of the situation, added to what I already know, we'll find those crates and get them out of this jungle and into the hands of those beautiful people who will pay any price we ask for them. I have every detail worked out now in my mind and on paper. And now I have all the equipment I need. I've been gathering it and stashing it safely away for months, and so has Keil. And thanks to Keil, I now have the soldiers, the equipment and another brain to work with me. With Keil's help—and your help if you decide to join us—I don't see how we could fail.

"You guys are totally nuts, Brent!" Harri said fervently.

"Maybe so, Harri," he agreed quietly. "But totally sane people don't win wars."

"Totally sane people don't start wars!" Harry blurted out angrily. "I would really like to know how you guys could even hope to defeat the terrorists on their own ground. Or how you could expect to get at those crates with the few men you have here. There are hundreds of terrorists in new Sangre De Lobo—there's no way we could win a war with them—short of nuking the suckers. Furthermore, I seriously doubt that they keep those crates on display in an amusement park, or that they have them wrapped and waiting for you guys to pick up at your convenience. I think the whole idea is ludicrous! Personally, I think we should get the hell out of here while we're all still alive . . . while we're still capable of getting out!"

"I would like very much for you to join us Harri, but I wouldn't want you to do something that you would personally find objectionable. I will even help you get out of here. I know people who would take you out tonight. So don't feel that you have to stick around to keep me or Keil happy. If you don't want to get yourself involved, nobody's going to . . ."

"I'm already involved Brent!" Harri interrupted. "Maybe more than you'll ever know. And I do understand your anger at the atrocities the terrorists have committed against the innocent people here. However, I believe there's another way to handle the situation. We could enlist the aid of outsiders. If other people in the states, or even here in Colombia, knew what was happening here..."

"No, Harri! You're talking about turning this into a political conflict. In the first place that would takes years. You know how hard it is to get the government to act on something like this. The people here would die of old age before help came. Nobody cares what happens to these people. Unless, of course, there's some way the demagogue can gain political power from their caring. The way we're doing it is the only way it will work for the people or for us. Even if we could get the government involved—which I doubt we could—it wouldn't protect the innocent from being slain, and we could forget about ever getting our hands on those crates. This way, we kill two birds with one stone. But like I said Harri, you don't have to get involved."

"And like I said, Brent. I am involved! I'll stick around and die with you guys—when is this raid taking place?"

"Three in the morning! And we're planning on winning—not dying!"

"Okay, I'll say no more. I suppose I'll have time to visit Old Villa Sangre De Lobo before we start World War III," Harri said quietly. "There's two people there that I must see . . ."

"I'll go along with you," he said. "There's someone there that I want to see before I leave the area."

"Would it be a young lady by the name of Stella?" Harri asked.

"It sure would," he answered, pushing her away from him, looking at her as if he believed her to be a wizard, or a sorcerer. "Is there anything that you don't know, Harri?" He asked.

She looked at him while searching for an answer to his question, then, smiling, she said, "I'm sure there is Brent, but at the moment I just can't think of what it might be."

CHAPTER 34

THE NIGHT WAS DARK, AND only a few stars were visible. The quarter moon that had offered a small amount of visibility was falling rapidly behind a hazy horizon. Brent pulled his truck to the side of the road and killed the engine. The other drivers lined up behind him and did likewise. All lights were extinguished.

Harri sat stiff backed and silent as she watched the men mill about, checking maps with penlights, and going over final plans. It was three in the morning. There was little she could say that hadn't already been said. The men in this party numbered forty-two. They were going against two hundred or more terrorist soldiers that were heavily armed and possibly waiting for them.

Both, Brent and Keil sincerely believed that their small army had the element of surprise on their side. They knew where the majority of the terrorists would be sleeping, and had already made arrangements to prevent them from ever waking.

Harri was not at all convinced that their small detachment had any advantage. When they left West Camp yesterday she had checked on the vehicle that had been hidden from view when she went in. It was missing. Someone had split the scene and could have by now alerted every terrorist in the jungle. True, the terrorists most likely would not be expecting an assault from such a small assemblage, even if the outfit had been watched by terrorist spies, at least not so soon after the West camp incident. The terrorists wouldn't expect that anybody could put together an army overnight. They would have no way of knowing that the army had been put together over a period of weeks; and that was their only advantage as far as Harri could see. But the truth was that nobody in this outfit knew for sure what the terrorists might know about this operation.

Brent was convinced that with the explosives, the assault weapons and the flame throwing equipment that he and Keil had put together over the past few months that they could easily take charge of the terrorists' villa in mere minutes. He and Keil planned on setting explosives at strategic areas in the villa while the terrorists slept, and they had definite plans for taking care of the guards. They even knew approximately how many guards they would be dealing with and when their shifts changed. They would have the villa under control before the terrorists knew they were there.

Harri knew, after talking with Brent, that he had been planning this for months—actually, since he learned that the terrorist had the valuable crates that had been taken from the crashed Cessna. But his most gratifying reason for the raid, the reason closest to his heart, stemmed from the fact that the terrorists they would wipe out this night were monstrous killers. They killed innocent people from other villas just for the fun of killing, and they captured and executed people without a trial. They had been terrorizing and killing the people of Old Sangre De Lobo in order to keep the more enterprising of those people under control. Brent wanted to stop the killings and the violence. He wanted to give the people of the nearby villas a rest and a decent shot at a normal life. They deserved better than they would ever get from these bloody terrorists. He especially wanted to help the older people and the very young children, and the teenagers such as Stella. None of those people would ever have a chance at a life; not without some outside intervention. And the very notion of trying to get the Colombian government involved here was a joke.

Brent had not entered Sangre De Lobo with any lofty ambitions, or with any moral or noble causes guiding his conscience. When he first began his campaign in the villa his sole intention was to locate the valuable crates. The only person Brent had wanted to help was himself. At that time, he was not even aware that Keil West had entered upon the scene. He would have been surprised to learn that Keil was working toward the same goal as he was…. locating and confiscating the crates.

Actually, Brent was surprised when he realized that his personal feelings for the innocent people had become a factor, gaining equal status with his main objective. But in spite of his original plans, his feelings had gotten involved. He had made the mistake of getting to know some of the people in Old Sangre De Lobo, and he couldn't just walk away from their devastating situation.

Brent told Harri that he had been working with the terrorists, posing as a negotiator for the release of prisoners. He had managed to gain the trust of many of the terrorists; and while he was gaining their trust, he was making plans to destroy them. But fate had dealt him a bad hand, and had changed his plans to a much greater degree than he could feel comfortable with. One of the prisoners that he had managed to get released recently, a man by the name of Jake Cox had worked with Brent's father at the dredge site for several years. When Cox discovered that Brent was J. C. Mathson's son, he told Brent that Keil West had been taken prisoner the day that Cox himself was released, and that Keil would be executed because there was nobody to pay the ransom that could get him released. Cox was going to try to reach Ward Holland with the news of Keil's capture, but he wasn't sure he could get to Holland in time to save Keil. Cox was sure that Holland would pay the ransom, but the ransom wasn't the big problem; getting to Holland in time was. However, he knew that if he talked to Holland in person, that Holland was sure to ask his help with Keil's release. Someone would have to get a message to the people who were holding Keil, and someone would have to be present for the actual exchange. Cox was the logical person to do it since he was familiar with the procedure. But Cox was determined to never again become personally involved in anything, at any time, that had anything to do with this damned jungle. He never again wanted to hear the name 'Sangre De Lobo,' or any other name that applied to any portion of the earth that lay south of San Antonio, Texas. When he departed from this hell, it was to be the end of his career as a mercenary.

Meanwhile, Brent had decided not to leave Keil's release to chance.

He knew that Cox most likely would never get a message to Holland in time. Brent began his own efforts to get Keil released; and cursed the fickle fingers of fate that was screwing up his well laid plans for obtaining the prized crates. Things would have to move along much sooner than he had planned. Worse still, if all didn't go according to plan, there was too much room for error; but that was just a bad beak he would have to deal with. Keil had to be freed. Brent knew if he couldn't arrange for the money in time to get him released affably by the terrorists, he would have to arrange for Keil's release in a manner that wasn't going to make anybody happy, including himself.

And, fortunately for them all, he had succeeded in freeing Keil and the other prisoner who were now his allies on this mission. So far things hadn't worked out too badly. He and Keil—and Harri—since she had elected to join them, were going to find those crates, and they were going stop the bloody terrorists and set the innocent people of old Sangre De Lobo free. This could be a history making moment for the three of them. There was not a doubt in Brent's mind about this invasion—it would go like clock work—it couldn't possibly fail. This whole operation had been planned to the N'th. degree.

The large trucks were once again moving slowly through the night. This time without lights. They were nearing the terrorist villa. They wanted to get as close as possible to the villa with their equipment. They were still operating on a time schedule, and everything had to be in place at the right time for this operation to work as planned. So far it was going well . . .

Brent was so high on excitement that he could hardly breathe. Nothing in his life would ever again equal this moment. He had Keil and Harri together again and they were going to be rich beyond their wildest dreams; and with Keil and Harri's help he was going to win a well-planned war. He was going to free hundreds of people from terror and degradation; he would give many a youngster a shot at a normal life. It just didn't get any better than this!

Harri sat staring straight ahead, telling herself that this couldn't really be happening. She couldn't be going into a terrorist villa with an army of soldiers that were far less in number than the terrorists in the villa they were planning to wipe off the earth. She knew Brent couldn't see the danger they faced, and she knew Keil would follow Brent right into the bottomless pits of hell. She remembered all too well, now that she had taken some time to think about it, the very day she had ceased to be the leader of their group. Brent had just taken over; there hadn't even been a contest, and nobody had drawn straws or held an election. It just happened. She hadn't even fought for her hard-earned position. Instead, she had become a disciple, without knowing or questioning how it had happened. From that time to the present, Harri had never totally regained her leadership position. She and Keil had shared it from the time they lost Brent. Now it looked as if she and Keil were once again playing the roll of followers. And while she couldn't speak for Keil, being a follower was not something she had written into her plans for her future. She would have to get that established as soon as this idiot raid on Sangre De Lobo was finished. She would be happy to walk beside Brent as long as his road was straight and aboveboard; but she would never again walk behind him—not ever!

Harri was happy about her decision, she would talk to Brent, let him know just how she felt about things. She turned now and looked admiringly at Brent's profile, a true work of the master's hand—except for that stubborn chin. At this moment that chin was set as if in stone. Brent was totally engrossed in this raid. He was living each second of it before it ever happened; playing and replaying each maneuver; leaving no rock unturned. This would be his moment of glory, and Harri knew, in spite of her doubts and misgivings about the whole affair, that she was glad to be in a position to share it with him. She even wondered if she would love him as much if he were just an ordinary man. If he was the type that would never launch an assault against a terrorist villa, if he was the type that would never permit her to join him in his battles and share in his ventures. If suddenly he should become just an ordinary intelligent and sound thinking man, would she still love him as much? She was afraid to pursue that question any further. She was afraid of the answer.

Harri caught a glimpse of movement up ahead and even before she could adjust her vision to the distance, she knew what it was. She caught her breath sharply and stared in disbelief as a large number of terrorist soldiers came out of nowhere and began firing on their trucks with rifles and machine guns. The crew in the trucks were caught by surprise, but all their weapons were ready and at hand. They jumped to the ground, rifles blazing. Many of them cursing the interruption in their plans, but still not taking the incident seriously enough to feel fear, or to believe that failure awaited them. This was far from what any of them, especially Brent and Keil, had expected, but they would work around it.

Somehow, after her initial shock, Harri wasn't at all surprised to find that the terrorists had been waiting for them.

It took several seconds for the crew to get organized into a defensive unit. They hadn't planned on being a defensive unit. Their plans had been to begin with an offensive assault and never slow down—not until the villa was totally under their control.

As the fighting raged on, none of them were anxious to venture far from the protection of their trucks. They were using the trucks as shields from enemy bullets. For several minutes they held the terrorists back and prevented them from using their grenades. The few that had tried had been shot before they could get the grenades out of their own hands. The grenades had done more harm to their own men than to the trucks. In spite of their losses the terrorists were slowly closing in. They had managed to get behind the trucks now, and had them completely surrounded. Harri wondered, as she fired steadily at the onslaught, if they stood a snowball in hell's chance of getting out of this alive. She knew that many of her crew were already dead, and the terrorists were using their grenades again. Keil's truck had just been blown to scrap metal. She hadn't seen Keil in several minutes and didn't have the time or the opportunity to search for him. Her only thought now was to stay alive as long as possible and to kill as many of these bloody terrorists as she could while she still lived.

The situation was looking more hopeless by the minute and she wondered what, if anything could be done to stop the assault. She felt pebble stones and other debris pelting her body as bullets kicked up the earth all around her. She could feel warm blood running down her arm and wondered if she had been hit; and if she had, why she felt no pain. Blood was running into her hand, causing her to loose her grip on the assault weapon that she was trying to hold onto. She wiped the blood on her pants and with a new grip on her rifle, she continued to fire at the oncoming terrorists, stopping only long enough to push new ammo clips into the weapon.

She could see them clearly now, in any direction she looked they were there, moving steadily toward the trucks and firing as they moved; and Harri kept firing also. There was nothing left to do but keep firing until it was over. She could at least have the satisfaction of knowing that she had taken out as many of the murdering pigs as she had time and bullets for. Each time she saw one of the suckers fall under her fire it increased her desire to keep up her own efforts even when she was certain that only a miracle could win this war for them, they could never win it alone. Harri wasn't sure at the moment that there was another living soul in her party. As far as she knew she was the last of her group. Then she saw Keil moving into the open, firing as he moved. He was obviously trying to reach her side. She wanted to yell at him, tell him to stay put, take care of his own skin. She knew she would be wasting her time and drawing attention to herself if she said anything to him. She kept her rifle aimed at the oncoming terrorist and held the trigger down as she moved the weapon from one target to the next, offering as much cover for Keil as possible.

Harri lost sight of Keil again as another half dozen of the terrorist came at her from another angle and she was forced to turn away from Keil in order to protect herself from the advancing terrorists.

Brent had climbed into the back of his truck and was trying to get at a flamethrower. He yelled for someone to help him with the fuel tanks and other gear. Harri lifted herself from her firing position and leaped forward, firing as she went. If she could help Brent get the flamethrowers in operation maybe there was a chance for some of them to survive this slaughter. She was reaching for the tanks and stopped short when she noticed the flashing lights advancing on the area from above. Helicopters were flying overhead, scanning the area with floodlights, and to her surprise, some of the terrorists were fleeing. Riflemen from the choppers were firing on the fleeing men. Harri watched that scene for a moment, totally confused as to what was taking place, and then she noticed an unusual scene up ahead. As she looked closer, she could see through the smoke of their own battle that the villa was going up in flames. Choppers were flying overhead dropping explosives on the villa.

Harri was brought suddenly back to the present scene when Brent handed her several pounds of gear from the truck. The two of them had the gear set up and within seconds Brent was spraying flames at the terrorists who had decided to fight instead of run. Some of them had taken refuge in the trees and shrubs and were determined to finish off the occupants of the trucks before they split the scene. Brent turned his flamethrower into an area that had unleashed a barrage of bullets at the trucks. As the flames caught at the trees and shrubbery, Harri could see the terrorists running, some of them with their clothes blazing. Grudgingly, she had to give some of them credit for their courage. As the area lighted up with flames she could see a dozen of the terrorists standing in the flames, pulling pins from grenades, getting ready to launch them at the trucks. She turned her weapon on the group and watched as they fell like freshly mowed grass, their grenades exploding around themselves. Harri began to feel confident that she, and whoever was left of their crew, might have a chance to get out of this hell alive.

When the action was over, the survivors of their small band gathered their dead and injured and headed toward the villa. As they drew near, Harri saw that the villa was surrounded by government soldiers. The soldiers were preventing anyone from leaving or entering the villa at the moment. Brent pulled his truck over to the side of the road and stepped out, waving to the following trucks to do the same. As the trucks filed into a line behind Brent's vehicle, he got out and walked toward the soldiers. Harri and Keil walked with him and listened while a soldier explained what was happening at Sangre De Lobo.

The Colombian government was executing this raid. It had been initiated by a Mr. Ward Holland, from the U.S. Mr. Holland had convinced one important member of the Colombian government that many of their people, along with some of his, were being held captive at Sangre De Lobo and that the U.S. would pay the Colombian government a handsome royalty for the release of the U.S. prisoners. Also, the U.S. would pay an even greater reward for two crates that belonged to U.S. citizens—crates that had been stolen by the terrorists.

The Colombian government had already been getting bits of news about the terrorists that were operating in this part of the jungle; they didn't need a lot of encouragement to move in on the operation.

Harri asked the guard, "Where is Mr. Holland now? Is he helping with this raid?"

"Yes, he is. He's right up there in that helicopter. He will be landing soon. If you wish, you may speak with him."

Keil and Brent walked slowly among the remaining crew, checking over the dead and injured bodies. Of the forty-three soldiers in their party, nine were now dead and two were severely injured. All of the crew had received from, insignificant to severe injuries. Brent had been hit pretty hard but his wounds were clean and would leave no permanent scars. All he had to worry about was infection. Keil hadn't been hit directly but had caught numerous pieces of shrapnel and some of his scars could very well be permanent.

Harri had been hit twice, but both hits were superficial and would heal quickly.

"Well," said Brent, ruefully. "I guess we're entitled to claim a victory here, but it's a damned sad victory. I never planned on losing those men!"

"People are always lost in wars," said Keil. "Death is an inevitable agent of war. Next time it could be us; even heroes die, Brent."

"Speaking of heroes, how come I don't feel like a hero," Brent asked. "And what makes you think there'll be a next time?"

Keil looked long at Brent, as if trying to decide on an answer to his question, then said, "Yes, Brent, there will be a next time! As long as you and I live there'll always be a next time for us, because that's who we are! We're stupid bastards that aren't smart enough to live any other way," said Keil."

"Would you be willing to try another way?" Brent asked.

"Any time pal! Any time!" said Keil, "There's really nothing wrong with being smart! It works for the best of men!"

After the smoke settled on the burning terrorist villa and all remaining terrorists had been taken into custody, Brent, Keil and Harri went in search for the crates. Since Brent already had an idea where they were stashed, locating them had not been a great chore. Getting them to the loading area where a helicopter waited had been more difficult.

Harri sat in the cab of the military truck and watched as her father walked toward the vehicle. As he drew near, she stepped from the truck and into his arms.

Ward hugged her close and shook his head, still in disbelief that his daughter was here. It was beyond his comprehension that she could take it upon herself to commit an act so totally reckless—that she would even consider taking on something this momentous. He wanted to hold her close and protect her from the world; but for now—just for this one moment—nothing would make him happier than turning her over his knee ...

Harri had to admit that her father had a reason to be angry. She could even admit that this raid on Sangre De Lobo was an act of stupidity. Even though she and Brent and Keil had learned a valuable lesson from it, the lesson had cost them nine lives. But the one thing that she would never admit to being wrong about was her original reason for being here in Sangre De Lobo. Facing the same situation, she would do it again—but she hoped she would never again be faced with such a situation. Harri wondered why her father had organized this raid on Villa Sangre De Lobo. She was almost positive that the only thing in the world that would inspire him to commit such an act would be to get her out of here safely. But she had learned just a few minutes ago that he wasn't even aware that she was here until he landed his chopper—what else could have inspired such a reaction from him?

"I tried to keep you from learning about Keil being captured and jailed here in Sangre De Lobo," Ward told his daughter. "I would have done anything to keep you from knowing. I learned about it from the two men who visited me at the estate, the ones who wanted me to lead their troops into this Villa. The day I left for Houston; it wasn't to gather supplies for the fourth-of-July cook out. I went there to meet with the people who would help me launch this assault against the terrorists who were holding Keil prisoner.

Harri, Brent and Keil watched as the crates were loaded into the chopper for their final trip to the U.S. The giant aircraft lifted slowly from the ground, leaving a blast of whirling hot air and flying debris in its wake. Simultaneously, Brent, Keil and Harri raised their hands into the air, bringing them together in a high five. Their personal war with the terrorists was over. They wouldn't even try to guess what the future might hold from this day forth. They were together again for now, alive and safe. For the moment that was enough …

Printed in the USA
CPSIA information can be obtained
at www.ICGtesting.com
LVHW080601031023
759759LV00050B/541